"I'm not going out with you..."

Ryan was more confused than ever.

Jo blew out a breath and explained. "Don't take this personally. I have a policy. No trying out my horses if you're not a serious buyer."

"I *am* a serious buyer," Ryan said. "*And* I'm willing to take you out."

"Willing?" Her dark eyes flashed. She took a step toward him, sharp chin jutting.

"Uh..."

"Like taking me on a date is a hardship?" Jo scoffed. "Have you been talking to my mother?"

Yes, and she warned me you were prickly.

"I meant I'd be *honored* to escort you to the Buckboard, all for the sake of creating a foundation of trust for this sale."

"You're not very good with girls, are you, Mr. Ryan?" That was Dean, one of her twin boys, serious as all get-out as he cast shade on Ryan.

Jo bit back a grin.

And Ryan sensed opportunity once more. "Admittedly, I'm not a ladies' man," he said slowly, easing forward. "But I could arrange a date for you...with my brother."

Dear Reader,

My ideas for books often start with one small kernel of an idea. In this case, I overheard two teenage girls talking about their high school crushes. And I had to wonder what they were going to think about their crushes years from now. Would they be over them? Or would they still be pining for those people?

Meet Joanna Pierce, who had a high school crush on Tate, the "nice" Oakley twin. Ryan, the other Oakley, was her high school nemesis. Over a decade later, Ryan wants to buy an expensive roping-competition horse from Jo, who still bears a grudge against him and harbors a crush on his brother. When Ryan tries to help Jo nab a date with his twin, things get even more complicated!

I had fun writing Ryan and Jo's romance. I hope you come to love and root for the cowboys and cowgirls of The Cowboy Academy series as much as I do. Happy reading!

Melinda

HEARTWARMING

A Cowboy Christmas Carol

—

Melinda Curtis

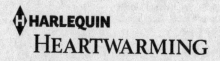

HARLEQUIN®
HEARTWARMING™

Recycling programs
for this product may
not exist in your area.

ISBN-13: 978-1-335-47554-1

A Cowboy Christmas Carol

Copyright © 2023 by Melinda Wooten

For questions and comments about the quality of this book,
please contact us at CustomerService@Harlequin.com.

Harlequin Enterprises ULC
22 Adelaide St. West, 41st Floor
Toronto, Ontario M5H 4E3, Canada
www.Harlequin.com

Printed in U.S.A.

Award-winning *USA TODAY* bestselling author **Melinda Curtis**, when not writing romance, can be found working on a fixer-upper she and her husband purchased in Oregon's Willamette Valley. Although this is the third home they've lived in and renovated (in three different states), it's not a job for the faint of heart. But it's been a good metaphor for book writing, as sometimes you have to tear things down to the bare bones to find the core beauty and potential. In between—and during—renovations, Melinda has written over forty books for Harlequin, including her Heartwarming book *Dandelion Wishes*, which is now a TV movie, *Love in Harmony Valley*, starring Amber Marshall.

Brenda Novak says *Season of Change* "found a place on my keeper shelf."

Sheila Roberts says *Can't Hurry Love* is "a page turner filled with wit and charm."

Books by Melinda Curtis

The Cowboy Academy
A Cowboy's Fourth of July
A Cowboy Worth Waiting for

The Mountain Monroes
A Cowgirl's Secret
Caught by the Cowboy Dad
The Littlest Cowgirls

The Blackwells of Eagle Springs
Wyoming Christmas Reunion

Visit the Author Profile page
at Harlequin.com for more titles.

PROLOGUE

September

"No PRESSURE. No pressure. No pressure."

"Steady now, Tate," Ryan Oakley told his muttering twin while guiding his fidgety mount, Suzie, into the heeling side of the team roping box.

How Ryan heard Tate amid the noise of the rodeo was a mystery only explained by the twin bond.

"Next up in the team roping competition are the Oakley brothers." The announcer's voice boomed in the covered arena.

Tate muttered about pressure again.

Ryan reminded him to be steady again.

And the announcer carried on. "Riding the header side is Tate, leaving the heeling to Ryan. These two are each in the running for third place in the Prairie Circuit and have an opportunity to beat out the Cole brothers. It all comes down to this last run."

Yep. It did. Ryan and Tate had never gotten

this far before. They were hungry for a place in the top three. Third place in the Prairie Circuit meant there'd be a national postseason, big purses and high-paying endorsement opportunities.

"No pressure. No pressure."

"Steady now," Ryan repeated in a soothing voice. He eased back on the reins with his left hand, flexing his grip on the throwing rope in his right.

"You boys ready?" Chet, the chute worker, asked Ryan, his white handlebar mustache twitching.

At Ryan's nod, Chet released the steer with a clank of the gate.

Out bolted several hundred pounds of compact Corrientes bovine intent upon hightailing it to the other side of the arena without being roped by horns or heels.

"Yaw!" Ryan kicked his horse into action. And even though Suzie leaped forward, the world slowed for Ryan.

In a few strides, Ryan and Suzie were almost ahead of Tate, which wasn't good. Tate needed to be leading. And the steer was veering to the right, into Ryan's path. Not good either.

Add half a second. Maybe more.

Neither one of them could afford more than that. Ryan couldn't throw his rope around the steer's heels until Tate landed his around its horns. They may call the competition *team* roping but they each were timed separately.

Ryan reined in his mount slightly, adjusting his speed to Tate's pace.

The steer adopted a drunken weave.

Ryan and Tate closed ranks around him, straightening his path.

Throw the rope, Tate.

Too many seconds were ticking past. They were thundering toward the arena's midline.

Throw the rope, Tate.

Finally, his brother gave it a toss. The lasso fell perfectly around both of the steer's horns.

Ryan was aware of Tate tying off, backing off, slowing the steer. But his body was switching to instinctive mode, feeling, not thinking—the twirl of his rope, the rhythm of the steer's heels, his lungs filling with air, his muscles bunching, gathering strength.

Ryan let the rope fly.

It was a good throw. A perfect throw.

And yet he knew…

He knew like he knew the sun was going to rise tomorrow.

They'd taken too long. They'd both come in fourth. Again.

CHAPTER ONE

December

"I'M QUITTING."

There was a ringing in Ryan's ears. And it wasn't from the clatter of dishes, the din of voices or the Christmas carols playing in the Buffalo Diner on a Sunday night in early December.

"Quitting?" Ryan very carefully set down his fork and stopped eating his pecan pie so that he could stare across the table at his twin brother. "We made a deal, Tate."

To keep competing in team roping until one or both of them placed high enough in the Prairie Rodeo Circuit that one or both of them would be invited to a postseason, big money, national event. Where they'd earn seed money for a spread of their own.

In fact, Ryan had asked his brother to dinner at the Buffalo Diner to discuss a strategy for moving forward next season. Moving ahead, not stopping. "We're not quitters."

Unlike their biological parents, who'd quit everything they'd ever set out to do, including raise their kids. Which was why Ryan and Tate had a foster family.

"It's just roping." Tate pushed around pecan bits on his pie plate, though most of his slice remained untouched. "You don't need me to compete."

That's an excuse.

Ryan searched Tate's face, gripping his blue jeans behind his knees.

For years, staring at his identical twin was like staring in a mirror. Same square jaw. Same strong nose. Same brown eyes, thick brows and black hair.

Lately, Tate had stopped shaving, claiming to want to grow a beard. For once, a stranger might be hard-pressed to see a resemblance between the brothers.

But Ryan saw more than a stranger would, beard or no. Ryan took note of a twitch in his brother's cheek, an indication of deep-seated worry. And he couldn't ignore Tate's reluctance to look Ryan in the eye, a tell that something important was being left unsaid.

Evie Grace approached their booth, planting her flashy yellow cowboy boots tableside. "Evening, boys." Despite addressing them both, Evie directed a practiced smile at Tate.

Ryan was used to being on the periphery of Tate's atmosphere. He rubbed his palms over his thighs, waiting for Evie to have her moment in Tate's sun.

"Evie." Tate acknowledged her with the nice, friendly smile he was known for, before glancing at her boots. "You must have a pair of boots in every color."

"Near abouts." Her smile grew. "I just bought a big-screen television. It's perfect for watching any sport, including the rodeo Nationals. You should come over."

"That's nice of you to offer." Tate tipped his hat, still looking as friendly as a well-fed puppy. "I'll let you know."

Ryan waited for her to make her exit before resuming their conversation. "Are you throwing in the towel because we didn't qualify this year?" They'd both had a slump midsummer and had never recovered their standing. "We almost made it."

"We did." Tate clenched and unclenched his rope-throwing hand, although not all the way. His fingers were still bruised and swollen from a recent ranch accident. "Our scores and rankings are separate, Ry. You can go on competing without me."

Ryan could but he didn't want to leave his

twin behind. "If you're worried about your hand, don't be. Doc said nothing's broken."

They'd taken test rides on a new bucking bull their foster father had purchased for his rodeo stock company. Test rides on bucking stock were nothing new. They'd been doing them for nearly twenty years for fun. But this time, Tate's fingers had twisted in the rigging when he was thrown, and he'd been fretting over the injury ever since.

Or he's worried about something else.

"Hey, Tate." Sophie Jean Godert, a pretty redhead, stopped by their table, smiling at Tate, receiving a smile in return. She gave Ryan a tentative glance.

Ryan ignored her. It wasn't him she'd come over to talk to.

"You've done something different with your hair," Tate told Sophie Jean, smiling at her as if she was his one and only. "Looks nice."

"You noticed." Sophie Jean tittered like a lark. "Are you going to be at the Buckboard on Saturday?" At his smile and nod, Sophie Jean said, "Save a dance for me?"

"I'll try." When she moved on, Tate showed Ryan his bruised fingers. "You see this? It's a sign."

"It's not a sign." Unlike their estranged biological mother, Ryan didn't believe in them.

If they hadn't been in a window booth at the Buffalo Diner and sitting in front of God and everyone in Clementine, Oklahoma, Ryan might have said the words louder. Instead, he tried to style a reassuring smile after Frosty the Snowman, currently on display as a pepper shaker on their table. "If anything, it means you should retire from recreational bull riding. Now, enough with the quitting. Let's talk about changes we should make for next season."

A group of cowgirls stopped at their booth.

Kiera Edwards artfully tossed her long blond hair over her shoulder. "Didn't see you two at the Buckboard last evening." The statement was directed at Tate.

Ryan sighed, ready to wait out the women vying for his twin's attention.

"It was poker night at the Done Roamin' Ranch." Tate gave each woman a smile and a compliment about their hair, their hat or their boots. "We'll be at the Buckboard next Saturday," he promised.

We.

When it came to the single Oakley brothers, the single women in town were only interested in Tate, the Oakley who was always open to their charms. And for the most part, Ryan was fine with that.

The ladies spotted a trio of friends and moseyed along. Tate set his elbows on the table and frowned at Ryan. "It wouldn't kill you to be nice every once in a while. It makes people feel good. It would make you feel good."

Ryan frowned right back at him. "And it wouldn't hurt you to think about the future every once in a while—to make *us* feel good. We're thirty-one. That's young in rodeo years but ancient when it comes to having a place of your own." They lived in the bunkhouse at the Done Roamin' Ranch, their foster parents' operation.

"You know what I'm talking about." Tate's frown deepened. "You spend so much time looking up to make sure there's a roof over our heads that you're missing out."

"On what?"

Tate waved his good hand around, possibly gesturing toward the single women in attendance, possibly indicating the holiday decorations in the Buffalo Diner, which were intense.

Christmas music played beneath the sound of the hungry dinner crowd. It was the season to be jolly, and most folks in Clementine, Oklahoma, were gushing with the holiday spirit.

An old memory surfaced...

Two Christmas tree sugar cookies lay on the coffee table, each with a wooden matchstick stuck in the middle. Ryan and Tate couldn't have been more than eight or nine years old.

"Jingle bells… Jingle bells…" Mom lit each matchstick. "Here's to having a roof over our heads at the holiday. Now, blow out your candles and wish each other a merry Christmas. Santa missed our house this year, but if you're really good, he'll find us next year."

Bah, humbug.

Santa had a bad record of finding the Oakley boys.

Yeah, Ryan wasn't much for the enthusiasm of the holidays given he'd been deprived of them during the first thirteen years of his life. And having grown up with so little, Ryan couldn't wrap his head around the expense of the Christmas season—decorations, cards, holiday sweaters. It was surprising to him that Tate didn't feel the same way.

But then again, Tate was more of a glass-half-full type of guy, while Ryan…

Inside, I'm as sour green as the Grinch.

Guarded. Standoffish. Hard to get to know. The cold twin.

Or so people used to say when the Oakleys first came to Clementine as foster kids.

Back then, Ryan lived in fear of his parents

arriving to take them back. And at school, he'd had to watch Tate's back as well as his own. You couldn't just make friends with anyone who returned Tate's carefree smile and naive trust. Kids took advantage. They wanted your lunch or your new shoes or to give you drugs or cigarettes. Foster boys couldn't be labeled as troublemakers, or they'd be sent to a new home. And since Ryan liked the Done Roamin' Ranch, Ryan had watched out for both of them. He still did.

So, yeah. Ryan was the guarded, hard-to-get-to-know, cold Oakley twin. But he was also the Oakley who planned for the future.

"There's more to life than roping competitions and rodeo dust." Tate's gaze roamed everywhere but Ryan's face. "I'm hanging up my competition spurs."

"We like the rodeo life," Ryan said with complete composure, although inside his stomach was doing a barrel roll. "And we like rodeo dust."

"Do we?" Tate stroked his beard.

Again, Ryan wondered what was really going on inside his twin's head.

"Are you quitting the D Double R?" The Done Roamin' Ranch was a stock company that provided roughshod livestock to rodeos inside and outside of Oklahoma, from Houston to Greensboro to Chicago to Denver. Ryan and Tate, and a dozen other ranch hands, drove cattle rigs and managed animals during rodeos, which was convenient since their competition travel expenses were covered by the job.

"I'm not quitting the Done Roamin' Ranch," Tate said in a hollow voice that implied he held back a word: *yet.* "At some point, Ry, we have to stop dreaming and be realistic." But Tate still didn't look Ryan in the eye, making his words land hard on the wrong side of the buzzer. "We're glorified ranch hands, not rodeo stars."

"That's not true." Ryan stabbed his fork into his pecan pie slice to keep himself from pounding his fist on the table. "What brought this on? Did some horse stomp your foot when you weren't looking?"

"No, of course not. And don't be such a darn fool." Tate slid out of the booth. "I'll see you back at the ranch."

"Hang on." Ryan caught his brother's arm when he would've walked past. "Give me one more year. I want to upgrade our mounts." But he'd hesitated broaching the topic since quality horseflesh was luxury-sports-car expensive to midranking cowboys like them. "We need better horses. That's the only difference between the Pierce brothers and us."

The Pierce brothers had come in first place in the Prairie Circuit this year. And last year. And the year before. Their horses were fast and smart with cows in the arena. If they wanted to make Pierce money, they needed horses like the Pierces had.

Just like they have.

"We can't afford better mounts." Tate stared at Ryan's hand. "Isn't that a sign?"

"It's not a sign. Look, at least think about it." Ryan let his hand drop. "Horses bred and trained for the rodeo will put us in the next tier of prize money."

"Enough to cover the cost of the mounts?" Tate shook his head. But at least he wasn't walking away.

"If we make the postseason, it will." It was a gamble. Ryan knew it. But it was a play he was willing to make. "We can do this. We can buy our own spread."

"By shelling out our savings to buy horses?" Tate said cynically. "How is money spent on horses for a dream any different than money thrown away on booze or cards?" The latter being the downfall of their parents.

"An investment in yourself is never money wasted," Ryan said, sounding like a fortune-cookie fortune. But he believed it. He believed in them.

A familiar red truck drove past their window, illuminated by the streetlights. Ryan trailed its progress to the feed store. "You wanted a sign? There it is."

Tate followed the direction of his gaze. "No."

"Why not?" Ryan downed his coffee and then got to his feet.

Tate gave him a look that said he thought Ryan was confused. "Not her."

"Yes, her." Joanna Pierce was a local horse breeder and trainer, the younger sister of the winning Pierce brothers and provider of their mounts. "I'm going to ask her to sell us a pair of horses. Do you want to come along?"

"Nope." Tate shook his head. "You're wasting your time. Those horses cost serious money and she's never liked you."

Ryan paused, frowning. "You mean she's never liked *us*." They'd always been something of a package deal.

"Not *us*." Tate shook his head again. "Jo Pierce doesn't like *you*. Have you forgotten the high school pranks you pulled on each other our senior year?"

"No. But that's just water under the bridge." Their rivalry had ended when they graduated high school. Ryan shoved his arms into his jacket, settled his cowboy hat on his head and grinned at his twin. "Wish me luck."

"You're gonna need it." Tate walked out.

Ryan settled up their bill, thinking about Jo and the pranks they'd pulled on each other. It had all been harmless fun...hadn't it? He hoped she thought so.

CHAPTER TWO

Ryan pushed through the door of Clementine Feed on a mission to buy a pair of horses.

Immediately, he was assaulted with a plethora of holiday greenery, sparkly ornaments, plush stuffed Santas of every size and shape and piped Christmas carols.

He craned his neck, searching the store for Jo. To his right, there were circular racks full of shirts and jackets for men, women and children. Wooden cubbies had been built along one wall for blue jeans. The opposite wall had hats hanging on display and boots on shelves.

No Jo.

On the other side of the store, you could find anything in the tall aisles for the care of pets and livestock. Tack, leashes, cat beds, mousetraps. He walked past row after row.

No Jo.

And at the counter behind it all, you could place an order for larger amounts of feed, fencing, lumber supplies or power tools.

Success!

Jo stood at the counter talking to Izzy Adams, who was working the cash register. Jo wore what was typical for winter ranch wear in Oklahoma—a gray hoodie underneath a maroon puffed vest, cowboy boots and hat, blue jeans. Except the hat that sat on her short brown hair was the wide-brimmed style few favored, and her jeans were tucked into her plain brown boots, also not a popular style. She'd always been…well…old-school. And she'd always been stubbornly proud of it.

Jo was accompanied by two miniature cowboys who were manhandling the gingerbread ornaments hung on the Christmas tree next to the counter.

The boy with the green jacket plucked a gingerbread man from the tree and took a bite, chewing open-mouthed as he laughed at his sibling. "I told you I'd do it!" Crumbs spewed from his mouth.

"Eww." The boy with the blue jacket shoved his brother back. "Mom! Max ate a dog cookie!"

And then both boys started to laugh.

And Ryan, being a twin who'd experienced his share of moments just like this one— *although not the dog-biscuit-eating kind—* chuckled along with them.

"Boys, behave." Jo spared them a stern glance that silenced all laughter in the feed store before turning back to Izzy to say, "Add a dog treat to my tab."

Jo was one of those no-nonsense, working cowgirls. Rough-and-tumble. Full of try and talk as a kid. And when she got older, as touchy as a spring bee. She'd done well at several sports in school, and during their senior year, she spoke her mind to the point she'd had a desk on reserve in detention, right next to Ryan's. Something of a rebel, she'd eloped with her high school boyfriend on graduation night.

Several months later, Jo had given birth to those two twin boys. Once she'd become a mother, she'd changed. Straightened out her life. Ditched Bobby and his last name. Took over her family's ranch operations and horse training, buying the small spread from her dad, making it into something. She became known around Clementine as a hard worker and someone who didn't put up with any guff.

For the life of him, Ryan couldn't remember how their high school rivalry had begun. The last few months of their senior year had been filled with pranks on each other, escalating until one final act before graduation— Jo had taken Ryan's motorcycle and put it in the old oak tree in front of the high school.

He'd been livid. She'd been expelled.

And that was the end of that.

Suddenly, a wave of doubt washed over Ryan. He and Jo weren't friendly nowadays. She might still hold a grudge. If she did, buying mounts from Jo wasn't going to be easy. It might, in fact, be nigh on impossible without some serious apologizing.

How badly do I want to win?

He didn't need to think twice: *To the nth degree.* Ryan wanted a place he and Tate could call home. He wanted to make sure they wouldn't just quit.

Jo's cell phone rang. She dug it out of her vest pocket and hit a button. "Ma, why are you doing a video call?" Jo held her phone at eye height.

From where Ryan stood behind Jo, her phone display was filled with a side view of someone's cheek and lips. There wasn't enough of a face to identify the caller, even if he knew it was Jo's mother.

"I didn't call you on video," Lois Pierce said, still holding the phone and its camera next to her cheek.

"You did call using video, Ma." Jo showed her boys the screen. "Can you see Grandma?"

"Yes!" Her kids chortled.

"You hit the video button. Again." Jo turned

the phone screen back to herself. "At least hold the phone in front of your face."

Ryan smiled. His foster father, who he endearingly called Dad, was similarly challenged by technology.

Mrs. Pierce's features came into view on Jo's screen—short brown hair, age-spotted face. "I was trying to do the loudspeaker thing. Can I help it if my little phone buttons are… *little*?"

The boys continued to laugh. The gingerbread dog biscuit Max had bitten into was handed over to the boy with the blue jacket, who took a bite. A gagging noise followed immediately.

"Dean! Boys! There will be no more dogbiscuit eating." Jo snatched the remains of the gingerbread man from her precocious son, tucking it in a vest pocket. "What do you need, Ma?"

"Replacement bulbs for the outdoor lights. The big, colorful ones." Mrs. Pierce craned her neck, as if looking for someone. Perhaps Ryan, since she appeared to be peering at him. "And a cowboy. Bring yourself one home."

"Ma…" Jo said in a tone that implied eye rolls were being made. "They don't sell cowboys at the feed store."

"But I see one," Mrs. Pierce singsonged, waving.

Jo turned and spotted Ryan, who was the only cowboy in the store besides the boys. She quickly spun back around but not before he registered a Christmas wreath on that sweatshirt of hers. "I'll see you at home, Ma." Jo ended the call and tucked her phone back in her pocket. The way Jo was hunching her shoulders made Ryan suspect that Tate was right—Jo still held a grudge against him.

Ryan didn't much care what folks thought about him. But with Jo...

Steady now.

He shifted his feet, as fidgety as Suzie before a roping run. A lot was riding on the next few minutes. But those hunched shoulders of Jo's meant the outcome was uncertain. And because of his early childhood, uncertainty triggered his fight-or-flight reflex.

Steady now. I need those horses. For the future. For Tate.

"Your mom is like my mom, Jo." Izzy laughed. "Unhappy while I was married to my ex-husband but perpetually unhappy with my single status."

"Yep," Jo agreed.

Ryan settled his nerves, picked up his feet

and sauntered up to the counter as if he was interested in feed. "Hey, Izzy... *Jo.*"

Jo spared him a chilly glance from beneath her wide-brimmed, white cowboy hat.

Just like old times.

Except Ryan's pulse increased and he had the strongest urge to smile, a reaction he associated with attraction to the opposite sex. But not to Jo Pierce. Never to Jo Pierce.

My wires must be crossed.

Definitely. His emotions were all tangled up by the possibility of Tate retiring and getting stuck as a ranch hand forever with nothing to look forward to but a weekly paycheck and the comfort of the bunkhouse.

"Merry Christmas, Ryan," Jo said dismissively. Her words were as cool as the weather, and her wishes early by his estimation. Christmas was still weeks away.

Bah, humbug.

He hoped to keep Christmas out of their transaction.

"Give Ludlow a few minutes before you pull up to the loading dock," Izzy told Jo, handing her a receipt for her purchases. "I'll be with you in a couple of minutes, Ryan." And then Izzy disappeared into the back room.

A few minutes.

Ryan hoped that was all he needed. Time to break the ice and test the waters. He smiled at Jo. "How about those Cowboys?"

Jo tucked a small wallet into her vest pocket and zipped it closed. And then she glanced at Ryan again. The ice storm descended, hardening her features just like they used to in high school. "Are you talking to me?"

"He is, Mom." One of her boys came to stand at her side, the one with the blue jacket. He had Jo's inquisitive brown eyes and Bobby Leith's dark brown hair beneath a dingy straw cowboy hat. "Which cowboys are you talking about, mister?"

"The…uh…football team." At their blank looks, he added, "The Dallas Cowboys?" Lots of folks in Oklahoma rooted for them.

"We don't watch football. Let's go, Dean." Jo placed one hand on Dean's back and glanced toward the other boy, who was still admiring the tree. Or the gingerbread dog biscuit ornaments. "Move it, Max."

Ryan's hopes sank. Although they both lived in Clementine, he realized they didn't interact at all. That was something he needed to remedy if he wanted to do business with her. The question was…how?

Tate would smile and make nice. Tate would be helpful.

"Don't lollygag, Max." Jo, and Ryan's chances, took a step toward the door.

"I guess you're an Oklahoma City Thunder fan, then?" Ryan eased into her path, trying not to look desperate. "Basketball?"

"Ryan," she said wearily. "I don't watch sports."

"No sports," Max told him, coming to stand next to Jo, a mirror image of his brother if not for the mischievous glint in his eyes.

"No sports except rodeo," Dean said proudly, hooking his thumbs in his belt loops, like a cocksure cowboy twice his age and half again his height.

"Why does *everybody* assume I watch sports?" Jo narrowed her eyes as she stared at Ryan.

He got the message. Today, *everybody* meant Ryan, and talking sports to her was a form of guff. He rocked back on his heels, both physically and emotionally. "I…uh…I was just trying to be friendly." Like Tate, who everyone gravitated toward and made small talk with.

"You and I aren't friendly." Jo's stare was as hard as a steer's horn and just as capable of wounding him. "And I'd like to keep it that way."

"There's no harm in mending fences with someone you might do business with." Ryan was past the point of backing down. "Or someone you have history with."

"I don't like our history." Jo dug in a vest pocket and drew out her truck keys. "And I'm not doing business with you, Ryan."

Her boys stared back and forth at the adults before them with open mouths.

"Why don't you like him, Mom?" Max gave Ryan a considering look, going so far as to poke Ryan's boot with the toe of his. "He doesn't look like he's out to steal our last dollar."

"I bet he wants to buy a horse." Dean sized Ryan up. "And you said we need to sell horses before Christmas."

Jo rolled her eyes and almost smiled. "Are you two my business managers now?"

"Yep." Max grinned.

"Do you have any money, mister?" Holding out his hand, palm up, Dean wasted no time on jokes.

"On me?" Ryan blurted.

"He's on the Prairie Circuit." Jo stared at Ryan as if this was his biggest sin.

"Oh," both boys said, crestfallen.

The mood among the trio turned as solemn as a funeral.

Ryan smiled harder. "Last I checked, roping in the Prairie Circuit isn't a sin."

She tsked. "I promised my brothers I wouldn't sell to anyone in the Prairie Circuit."

That explained so much. And posed a problem that gave Ryan pause.

"Merry Christmas, Ryan." Jo moved around him toward the door, pointed chin held high.

Forget her body language. That was two Christmas wishes in the last five minutes. More goodwill than their history might warrant. He couldn't give up now.

"Hang on. If you need to sell a horse and I'm in the market to buy a pair," Ryan said plainly, no guff intended, "we should set up a time to…"

She stopped, fixing Ryan with a questioning look, cutting him off without actually saying a word.

They stared at each other. Again, Ryan's pulse ticked up a notch and his smile came more easily, the way it did when he was interested in a woman.

But not Jo. Never Jo.

Nope, nope, nope. It's because of old times.

Their rivalry had been…invigorating. *Invigorating?*

Jo shook her head.

"Why not?" If it was something Ryan couldn't get past, he'd look elsewhere. It was just that he'd set his sights on her horses. And once he set his mind to something, he was as stubborn as a mule about getting it. "Why not sell to me, Jo?"

Her cheeks flushed with color.

Max elbowed Dean, giving his twin a trouble-making grin. "Mr. Ryan, don't you know you ain't supposed to ask *why* when Mom's already explained it once?"

Dean nodded solemnly, staring up at Ryan with pity in his young gaze. "I'll say it again so you can remember it." The kid cleared his throat. "Mom promised our uncles not to sell to Prairie Circuit team ropers."

"Plus, she doesn't like you," Max added, grinning gleefully.

"I've gotten past worse obstacles than this," Ryan told them, hanging on to his smile and the impulse to say he could remember a lot.

"Boys, wait in the truck." Jo's voice was brittle, her stance solid. Only that cheerful holiday wreath on her sweatshirt indicated softness.

"You're in for it now, mister," Dean prophesied, taking a step back.

Max placed his hands over his ears, exchanging a grin with his brother.

"Stop that, boys." Jo's brittle facade cracked with a hint of a smile, a thin ray of warmth. "Ryan is going to think I'm an ogre."

"Never." Ryan leaped at the opening, no

matter how small it might be. "Let's just by-pass all the hoopla and make a date."

Jo froze again, mouth forming a little O.

"My mom doesn't date." Max's eyes were wide. His smile gone.

"She says her love of horses is enough." Dean nodded.

They think I want to date Jo?

"Uh…hang on." Ryan tried to backpedal, but he wasn't fast enough.

"Grandma wants her to date," Dean said solemnly.

"And Miss Ronnie says she knows Mr. Right," Max added. Miss Ronnie being Jo's friend, a school secretary and a part-time matchmaker for ranch and rodeo folk. "That can't be you, though, 'cause she doesn't like you."

"Uh…" Ryan said, mind blank. He couldn't even muster a smile Tate would be proud of.

"If you could get Mom to date you, she might sell you a horse." Max looked Ryan up and down judgmentally. "Do you like the look of him, Mom?"

"He's all right, I suppose," Dean said, giv-ing Ryan a similar inspection. "But if you want a horse, you have to date Mom more than once. You think you can do that, mister?

Grandma says she's as prickly as a dried-out tumbleweed."

"Boys." Staring at her boots, Jo rubbed her forehead. "Please go to the truck."

Again, the twins didn't budge.

Relieved, Ryan tried again. "When I mentioned a date, I was…asking when I could look at those horses you want to sell. Not…"

"I know." Jo settled her cowboy hat on her head, blew out a breath that seemed blush erasing and got right down to business. "Even if I would sell to you—*which I won't*—you can't afford my prices." She leaned forward and gave him a number. "That's per horse."

Forty thousand dollars per horse?

Ryan held his breath. Her prices had gone up since last he'd heard.

A part of Ryan—*the responsible part*—passed out on the floor from shock. But somehow, he stayed on his feet. And somehow, he managed to smile and say, "So, when should I come by?"

He should have expected her response.

"Never."

CHAPTER THREE

"Mom, why do Uncle Ty and Uncle Eric get a say in who we sell our horses to?" Max asked as Jo pulled away from the feed store.

"Is it because you won't let them ride anything but our horses?" Dean asked.

I wish that was the case.

What might better be wished for was a reduction of curiosity. Her eleven-year-olds had started asking questions when they were three and hadn't stopped since. Most days, Jo welcomed their inquisitiveness as an educational opportunity. But today, she could have used a little less curiosity toward her least favorite cowboy in Clementine.

"We're family. And family support one another." Jo repeated what her older brothers had told her years ago, when she'd agreed to their demands in order to keep peace in the family the way Ma wanted her to. But her brothers' words didn't hold water when there were bills to pay and team roping buyers on the Prairie Circuit at her door. Buyers like Ryan Oakley.

Ugh. Had she really sunk that low that she'd consider selling to her high school nemesis?

Her good-looking, sexy-just-breathing, archenemy?

He's not Tate...

But that didn't answer the question.

The question she needed to be asking was of her brothers and their request that she limit her business, of which they had no part in.

Maybe I should just tell them I'm going to start selling to folks on the Prairie Circuit.

That wouldn't go over well. And she didn't want to rock the boat until after Nationals in Las Vegas, where Ty and Eric's performance might create a much-needed boost in demand for her horses.

"Our uncles only win on our horses," Dean said, yawning.

"Can we drive by the Christmas houses before we go home?" Max caught the yawning bug, too. "I love Christmas."

"Me, too," Dean said sleepily.

"Me, three." Jo loved the pretty lights and festive packages beneath a colorful tree. She always looked forward to traditions, too, like holiday shopping with her girlfriends and Clementine's Santapalooza, a parade of over one hundred riders dressed as Santa on Christmas Eve morning.

Jo made a turn to drive down Jefferson Street, which was filled with some of the oldest homes in Clementine and some of the biggest displays of holiday cheer—festive lights, lawn displays, outdoor Christmas trees. One house even had a miniature steam train running along a track on the driveway.

"I've seen Mr. Ryan before," Max said slowly. "At the rodeo and at the Done Roamin' Ranch."

"I like him." Dean sighed heavily, the way eleven-year-old boys did after a long day running around a ranch. "I hope we sell him a horse and he wins."

"You want him to beat your uncles?" Jo grinned.

"Maybe just once," Dean said slowly.

"If he asks you out," Max added.

Date Ryan Oakley? Jo struggled to grasp the concept.

Back in their senior year of high school, she and Ryan had been too much alike. Obstinate, defensive, angry. And always in detention together.

She'd been that way because that was the year her father began an affair and flaunted it all over town. When he was home, her father was always trying to pick a fight with her mother and wanting the kids to choose sides. Dad had won over Ty and Eric, leaving Jo to defend their mother, who refused to fight in the name of trying to keep the family together. Somehow that fall, she'd become defensive about anything and everything with everyone and had been unwilling to keep all that vulnerability bottled inside. She'd risked friendships, a high school diploma and her future. She hadn't cared.

Where had that ornery Jo been when her brothers proposed she not sell to their competitors?

Ryan Oakley would never have agreed to such a demand. He was one of the Done Roamin' Ranch fosters, one of the prickliest of the lot. Back in school, no one had seen or heard anything about his and Tate's parents. They'd come from the next county over. Unlike Jo's parents, who were the talk of the town. And somehow, in the midst of her own problems, the mystery of the Oakleys had made Jo curious.

The first time she and Ryan had been in detention together their senior year—Jo for sassing a teacher, Ryan for incomplete assignments—Jo had worked up the nerve to ask him, "Where are your parents?"

His sharp stare had practically drilled a

hole between her eyes. "My dad didn't cheat on my mom, if that's what you mean."

"Now I see why they say Tate is the nice Oakley," Jo had snapped back. And that might have been the end of their skirmishes if not for an incident a few weeks later.

It was a tradition at Clementine High School for kids in each class to draw names in December for a week of Secret Santa gift giving before the holiday break. Jo had drawn Tate's name. The first gift she'd planned to give him was sugar cookies with peppermint icing. She'd bribed his ex-girlfriend for his locker combination and had come extra early Monday morning to plant them in his locker. And then she'd waited down the hall for him to arrive, wanting to see his reaction, imagining the smile on his face, a smile she'd have been responsible for.

But it was Ryan who opened the locker. And Ryan who took her plate of cookies and dumped it in the trash. And Ryan who'd broken the last straw inside Jo, making a declaration of war. Over the next six months, she'd pranked him endlessly, ruthlessly and without regret.

Instead of taking it lying down, Ryan had given back as good as she'd dished out.

And now he had the nerve to ask to buy a horse from her?

Never.

Never?

That was pride talking. The voice inside her head that kept track of things like the balance of her bank account and the due date of mortgage payments… That voice had a different reaction.

Sell. Sell many. Sell often.

She couldn't afford pride.

Jo took the road out of Clementine, trying to convince herself that selling to a man she didn't like was the adult thing to do. Oh, but that was a tough internal conversation to hold. And she had to hold it in silence. The boys had fallen asleep in the back seat.

She let them, thinking more about the logistics of Ryan's unexpected request. It opened a can of worms with Ty and Eric, but it was a can she'd been avoiding for the past few years.

There were thirteen PRCA rodeo circuits in the United States and Canada, of which the Prairie Circuit was one. During the main rodeo season, cowboys in the market for a competition horse had to be able to swing by Clementine. Remote as she was, it was hard to promote and sell her horses, especially when her brothers had limited her nearest market for sales. She'd supplemented her income by training horses for others, buying horses from pleasure riders and training them to be ranch mounts and generally watching every penny. But now there was a balloon payment coming due on the ranch, owed to her estranged father. Two horse sales had fallen through last month, plus there'd been the return of another.

Jo sighed. She needed to find funds somewhere. Inquiries continued to trickle in, but no one wanted to visit or purchase a horse until after the New Year. After her balloon payment was due. Her father may have personally financed the ranch mortgage, but he was rabid for her to fail.

Jo turned into the driveway of the Pierce Ranch. The Christmas lights outlining the house had come on automatically. Their bright red, blue, green and yellow bulbs welcomed her home. Behind the house, the large roof of the first barn rose up into the dark night sky. She drove past the house and to the barn, then set about unloading the hay bales and feed supplements.

Blue, their ranch dog, came out to offer moral support, happily wagging his whiplike tail. He was a leggy, short-haired dog of uncertain lineage with a heart of gold and was delighted to eat the rest of Max and Dean's gingerbread dog biscuit.

When Jo was done, Blue hopped in the truck with her. She parked in the attached garage and tried to rouse the boys.

"Carry me, Mom," Max mumbled, eyes shut tight.

"Carry me," Dean echoed.

They may have just turned eleven, but they were still young in many ways. A part of her didn't want them to grow up. So she caved.

"We're back." Jo entered the kitchen, carrying a groggy Max in a saggy piggyback position.

"You're just in time," her mother said, patting Blue on the head when he came to beg for treats in the kitchen. Her brown hair was shorter than Jo's, bangs covering her eyebrows but not the nape of her neck. Her nails were short, too. Everything about the Pierce women was utilitarian. "I tried a new apple pie recipe and it's out of the oven. Let's sit and have a slice."

"I need to do my rounds first."

"Okay, but I want details about that cowboy in town," her mother called after her. "He looked like one of those Oakleys. I know they're single."

"I'm not looking for a man, Ma." Especially not Ryan Oakley. "You know, I'm in a relationship with my horses."

When she returned, her mother had spread silver, velvety material over the kitchen table and was pinning a paper pattern to the fabric. "Only a few more Santa costumes to make before the annual Santapalooza parade." A ride where folks of all ages dressed up like St. Nick and rode their horses through Clementine. Ma was on the organization committee and made costumes for the event.

"In silver?" That gave Jo pause. "Doesn't Santa wear red?"

"I thought Santa needed to shake things up this year. I'm only making a couple, but it might give us a boost in terms of social media if Santa dressed out of his comfort zone."

"We don't need to make the event bigger, you know." Jo grabbed a fork and stole a bite of warm apple pie, which was just as good as it smelled—sweet and cinnamony. "I like knowing who all the Santas are."

"Including which cowboys don't like to don a white beard at the holidays?" Ma chuckled.

"It's not a crime to have a list of requirements for a man I date." Jo stuck her nose in the air. The next time she got serious about a man, he'd be nice, love his family and adore everything about Christmas the way she did. Even strained families came together at Christmas.

"Which Oakley was in the feed store?" Ma smoothed a pattern piece that didn't seem to lie right. "The one who rides in Santapalooza or the one who doesn't? Not that it matters. They both have such handsome, expressive features."

"It's the eyebrows." They were dark and thick. And when they were younger, an Oakley eyebrow waggle—mostly Tate's—had caused many a swoon. Jo wasn't immune. But she was Team Tate when it came to the Oakleys. Tate was the good-natured twin, the one she'd never had an unkind exchange with, the only man she ever so much as dreamed about dating.

Not that Tate knows I'm alive.

Jo stepped over Blue and headed toward the garage. "It was Scrooge Oakley at the feed store. And before you head down the hearts-and-flowers road again, you know I could never be with a man who didn't love Christmas." Everyone in town knew Ryan only reluctantly participated in the holiday.

"I could sway him to the jolly side." Ma fiddled with a straight pin to reduce fabric pucker. "Everyone should have a merry

Christmas. And everyone should find their forever love."

"Here we go again."

Ma sniffed, picking up her prize fabric scissors. "I just don't want you to be alone."

"You're alone," Jo pointed out, hand on the cool garage doorknob.

"That's different. I like being a footloose, single grandma." Although Ma's tentative smile hinted otherwise.

"Maybe I like being a footloose, single mom," Jo countered.

"You said *maybe*." Ma pounced on Jo's error. "And everyone likes a redeemed Scrooge."

"Not me. I talked to Ryan about selling him a couple of horses. That's it. End of story." Jo made her exit, shutting the door before her mother could make any more suggestions about her love life. She returned to the house giving a half-asleep Dean a piggyback. "These boys are getting too big for me to carry to bed."

"That's right. You're not getting any younger," Mom said, softening her words by rubbing Jo's shoulder as she passed. "But neither am I."

"You stole the words right out of my mouth." Jo headed down the hall to put Dean to bed.

A few minutes and another bite of pie later, Jo strode to the outbuildings to close them for the night. The barn cats were up and about, ready to pounce on vermin or Blue's wagging tail. Having been pounced on before, the big dog stuck close to Jo's side as she checked on each horse, every filly and colt.

"You talk a good game about being brave, Blue." Jo gave him a reassuring pat in between picking up a lead rope that had fallen from a hook. "But if one kitten looks at you wrong, you make for the hills."

Jo glanced around the barn as the wind pressed against the outer walls. She'd added those walls during the first few years of ranch ownership. Before that, there'd been a roof over the open-air stalls and a metal shed where tack and feed were stored.

When she was little, she could remember running after Eric, Ty and her father in the aisles between stalls, listening to Dad's lectures about horse training, her telling them that she could help, that she could rope, that she was going to be a great horse trainer and run the ranch someday. For the most part, they'd ignored her. But that hadn't deterred Jo. She'd just tried harder to do what her brothers did, to garner her father's attention, to earn his praise.

Thankfully, Eric, who was only three years older than Jo, had taken her seriously when she was eight or nine. Or at least, he'd been willing to mentor her horse training and roping skills. She'd ridden as the header roper while he rode heeler. It had given Eric more time to practice. It had given Jo an insight into how the small things about a horse and rider's performance could make big gains.

Not that her father felt the same way. He'd been raising and training horses part-time back then. The quicker he trained them, the quicker he could make money. He had no patience for refining a horse or rounding out their skills. In hindsight, he preferred to break a horse's spirit to nurturing the animal's drive to compete and win.

Jo could relate. He'd tried to break her spirit, too, but she'd refused to be cowed. She supposed the experience had made her stronger. And yet there was still a little girl inside of her who yearned for her daddy's praise.

Blue had his nose to the ground at a stall door. He whined and scratched the floor. A black cat paw took a swipe at him from the gap beneath the stall door. Blue leaped back.

"Come on, boy," Jo called, shaking off the memories. "Lots to do before bed." Which always came too late, and the morning too early.

They walked out of the first barn and toward the newest one, passing by the wagon waiting to be decorated for Santapalooza. The wagon gave those who didn't have a horse or couldn't ride a way to participate. She and Ma decorated it differently every year. They hadn't decided on a theme for this year and the twenty-fourth was fast approaching. But Jo's to-do list seemed to be growing, not shrinking.

Stress gathered in her chest, quickened her breath, slowed her steps.

Is this the year it all falls apart?

The year she didn't make the mortgage. The year she let the Santapalooza ride and everyone in Clementine down. The year she had to pack up and move on to work for someone else, uprooting the boys and selling off the horses she'd invested her heart and soul in.

Blue woofed and bounded ahead with a carefree, powerful grace that lightened her spirits.

"One step at a time. Right, Blue?" She followed the dog into the second barn, where the horses at the later stages of training and Jo's breeders were kept, repeating her good-night ritual with every horse.

She paused at Tiger's stall near the end of her rounds. The stocky chestnut ambled up to her and submitted to a bit of petting. "What am I going to do with you?"

He blew a raspberry, as if trying to say that the buyer who returned him was full of stuff and nonsense.

"That's enough attitude, mister. If I'm hanging on to you, you need to earn your keep." And since he'd been gelded, breeding wasn't an option.

Breeding… Romance… Love…

Jo moved on, thoughts turning to her dateless life as she finished locking up. Who needed love? Jo had nothing to complain about. She had a social life with her girlfriends. She had family. And two barns full of horses that gave her varying degrees of affection.

But it would be nice to have a man's arms encircle her, to lean against a strong, warm chest, to lift her face and stare into someone's eyes as she waited for a tender kiss.

Jo stared up at the night sky, catching sight of a falling star and making a wish, a young wish, a foolish wish.

For love.

When Ryan pulled into the yard at the Done Roamin' Ranch after talking to Jo, his foster brother Wade was walking his fiancée, Ronnie, to her little green Volkswagen.

The couple were both dressed in jeans, boots and cowboy hats, and bundled into thick winter coats. They spoke quietly, intimately, as they neared Ronnie's car.

Something panged deep inside Ryan. Something he didn't want to name.

He glanced away, attention immediately claimed by the huge Christmas tree in the large window of the main ranch house. His gaze shifted to the inflatable set of reindeer on the lawn, then to the pulsing, colorful lights outlining his foster parents' home. His family went all out on the holiday. Or rather, his foster mother. She was probably inside decorating the interior or making cookies, singing Christmas carols off-key and checking her gift list twice.

Wade opened the car door for Ronnie, one of Jo's closest friends.

Duh. Ryan hopped out of his truck. "Hey, Ronnie, do you have a minute?"

"Sure." She snuggled closer to Wade, jingling her key ring. "What's up?"

Ryan jogged up to them. "I want to pick your brain about Jo Pierce."

"About Jo?" Ronnie, a budding matchmaker, frowned slightly. "If you're looking to date her, you've got a lot of prep work to do first. And I mean, a lot."

"You like Jo?" Wade took a dramatic step back, clutching his chest, teasing the way close brothers did with equal parts affection and mischief. "Yikes. Memories of your senior year. If there was a category in the yearbook for Best Rivalry, they would have put yours and Jo's pictures there. I can't believe there are sparks between you two."

Ryan couldn't either.

But before he could say so, Ronnie weighed in. "I can put my mind to who'd be more open to your charms than Jo, Ryan." As if no women immediately came to mind.

"He has charms?" Wade laughed.

"I'm datable, Wade," Ryan said with strained patience. "I just don't want to date Jo. I want to buy a horse from her and move up the leaderboard."

"Oh," they both said, quieting.

A brisk prairie wind tested the stakes holding the inflatable reindeer to the ground.

"Unfortunately, Jo…" Ronnie began apologetically. "Well, the mere mention of your name makes Jo tense. She hasn't forgotten high school."

The lights outlining the main house's front porch strobed to an instrumental version of "Jingle Bells."

Ryan closed his eyes, pinching the bridge

of his nose. But that couldn't stop the image of his biological parents drunkenly singing along to the same tune as they walked to the car where they'd left their boys on a cold winter night.

He opened his eyes and turned his back on Christmas. "What can I do to convince Jo to sell me a horse?"

"Offer her more than she's asking." Wade wasn't joking.

Jingle bells... Jingle bells...

Ryan's shoulders twinged as if straining under the burden of carrying everything needed to ensure his and Tate's future wouldn't look like their past.

Ronnie nudged Wade with her elbow. "Be nice." She moved away from Wade and took Ryan's hands with her warm ones. "That goes for you, too, Ryan. Be nice to her. Show Jo that you've changed."

"That *I've* changed?" Ryan very nearly shouted the words.

"What are you all doing outside in the cold?" Ryan's foster mother appeared on the porch of the main house, holding a large wreath. "Are you admiring my Christmas display?"

"We are," Ronnie told her. "It's beautiful, Mary."

"And besides admiring all your hard work,

Mom," Wade said cheerfully, "we're giving Ryan advice about Jo Pierce."

And now the cat was really out of the bag.

Mom set down the wreath and descended the porch stairs, smiling with her entire being, most likely because she'd heard Ryan's name and a woman's in the same sentence. Having been unable to have children of her own, she loved all her foster boys. And now she wanted those grown fosters to find love and family. "Are you talking about that slip of a girl Ryan was sweet on in school?"

"I wasn't sweet on her, Mom." Jo had been Ryan's biggest annoyance. She'd gummed his pens with clear nail polish on test day. Gifted him a hollow chocolate heart filled with spicy mustard on Valentine's Day. Glued a pink, plush bunny to the back of his motorcycle for Easter.

"Pfft." Mom smiled, hugging herself against the chill as she joined them in front of Wade's house. Her short gray hair danced in the wind. "Jo occupied your every thought when you were younger."

"Because I was trying to outdo her pranks!" Back then, Ryan wasn't one to let a slight or a jab be overlooked.

"Jo beat you on all counts." Wade draped his jacket around Mom's shoulders. "Your heart was in it, but you were always so stiff and standoffish. It stifled your creativity when it came to that feud. And before you argue, you're still stiff and standoffish."

The cold Oakley.

The name didn't use to rankle.

"Ryan isn't stiff and such with family," Mom said staunchly. "And that's what counts."

"Thanks," Ryan mumbled.

"Bested or not, Ryan, you were sweet on her. I could see it in your eyes," Mom insisted, giving Ryan one of the all-encompassing, heartfelt, supportive hugs she was known for. "You couldn't stop talking about her."

"Because…" Ryan blew out a breath. What was the use in arguing?

He stepped out of Mom's embrace, closed his eyes and counted to ten while his family continued to make outrageous statements about him and Jo. And when counting didn't change the way he was feeling or stop the ribbing, he took Ronnie by the arm and said, "Help me make peace with Jo."

She studied his face with those big, dark eyes of hers. "You're serious about this? I don't want you to hurt her like you did before."

"Me? Hurt her?" There was irony. Ryan shifted, turning his back on the lawn display.

"You should take her dancing at the Buckboard," Ronnie began. "And bring her doughnuts on the weekends. I bet those boys of hers eat their weight in sugar."

"This sounds an awful lot like dating." Ryan was beginning to regret asking for advice. "Focus, Ronnie. Be a friend, not a matchmaker."

After a moment, Ronnie nodded. "Okay. She picks up coffee every morning at Clementine Coffee Grinders after she drops the boys at school. Get there before eight and don't talk about her horses."

"Don't talk about…" Ryan tossed his hands in frustration. "Then what *am* I supposed to talk to her about?"

"Admit you had a crush on her in school," Mom suggested warmly. "And then apologize for being overzealous."

"Apologize? But…*she* started it!"

"And you kept it going," Mom said in her wisest tone of voice. "Despite us telling you to be a bigger person and let it go."

"Ask her for advice about *your* horse." Wade smoothed a lock of Ronnie's hair behind her ear. "Tell her you've given up on buying one of her horses."

"I think Wade's onto something." Ronnie rubbed Ryan's arm, smiling encouragingly.

"Offer to buy her cup of coffee in exchange for her opinion."

"In other words, act like a gentleman," Mom said crisply, handing Wade his coat before turning back toward the house. "I know you've got it in you."

"And if that doesn't work?" Because Ryan doubted it would.

"I've found kissing has a way of changing a woman's mind." And to prove it, Wade wrapped his arms around Ronnie and kissed her as if no one was watching.

"I don't want to date her," Ryan reiterated, although no one seemed to be listening.

Mom laughed, calling over her shoulder, "I think you protest too much."

CHAPTER FOUR

THE BUNKHOUSE WAS QUIET.

Days began early on the Done Roamin' Ranch. Griff and Tate were already asleep. Griff snored softly. Tate breathed deeply. Ryan tossed about in his bunk. The other ranch hands had left to spend the holidays with their loved ones.

Since they'd grown up on the ranch, the bunkhouse represented independence. Foster boys stayed in the main house first until they'd settled in and earned the trust of Frank and Mary Harrison. Back then, the other ranch hands had lived in either the original farmhouse or what was now called the foreman's house.

The bunkhouse was set up like a barracks. There was a kitchenette, a large dining room table, rows of bunk beds separated by dressers, a small living room and television. The bathroom was large and communal.

Having lived in the bunkhouse for more

than seventeen years, Ryan and Tate were ready for a place of their own.

Jingle bells... Jingle bells...

Ryan turned to his side, facing the wall of his bunk. But he could still see the reflection of lights dancing to the holiday tune.

The outdoor Christmas display in front of the main ranch house was still on, despite it being after ten. Most likely, his mother had plugged everything but the timer in.

If they didn't go off in fifteen minutes...

If Ryan wasn't asleep in fifteen minutes...

He'd get up, unplug them.

Jingle bells... Jingle bells...

The lights strobed, creating shadows on the wall. The tune went on.

The lights and music reminded him of sitting in a bare apartment while Tate slept next to him. Ryan would be on the lookout for their parents, watching the light displays on apartment balconies and through windows, telling time by when lights went dark. Wishing instead there were lights on a Christmas tree for him to look at, with presents underneath.

We need better horses.

If not Jo's, then someone else's.

Merry Christmas, Ryan.

Jo's voice returned to him. He hadn't heard

her speak in years. And yet there was something about her voice that was comforting and somehow uplifting. She believed in the holiday enough to wish good tidings to others.

Merry Christmas, Ryan.

He almost felt guilty for not wishing her the same.

He'd much rather have heard her say, *I'll sell you a horse, Ryan.* Even if it was a stretch for him to find financing for the deal.

His body tensed, filled with worry over the unknown.

Jingle bells... Jingle bells...

At this rate, he'd never get to sleep.

He closed his eyes, breathing deeply, trying to relax and find a place inside of him that was devoid of worry, of the sounds of Jo's voice and Christmas. And he did find that place. But Jo's voice... He couldn't shake her. And so, despite his best intentions, he dreamed...

Ryan couldn't get used to the crisp feeling of new blue jeans. When he was standing, he'd put his hands in his back pockets. When he was sitting, he'd cling to the material behind his knees. The stiff, strong material was like a reward for Ryan being tough the first thirteen years of his childhood.

He clung to the backs of his knees as he

sat in the stands at a rodeo arena for the first time. The dust. The nonstop activity. The noise. There was too much...everything.

He didn't know where to look or what to be on guard for. While Tate... His twin blended in, the same as always, so trusting. As if he'd never worried where their next meal came from. Ryan was slower to trust, quicker to catch on to things that might help him later in life, like throwing a rope or riding a horse without falling off.

Clementine's high school rodeo team was holding their annual Fun Day, where they invited kids as young as eleven to compete in a junior rodeo. It was May. Ryan and Tate had only been living at the Done Roamin' Ranch since January. They were new to riding and roping, new to full bellies and warm beds, new to having a posse of boys looking out for them.

A stream of cowboys flashed before his eyes, wearing big belt buckles and telling Ryan to dream big.

And then Ryan and Tate were sitting on horses on opposite sides of a cattle chute. Tate looked nervous. He'd thrown up earlier. There was a lot of pressure on Tate. If he missed roping the horns of the steer or fell

off his horse—which he did on the regular—
Ryan couldn't rope.

"You got this," Ryan told him. "Steady now."

"No pressure." Tate gritted his teeth.

The cattle chute opened, and everything
went in slow motion.

Tate and his horse leaping forward.

Ryan a pace behind.

Tate was taking too much time to throw. Al-
though, miraculously, his rope landed around
the steer's horns when he finally let it loose.
Ryan's subsequent throw was quick, instinc-
tive and looped around the steer's hooves.
The boys from the Done Roamin' Ranch had
cheered. His foster parents had given them
hugs afterward.

Later, they sat in the stands watching oth-
ers compete in different events. Ryan clutched
the backs of his new blue jeans pants legs and
wondered how long they'd be allowed to stay.

A little cowgirl with brown pigtails and a
chocolate chip ice cream cone came to sit be-
hind them. "You're a good roper."

Ryan elbowed Tate. "She's talking to you."
Strangers never approached Ryan.

"Nope." The little cowgirl with inquisitive
brown eyes shook her head. "You're the bet-
ter roper. The heeler is the hardest job, if
you ask me."

Ryan didn't know what to say. He'd seen the girl at school. She wasn't in his class, and he didn't know her name.

She licked the drips from her cone. "I like to rope."

"Aren't girls supposed to do barrels?" Where had Tate gone? He was good with people, unlike Ryan.

"Girls can do anything." Her little pointed chin went up. "Your brother thinks too much when he rides. Good ropers don't think. They do."

She made it sound so easy. Ryan had been trying really hard to fit in so that when his biological parents showed up, his foster parents would say he had to stay. He was a cowboy now. He wanted to belong to the D Double R. The little cowgirl's praise and advice were welcome. Reassuring. They gave him hope for the future.

"I gotta go." The little cowgirl stood, her ice cream gone. "My mare Gumball is gonna have a baby today. Don't forget what I said. You're good."

She left him without him thanking her.

Jingle bells… Jingle bells…

Things got fuzzy before coming back into focus.

His little cowgirl was older now. She had

braces. Her brown hair was no longer in pigtails. It hung in stringy strands from beneath a battered and bent straw cowboy hat. She wore a brace on her wrist. "I heard you broke your arm riding a bull."

"I didn't ride so much as get thrown." His arm was in a sling made of Christmas-patterned flannel his foster mom had made for him, which was embarrassing. But Ryan would deal with embarrassment if it meant staying at the Done Roamin' Ranch.

He and the cowgirl stood in the halls of the high school outside freshman gym class. They weren't participating because of their injuries.

"Did you cry? I got thrown from my colt Gumdrop. I cried. And I didn't even break my arm. It's just a sprained wrist. Did you try out for the rodeo team? I heard you're still a good roper. Does your brother still think when he throws? I love to rope. Dad rented some cattle from Mr. Terence just for roping. Dad said we need fresh cows because me and the boys practice roping so much. But you have to practice a lot if you want to sell a good roping horse. And that's what I want to do. Train and sell good roping horses. Or barrel horses."

She didn't stop talking or seem to care that

Ryan didn't answer. It was as if she didn't know that the other kids called him the cold Oakley and gave him a wide berth. It was... nice.

"I hope you make the rodeo team. My dad won't let me try out. He says we all have to pull our weight on the ranch. I want to be on the team, but Dad says the odds of me winning a cash prize is less than the odds of selling a good horse to a foolish cowboy. I don't know what that means 'xactly. But I do understand it means no rodeo team for me." She sighed heavily.

She was an absolute mess. And adorable in an odd way. If he overlooked her green sweater with candy canes knitted on the front. It had the look of something handmade. The little cowgirl had something of a reputation as a frump, although he'd heard her talk back a time or two to anyone who laughed at her homemade wardrobe.

He never praised her. He never so much as singled her out with a smile of support. It wasn't in his nature. That was Tate's department.

Jingle bells... Jingle bells...

Things went out and back into focus again.

Something was wrong with the not-so-little cowgirl. She'd changed. Completely.

She cut her hair. She didn't talk nonstop. She sat in the back of class instead of the front. She flung open doors so hard they banged into walls. Or she slammed doors shut so fast that the walls shook.

It was senior year. Ryan watched her. Not because he wanted to ask her out but because he was curious about this change. Her brothers had already graduated, and she had no one to look out for her.

Things were changing in Ryan's world, too.

Tate was dating a girl. Nia Plevins was trouble.

Tate refused to listen when Ryan warned him that she was interested in any guy who she could capture and control. Ryan worried about it. He didn't sleep.

The school hallways were filled with Christmas music. A school holiday dance was fast approaching.

Again, Ryan tried to tell Tate that Nia was out to ruin his future—he'd heard the whispers about how she'd dump Tate if he didn't do whatever she wanted when she wanted it. But his twin wouldn't listen. Instead, he put a Santa hat on, let out a jolly ho ho ho and told Ryan he was paranoid.

It was during December that he heard someone say the little cowgirl's father was having an affair. About the same time, his mother showed up, claiming Ryan's father was in prison again and she needed her two boys to help keep a roof over her head.

Tate, being Tate, ran to the bank and gave their mom the money he'd managed to save, despite Ryan trying to stop him. She'd passed through town singing the same song before. But this time, she didn't move along after getting the cash.

Their mother found a place to stay in town and petitioned for custody. Tate broke up with Nia because their mother required all his spare attention and spending money. Again, Ryan tried to talk sense into Tate, this time about their mother. The only reason she stayed and was petitioning for custody was to get the money they'd made working part-time for their foster parents. What good was custody now? They were practically eighteen.

Finally, Ryan gave up arguing. He gave up on a lot of things while sitting in the courtroom listening to his mother present her case. One of the things he gave up was homework, which landed him in detention next to the little cowgirl, where she asked about his parents.

And because Ryan was scared and angry at the world, he told her the meanest thing he could think of. And then he regretted it. But not enough to apologize because he had bigger things to worry about, like Tate derailing his future with some selfish girl who didn't truly care about him, or their mother derailing their future by laying legal claim to them.

Jingle bells… Jingle bells…

Ryan jerked awake. He was sweating. Snatches of the dream came back to him. The stress of fitting in…the worry of wanting to stay…the fascination with a little cowgirl… *Jo.*

He wiped a hand over his face. He'd forgotten they'd known each other in passing when they were younger, only remembering those last few months in high school. He wasn't sure if that made him more or less nervous about seeing her in the morning when he tried to make friends.

She'd meant something to him once, although he couldn't put a name on what that was.

Outside in the ranch yard, the holiday performance of lights and music was still going. It was after midnight. Ryan got out of bed and went to put his boots and a jacket on.

He had to turn off Christmas and finally get some sleep.

CHAPTER FIVE

"MORNING, JO."

Jo glanced up as she approached Clementine Coffee Grinders on Monday morning.

Ryan stood holding the door for her. He was smiling the way his brother Tate sometimes smiled at her. It was a friendly smile. A happy-to-see-you smile. A platonic smile that always managed to break her heart a little.

Or it did when Tate smiled at her like that. But when Ryan flashed those pearly whites?

Jo bit back the smile she hadn't known she was making.

It does nothing for me. At least, that's what she tried to tell herself.

She cleared her throat and stopped drooling over the wrong Oakley. "Morning."

Jo entered the coffee shop, breathing deeply. This was her second cup of the day and the time she savored for self-care and silence while she drove back to the ranch.

"About last night…" Ryan was hot on her heels. He wore a blue jacket over a red hoodie.

She imagined that shade of red was on her cheeks, too.

"I'm not selling to you," Jo said. He was invading Jo's space and destroying her morning ritual. At the rate he was going, she'd want to prank him before the first sip of her coffee order.

"I know you aren't selling, Jo. I wanted to apologize for the past."

Jo did a double take. Ryan looked sincere, from those earnest brown eyes to the absence of an up-to-no-good grin. He stared at her as if really seeing her—Joanna Pierce. Not the troublesome, smug cowgirl she'd been in their senior year of high school.

Her heart *ka-thumped*.

Again, she chalked it up to Ryan looking like Tate.

"I never thanked you for the kind words you gave me when I needed them. I never offered you support in return." He looked pained. "And I could be…cruel."

"Oh." His apology covered a lot of ground. She wasn't entirely sure what it covered. "Okay."

But Ryan wasn't done. "Neither one of us had golden childhoods, and looking back…" He swallowed thickly, as if mending the rift between them was important to him. "It feels like we might have taken our frustrations out on each other. In high school, that is."

That was big of Ryan to say. And most likely true. Jo vaguely remembered him before her senior year. He was quiet and closed off. She'd even talked to him once or twice. She'd been a talkative kid before Dad had his midlife crisis.

"Jo?" Ryan was staring at her while she had a back-in-time moment.

Since he was being magnanimous, it made Jo feel small to hold on to hard feelings. She gave him a brisk nod. "I accept your apology and offer one in return."

His smile grew back to its original size, the smile he'd given her at the door. Such a friendly, happy-to-see-you smile…

Jo caught herself from being swept away to Tate-wishing territory. They may be declaring a truce, but Ryan wasn't, and would never be, Tate. Tate wasn't guarded, distant or sabotaging. Tate didn't tell her to stop the pranks or else. Tate always had a kind word for everyone.

"I came here this morning because I was wondering if you could give me some help with Suzie."

"Suzie?" Something akin to a stab of jealousy had Jo facing Ryan squarely and planting

her boot heels. "If you're looking for match-making help, call Ronnie."

"Suzie is the ranch horse I ride in compe-tition," Ryan said, confusion evident in the bunching of his thick, dark brows.

"Oh." Jo frowned at Ryan, at her tall, hand-some cowboy. He had broad shoulders and... He wasn't hers. Not by any stretch. She blinked, trying to focus on what Ryan was saying.

"Since I can't buy from you—"

"That doesn't mean you can't buy from someone else," she said quickly, testily, back-ing up a little.

"—maybe some training would help shave time off my scores." He signaled the barista. "I'll pay for whatever the lady is having—"

The lady?

"—and a black coffee, two sweeteners." Ryan's handsome features were unfamiliar in their lack of a frown or a suspicious ex-pression.

"You don't need to pay for my drink, Ryan." Jo requested a brown-sugar oat-milk espresso from the barista. "There's a horse trainer north of Tulsa who probably has what you're look-ing for." A lower-priced roping horse.

She'd thought a lot about Ryan's reaction last night to her telling him the asking price of her horses. She'd thought about it too much, actually. As much as he'd tried to hide it, he'd practically recoiled. As much as she needed a sale, it wasn't going to come from him.

The barista filled a cup with ice.

"I'm looking to win big, Jo." Again, Ryan spoke without disdain or superiority, which were basically the only memories she had of their interactions. "You have six horses across five circuits competing with their riders at big events this month. You make winners."

Actually, it's eight horses.

His flattery was hard to brush off. Jo was exceedingly proud of her horses.

Still, she wasn't comfortable doing what Ryan asked. "I can't just give you tips." That implied…something like friendship. They weren't friends. She wasn't even comfortable letting him buy her a coffee. If Ma found out, she'd never hear the end of it. "Why listen to what I say when I haven't seen you on Suzie?"

He shook his head, smiling ruefully. Apparently, he had an arsenal of smiles. Apparently, she was here for it.

"I know you've seen me compete," Ryan said. "You've been at several events this past year."

She nodded. She had. And she had her opinions, even if she kept most of them to herself. "I could give you some general tips."

Something that could be imparted in five minutes or so. "But that's all."

Because when it came to Ryan, she wasn't sure she could take him at face value.

Even when faced with his welcoming smile.

"I HADN'T REALIZED Suzie not being fidgety in the box before a run could impact my time." Like Tate, the mare got anxious in anticipation of a cow's release, which meant Suzie wasn't always ready to go when the gate opened.

He and Jo had been having a nice conversation, sipping coffee and talking horses. It was…surprisingly *not* unpleasant.

That was, if Ryan didn't listen to the holiday music and didn't let his gaze drift to the large Christmas tree in the corner. And if he didn't dwell on the fact that this was Jo Pierce he was talking civilly to, a woman wearing another holiday-themed sweatshirt, whose gaze warmed when she stared at the Christmas tree.

"Let Suzie burn off some of those nerves. You're allowed that time to get set in the box. You should use it." Jo had a steady, brown-eyed gaze. And a steady stream of advice when he asked directly. She didn't offer up anything unprompted. She wasn't the little, chattering cowgirl he'd first met years ago.

After having dreamed of her last night, he kept looking for signs that the little, chatty cowgirl was still there, somewhere inside of Jo.

Not that I'm interested in her like that.

He was curious—that's all.

Ryan realized he was gripping his blue jeans behind his knee and set his hand on his thigh.

"Hey." Cooper Brown, owner of the local brewery, entered, stopping just inside the door to wipe his boots on the mat. "I didn't realize you two were on speaking terms. Did Ronnie set you up? She sends a lot of her matches here for coffee."

Both Ryan and Jo hastily assured him they weren't on a date.

Cooper scoffed as if he didn't believe them. "This explains a lot about our senior year. I guess Ryan will finally ride in Santapalooza."

Not a ho-ho chance in Hades, my friend.

Jo had her palm over her forehead and color in her cheeks. "I should go."

If Jo left under these circumstances, she might never sit and chat with Ryan again.

"Okay," he said quickly, making no move to get up. "Thanks for this. It's funny to think about how you were when you were younger. A real talker. And now you parcel out your words the way I measure oats, as if each ounce counts and isn't to be wasted."

That got a smile out of her, small though it was. The accomplishment gave him the oddest feeling, as if he'd done something monumental to earn that tiny smile.

"You were the one parceling out words when we were young, which is why today feels so odd." She rested her elbows on the table and leaned forward, studying his face. "Are you really Ryan Oakley? Not Tate?"

He knew she meant it as a joke, but her question smarted nonetheless. The mantle of being the grumpy, cold twin to her seemed wrong. "Was I that bad? Back in the day, I mean."

"I think we were both unhappy and acting out," she admitted, shifting uncomfortably in her seat.

Ryan didn't normally try to put folks at ease, but he wanted her to be at ease with him. So, he kept talking. "Most people want to go back and redo their high school experience, but not me. It had its low points. But there were some high points as well. Being on the rodeo team. Going to a dance or two." Being accosted by a chatterbox. He gave her a smile that encouraged her to respond.

Which she didn't. She lurched to her feet.

"So, to recap, you need to take Suzie on some pleasure rides, give her some nonworking attention. Ranch horses are used to work, but I believe competition horses need to feel they're your partner in all things, work and play." She drained her coffee before tossing the cup in the trash.

Ryan took her cue and stood. "Thanks for taking the time to talk. This morning has felt like you and I are just…" *Friends?* Not hardly. He searched for the right words, staring at her no-nonsense wardrobe. "That you're just one of the guys."

"Right." Jo practically made a run for the door.

He barely managed to open it for her. "Did I say something wrong?"

"No. Nothing I wouldn't expect *Ryan* Oakley to say." And in a flash, she'd reached her truck and shut him out.

Leaving him wondering where he'd gone wrong.

Just like one of the guys.

Jo gripped the steering wheel tight all the way home, driving too fast and telling Ryan Oakley off in her head.

Just because I don't wear dresses doesn't mean I'm one of the guys.

She frowned. That was defensive. She should have flung a comeback that hit harder than that. It was just that she couldn't think of one. It couldn't be because in the moments before he'd said that he'd been staring into her eyes the way she'd always dreamed Tate would do, talking about the good days in high school with the rodeo team and dances.

Nope. That wasn't it. She hadn't been allowed to try out for the rodeo team and no one had ever asked her to a dance.

In a bad mood, she rolled up to the main house and a familiar truck parked out in front.

"Dad. What a surprise." And not a good one. Jo got out of her truck just as her father was leaving the house, all thoughts of Ryan Oakley vanishing.

Her old man strutted when he walked. He was built like a bull, barrel-chested and broad. And his personality matched his appearance. He fixed her with an emotionless stare. "Taking the morning off, Joanna? It's no surprise that you owe me a good sum of money."

She refused to rise to the bait. "A sum I have every intention of paying you on time." Not early, sadly.

"Your mother believes otherwise." Her father made a stand, blocking the path to the front door. "She's worried."

Only about my relationship status.

"Mom isn't worried about the finances." Or not nearly as much as Jo. "You'll have your money by Christmas." She hoped.

Dad laughed, a grating sound that was chillier than December's harshest prairie wind. "We were married for more than twenty years. I know when that woman is hiding something from me." He peered at Jo. "And you look much the same."

"Me? Worried?" Jo tried to laugh and nearly choked on the attempt. "I've just come from a meeting with a cowboy looking to buy a pair of horses." *If only.* Jo's stomach knotted.

Her father considered her and those deceitful words, chewing on the inside of his lip. "I admit, you always manage to scrape by. Now, the boys—"

"Wouldn't be as successful if they didn't ride on horses I bred and trained," Jo pointed out. It was hard to believe that once upon a time she'd doted on this man. He'd found bitterness in his midlife crisis and embraced it like a second skin. She'd spent the time since then trying to prove to him that he should be as proud of her as he was of Ty and Eric.

Dad chuckled, expression turning smug.

"You haven't talked to your brothers recently, have you?"

Worry-induced nausea swirled in her belly. "I haven't talked to them since last week. They're in Las Vegas preparing for the Nationals and—"

"They *aren't* riding your horses." Dad hitched his pants and strutted past her.

And Jo had no comeback to that news. If it was true, her best avenue of promotion was lost, along with her hopes of some end-of-the-year sales. Mutely, she watched her father walk to his truck.

Dad opened the door, pausing for one last salvo. "I've been telling Ty and Eric for years that they'd place better nationally with higher-quality horseflesh."

Only because you want to sabotage me to get the ranch back.

Jo didn't bother arguing. She reached for her phone and bolted inside the house, locking the door and placing a call to Eric's cell phone.

"That man…" Ma stood in the living room in front of the Christmas tree and a stack of Santa costumes on the couch. She clung to the hem of her bright red Christmas sweater, looking stunned. "He measured the master bedroom for new carpet. Just barged in there as if he owned the place."

And, of course, her mother wouldn't protest. She never did.

"Technically, he does own the place." He'd financed Jo's mortgage ten years ago. She had just over five years left. But that included six balloon payments, one every December.

"Hello, sis." Eric's voice crackled through her cell phone. Voices and an announcer calling out a time further muddied the clarity of the call. "How are you doing?"

"Is it true?" Jo demanded, dry mouthed, staring at a picture of her and her brothers as kids, all sitting atop a brown draft horse they used to own.

"Oh, you talked to Dad." Eric might have sounded regretful. There was too much background noise to tell. "Yeah. We've been thinking about a change. You know we're in a slump."

"You won the Prairie Circuit three years running." Jo's hands had begun to tremble. "That isn't a slump." She turned the family photo over.

"But we haven't placed in the top ten in any of the Triple Crown postseason events. Dad thinks it's because we need a higher class of mounts."

"If you wanted a higher class of mounts, you could have bought Prince and Pauper from me." The best pair of ropers she'd ever trained.

"Ty said you'd get all emotional." Eric sighed. "This is why we wanted to wait to tell you."

Until I found out by watching you compete?

Jo was frustrated and afraid, two breaths shy of letting the two emotions morph into anger. Two breaths shy of losing her composure and making the situation worse.

She bit her lip, took a deep breath, held on to her mother's sweaty palm. "What are you going to do with the horses you bought from me? Do you have all four with you?"

"We only brought Laurel and Hardy."

"Are you selling them? Or Fred and Ginger?" If they did, she might not be able to sell Prince and Pauper. There would be too many "Jo Pierce–trained horses" on the market.

"We're not going to sell any horses until we do better with this pair we're trying out."

"Nobody *tries out* a new horse at Nationals, Eric. That's just foolish," Jo snapped, losing it. Not only were her brothers gambling in a high-stakes competition, but they'd also rolled the dice and given her snake eyes.

"When you're competing, you can make

your own decisions, Jo. But for now, it's our show," Eric snapped back at her.

"Stay calm," Ma whispered. "It's not worth upsetting the apple cart over."

But it was.

Jo released Ma's hand. "I guess this is an end to our agreement, then. Good thing, too. I've got offers from a team of ropers in the Prairie Circuit."

Eric hung up, leaving her counting the days until the Nationals were over and she could consider her options and send up a prayer for a Christmas miracle.

But no matter what she thought of, her best bet was making a sale to Ryan.

"YOU LOOK LIKE you did the day Jo treed your motorcycle," Tate greeted Ryan in the tack room at the Done Roamin' Ranch, where he was oiling a pair of reins in front of a space heater. He tapped his phone, ending a cheerful Christmas carol coming out of a Bluetooth speaker. "Strike out with Jo again?"

"No." Ryan set his wallet and truck keys on a shelf before grabbing Suzie's bridle. "Jo just called. I'm going to see a pair of her horses tomorrow afternoon." What a surprise that call had been. He'd been too shell-shocked to ask her what had changed her mind since she'd bolted from the coffee shop earlier. Ryan breathed deeply, taking in the comforting smell of leather, hay and horse. He ran his hands along the thin strips of leather that made up Suzie's head stall. "Want to come along?"

"Jo set up a sales ride?" Tate lowered the cleaning cloth, shaking out his bruised fingers while studying Ryan's face. Beneath that beard, Tate's cheek twitched. "For real?"

"Yeah. That's a sign, right?" Ryan tried to sound positive. He hadn't told Tate what Jo's prices were, and he hesitated to do so now. They'd need loans. But luckily, one of their foster brothers was a bank president. "This could be the final piece we need to put us in the big money. We could save for a large down payment on a small ranch and not worry about making a high mortgage payment. Come with me."

"Tomorrow? I can't. I promised Dad I'd drive to Friar's Creek to check out another bucking bull. And before you say anything..." Tate held up his colorfully bruised fingers. "The seller is going to ride the bull, not me or Dad."

"But you'll come later this week," Ryan pressed. "If I like the horses and can work something out with Jo and the bank." A lower price. A payment plan. Something.

"The bank?" Tate pulled a face.

"We need to think of this like we would buying a pair of trucks. We'll need a loan."

Their foster brother Griff came in, setting a saddle on a rack and hanging a bridle on a hook. He took in Ryan and Tate with a cynical eye before grinning. Life was mostly a laugh to Griff. "Ryan, you look like you're cooking up a surprise for Christmas, which is unusual since you never do the annual Santapalooza ride, and you always give gift cards to the feed store as presents. You're as predictable as an annoyed rattler."

"Knock it off." Tate fired his towel at Griff, missing by a mile. "He's looking into buying us a pair of finer-quality roping horses from Jo Pierce."

Ryan breathed a sigh of relief. That was the first time Tate had seemed to really buy into the idea.

"Horses? From Jo Pierce?" At Ryan's nod, Griff laughed boisterously and overly long. "Did you sign a peace treaty? Back in the day, you two were like a pair of billy goats in the same pasture."

"A pair who butted heads more often than not." Tate laughed awkwardly, as if grateful for a change in subject. "If she saw you coming, she'd step into your path."

"We had a…a healthy rivalry is all." Ryan lifted his saddle. "We're moving on, like I said."

"You should move on with other people," Tate said softly, all traces of humor gone.

Other people? Like our parents? Not a chance!

Ryan held Tate's gaze, shaking his head a little. "I'm going for a ride." He stepped toward the door.

His attention was firmly on the future. All he needed was to keep working on moving forward to even better days and forget about looking back to those dire, uncertain times.

CHAPTER SIX

"WHAT ARE YOU DOING?"

Ryan sat in the large, six-bay garage at the Done Roamin' Ranch on Tuesday morning, his motorcycle in front of him. He stared up at his twin. "Isn't it obvious? I'm going to try and get my motorcycle looking good again." He was polishing the engine, having gotten it to start earlier.

"Are you going to sell it?" Tate folded his legs and sat down nearby. He tipped back his cowboy hat and grinned. "Or is this an early midlife crisis?"

"I might take it for a ride a time or two," Ryan admitted, wiping a bit of polish from a crevice. He had many happy memories of riding around on his bike. Seeing it hanging from a pulley system in an oak tree in front of the high school wasn't one of them. "But I want to sell it. Buying a competition horse takes money. And there are a lot of things in here that I don't use."

Tate glanced around. "I suppose we don't

use those golf clubs. Or the two-person kayaks. There are some old video game systems on a shelf back there. I hadn't realized how much stuff we accumulated since we've been here."

"We wouldn't have any of this stuff if we hadn't come to live at the Done Roamin' Ranch." Ryan applied more elbow grease to a stubborn spot of grime.

Tate didn't say anything.

"You have regrets?" Ryan lowered his rag and stared at his brother, taking note of the twitch in his cheek where his beard began. "You don't believe that coming here was the right thing for us? The best thing?"

Tate shrugged. "I realize that our biological dad was a lost cause. But Mom needed us. She had no reason to be sober after what happened that last Christmas we were together."

"We weren't together and I won't apologize." Ryan twisted and turned the rag in his hands until it was as knotted as he was inside because he'd been the one to reach out for help to a teacher and get them into the foster system. "You had a fever. We were hungry. And we hadn't seen Mom or Dad for days."

"I know. I get it. In here." Tate tapped his temple and then resettled his cowboy hat on his head. "But in my heart, I know she needed someone. And I wish that could have been us."

There was no way Ryan would ever change his softhearted twin's mind about that. And vice versa.

"Anyway," Tate said briskly after too long of a pause. "There's probably a lot more things you can sell in here. Maybe Griff will donate his electric bicycle to the cause."

Ryan's spirits lifted at his twin's comments. "You're really getting behind the idea of buying horses, aren't you?"

He shouldn't have said anything.

"I like the idea. But the money... I'm retiring, remember?" Tate got to his feet. "I'm just pointing out that Mom and Dad would probably appreciate us getting rid of the clutter."

That wasn't it and Ryan knew it. "This would be so much easier if you'd tell me what's going on in that head of yours."

"It's my head, Ryan," Tate said before he disappeared out the door.

It was Jo's turn to pick up kids after school.

Dean and Max piled in first after the bell had rung, slinging backpacks inside, shedding jackets and tilting back cowboy hats.

"Boys, where are your manners?" Jo gestured toward Piper and Ginny, girls their age, in their class and in their car pool. The pair was headed toward the truck. "Gentlemen always let girls decide where to sit first."

"Gentlemen? We're cowboys." Max's shoulders fell and he stared open-mouthed at the ceiling as if this was the end of the world. "And Piper always wants the front seat."

"She doesn't always," Dean said. But he moved to the middle seat in the back as if anticipating that fact plus the desire of Max and Ginny to sit next to a window. Dean was her little peacemaker.

Max opened the front door and slid out of the front seat as if he was melting, turning slowly while still leaning against the seat cushion, letting all the cold air in. "Girls, where do you want to sit?"

The girls stopped a few feet away and whispered.

Piper was from the Burns Ranch, located next to Jo's spread. She wore blue jeans, a pink button-down shirt and red jacket, along with a straw cowboy hat. Ginny lived on the Done Roamin' Ranch with her daddy, Wade. She wore a pink cotton dress under a white jacket. Her red cowboy hat coordinated with her red leggings and boots. Looking at the two girls was like looking at herself and Ronnie when they were little—a girlie-girl and a tomboy.

"We're gonna sit in the back on either side of Dean," Piper announced, strutting forward as if she ran the world.

Max climbed back into his seat. He stared straight ahead while closing the door, as if he'd been delivered the biggest shock of his life—discovering that he wanted some of that feminine attention his twin was about to receive.

A glance in the rearview mirror revealed Dean looking the same way he did anytime he was with the other two girls. Relaxed. They were just his friends, not yet *girls*.

"Miss Jo, can we stop by Clementine Coffee Grinders?" Piper asked in a sweet voice.

"For coffee? Not a chance." Plus, she had to get ready for Ryan's visit this afternoon. She drove past the high school, noticing how sturdy the oak tree in front looked.

Strong enough to hoist another motorcycle up there.

Jo smiled. "Why would you want to go to the coffee shop?"

"They sell hot chocolate and smoothies," Piper explained as if Jo had never been there before. "Plus, you can sit at a table and talk."

"Miss Ronnie told me you went there with Uncle Ryan," Ginny said in an all-knowing voice. "She said you sat and talked. She said—"

"That you were dating, I bet," Max groused. "That's all Miss Ronnie talks about is dating."

"She's a matchmaker." Ginny was a staunch defender of her soon-to-be mama, having lost her birth mother a few years back to cancer. "Matchmakers make people date."

"Make people date." Max tossed his hands about. "She can't make me date nobody."

"Hang on. Can we rewind?" Jo tried to catch Ginny's eye in the rearview mirror. "How did Ronnie know I had coffee with Ryan? I bumped into him yesterday morning and haven't talked to Ronnie since." Although she'd been seen by Cooper Brown, lover of town gossip. And she supposed Ryan could have mentioned it to Wade, Ronnie's fiancé. She reached over and nudged Max's shoulder. "I bumped into Ryan, Max, same as we did at the feed store. I wasn't on a date."

"So you say." Max stared out the window. He was in a preteen funk and would need a few minutes to shake it off.

Back to the investigation at hand. "How did Ronnie know I had coffee with Ryan, Ginny?"

"I don't know." Ginny shrugged. "Uncle Ryan tells Miss Ronnie stuff, I guess. But now we know what you do at the coffee place. You sit and drink coffee and talk to folks you like."

"That's right," Piper seconded.

"Who do you want to sit and talk to at the coffee place?" Dean asked, adorably innocent.

"You and Max, of course," Piper said primly.

Jo swallowed the urge to chuckle, setting aside how everyone in Clementine knew everyone else's business for this lighter moment. The kids were in the fifth grade now. The innocent age of asking someone to go steady and then ignoring them completely if they said yes. Just being able to claim you had a boyfriend or girlfriend gave you social status. No talking, hand-holding or kissing required.

"You've been talking to us all day," Dean pointed out, a future sober scientist in the making, clueless about social settings. "We're in the same class. What more can you have to say?"

Piper and Ginny leaned forward, exchanging glances around Dean. And then they sat back in their seats and giggled.

Next to Jo, Max crossed his arms over his chest and sank into his seat. His cheeks were growing red. Unlike his brother, he knew what was going on.

Jo took the turn toward the Done Roamin' Ranch. Soon, they were passing fields of grazing cattle, tufts of grass bending in the prairie wind. A hawk sat on a fence post looking for a meal. Another circled above against the clear blue sky. It looked like any other day in Oklahoma—spring, summer, fall. Only the temperature was different.

"Miss Jo, how is the Santapalooza float going to look this year?" Ginny asked from the seat behind Jo.

"She can't tell you," Max said too quickly and too sharply, still in his funk over being ignored by the girls in favor of his brother. "It's always a surprise on the day of the ride."

"Not to good friends," Piper said with all the authority of a girl accustomed to being the boss at home, which she was. "And we're all good friends."

"Yep," Ginny seconded. "We've been friends since we were babies, and our mamas were friends since they were babies."

That last bit might have been a stretch.

"She's still not going to tell ya," Max predicted darkly.

"I can't tell anyone." Jo jumped in, trying to ease the tension in the cab. "Mostly, I can't tell because we haven't decided. Last year, we made the wagon look like snow by covering hay bales in white fabric, and then we put a reindeer on the front."

"Rudolph." Dean nodded, catching Jo's eye

in the rearview mirror. He was smiling. "I painted his nose."

"We did elves the year before that," Max added, not to be outdone by his twin. "Grandma made them, and we stuffed them like scarecrows."

"It was Christmas trees the year before," Dean said in his most helpful voice. "We frosted them with fake snow."

"And an inflatable snow globe the year before that." Max glanced back at Dean with a genuine smile, funk broken. "That was easy, wasn't it?"

"Maybe we'll do something easy again," Dean said in a hopeful voice. "We got plenty of chores."

Amen to that. Jo needed to put the finishing touches on a bay she was training for a rancher south of Tulsa.

"Does anyone have any ideas?" Jo was open. She turned onto the Done Roamin' Ranch's wide driveway, wondering if she'd see Ryan or Tate when she dropped Ginny off. Wondering if she should talk to Ryan if she did see him. Deciding she'd just wave.

While she'd been having that internal debate, the younger occupants of the truck had fallen silent, possibly applying some brainpower to the issue at hand. Possibly thinking about coffee dates at Clementine Coffee Grinders.

"Wreaths." Ginny broke the silence, pointing past Jo's shoulder to the main ranch house. "Grandma put a big wreath on her front door."

"Candy canes would be fun. Everyone likes candy canes." Piper sounded certain.

And maybe she was right. As Jo pulled up in front of the white farmhouse where Ginny lived, her boys were nodding. If only she knew how to make oversize candy canes.

Ginny collected her things, said her goodbyes and got out. Her daddy, Wade, emerged from the barn, waving to Jo as she turned around and drove off. There was no sign of the Oakley twins.

Jo was disappointed, which was silly in too many ways to count.

"What are you doing?" Piper asked Dean, who'd unclipped his seat belt and was moving behind Jo. "You don't have to move. You can sit next to me."

"Why?" Dean asked naively while his brother silently went back to fuming in the front seat.

CHAPTER SEVEN

"I BROUGHT THE boys doughnuts." Smiling, Ryan stood on the front porch of the Pierce Ranch Tuesday afternoon. He offered a pink box of doughnuts from Betty's Bakery to Jo's mother, who was wearing a red apron with lots of padding over her stomach, almost like a baby bump. "Did I come at a bad time?"

"What? Because of this?" She held out the apron, extending the padding toward him. "It's a Santa belly-maker. Can't try on Santa suits without it."

"Mrs. Pierce, I…" What did he say to that? He glanced over her shoulder.

There was a Christmas movie playing on the muted television. A fully decorated tree stood in the corner, lights aglow and an angel tree topper turning to and fro. There were a few presents wrapped and adorned with bows beneath fir branches. The sweet smell of baking filled the air.

This was a household that loved Christmas. If ever there was a sign that he didn't fit in…

I should go.

As if she heard him, Jo's mother frowned at Ryan, arms crossing over her padded bowl full of jelly. "First off, I'm not *Mrs.* Pierce anymore. No need to call me missus. You can call me Lois. Second, don't stare down upon a woman's Christmas decorations with a jaded look in your eye. Folks will think you don't like the holiday, which I've heard you don't but I don't believe that."

Oh, she should.

"And third, it's three o'clock. If I let my grandsons have sugar, they'll be bouncing off the walls all night."

"I'm sorry. I can take the doughnuts home with me." Ryan drew the box back. He could have ridden over on his motorcycle if he hadn't needed to stop for those doughnuts.

Lois plucked it from his hands. "That's all right. I'm meeting with the Santapalooza organizing committee tonight." She gestured toward a stack of fur-trimmed costumes on her couch, expression softening. "These doughnuts will be much appreciated, along with you saddling and suiting up for us on Christmas Eve morning. We're trying to protect our record for a parade with the most Santas on horseback. There are copycats all over the United States. We can't rest on our laurels."

"You can always rely on my brother Tate." Ryan deflected the invitation. His twin always rode in Santapalooza. His twin volunteered for anything for which he was asked.

"But you're here and…" Lois brightened, as if struck with inspiration. "I could use a model for some of these Santa suits. I never really know where to hem the slacks." Lois took a gander at his legs. "And trying on a Santa costume might give you a boost of holiday spirit."

"My spirit is just fine." Nonexistent, just the way he liked it. Ryan backed away. "Glad the doughnuts will help the cause."

"Ah, you are a project, aren't you? Now, listen." Lois set the doughnut box on a narrow table next to the door. "You may not know this, but my daughter is single."

Ryan suppressed the urge to hightail it out of there.

"Jo is choosy and hard to get." Lois gave Ryan's bicep a strong squeeze. "But even through your coat, I can tell you're a strong man who'd rock a Santa beard. Jo loves a man in a Santa suit."

"I…" Ryan choked on the simple syllable and all Lois's statement implied. "I'm just interested in a pair of horses."

"Pity. I could have put a good word in for you with Jo." Lois looked him up and down, which seemed to be what the Pierces did to him. "Jo and the boys are in the second barn. You can head around yourself." She gestured toward the driveway that went past the house. "Just remember not to be put off by her gruff manner. My girl has a heart of gold."

"I'm sure she does." But Ryan was interested in her horses, not her heart.

He walked around the house to the first barn. It was painted a bright red outside and had a wide breezeway intersected by smaller aisles. Curious about the stock in Jo's possession, Ryan eagerly walked in, glancing down different wings. There had to be over thirty stalls. Young horses extended noses over doors, colts and fillies in striking colors— grays, jet-black, paints, palominos. Rodeo folk paid extra for well-trained, flashy horseflesh, and Jo certainly understood her target market.

Ryan went out the back and traversed a yard with a cool-down walker, an old wagon and a place to bathe horses. To the west of the barns, there were two arenas. One was covered. One wasn't. Beyond that was a large pasture. The Burns Ranch buildings on the next spread over were visible in the distance to the east.

In Clementine, the Pierce Ranch was referred to as a ranchette, perhaps because other ranches, like his family's Done Roamin' Ranch, were one hundred acres or more. Ryan estimated Jo's ranch to be somewhere around twenty acres.

He entered the second barn, which was just as large as the previous one. Christmas music played from somewhere. A tall, slim dog with short, bluish-gray fur trotted up to Ryan with a happy face and an energetic tail wag. Ryan gave him a friendly pat.

Jo stood at the far end of the breezeway, looking into a stall and shaking her head. "I knew I should have dropped you boys off at the Burns Ranch after school."

"You're not showing him Tiger." An indignant boy's voice.

"He's ours," a similar voice chimed in.

"How many times have I told you two not to get attached to horses I train?" Jo asked in a good-natured voice.

"A gazillion?"

"A gazillion trillion?"

"Sounds about right." Jo chuckled. "But you're lucky. In this case, you can rest assured. I'm not showing him Tiger." She noticed Ryan and called out a greeting. Tapping the closed stall door with a hand, she said, "Boys, I need you on your best behavior." She turned away from them and walked toward Ryan in her usual attire—gray hoodie with Rudolph on the front, maroon puffy vest, wide-brimmed white straw hat, blue jeans tucked in plain brown boots.

A long-forgotten image came to mind, one of Jo walking through a school hallway directly toward him, Santa hat on, nose in the air, not moving out of his way. The memory warmed him the way images of Christmas seldom did.

Other horses followed her progress through the barn, some poking heads over stall doors, others just peering at her between the bars. All the horses in this barn seemed older and large enough to be saddle ready.

"I see you've met Blue." Jo patted the dog before stopping near two stalls. She gave Ryan a small smile, nothing like the haughty expressions they'd exchanged in their youth. "The horses I had in mind for you and Tate are Prince and Pauper. They're brothers and I've been training them since they were born." Pride rang in her tone. Pride, not the gruff manner her mother had warned him about.

The burden on Ryan's shoulders lightened, but he didn't dare show it with a smile. That might destroy the truce between himself and Jo.

The stall with Prince's placard contained a stocky gray horse with good lines and intelligent eyes. Pauper was a mirror image of his brother except he had a white star on his forehead. They had the build of good cow horses. Average height with sturdy-looking legs and muscular hindquarters, an indication that they might have shorter strides and the ability to wheel about on a dime.

Pauper extended his nose, gumming the brim of Ryan's hat before Ryan playfully pushed the gelding's head away. "Their lineage?" At the prices she charged, Ryan wanted horses that weren't just built for roping but also had the smarts for it.

"The same sire as Ty and Eric's horses. Regal Robert." Jo didn't just speak with pride; she glowed with it.

Ryan wasn't used to seeing her exude such confidence, such…magnetism.

He rubbed a hand around the back of his neck and tried to focus on what she was saying.

"Regal Robert is my best stud." Jo gestured toward a gray horse in a stall on the other side of the breezeway. "When I started a breeding program here ten years ago, I wanted to be known for horses bred for rodeo and ranch work—compact, strong and quick—with intelligence and competitiveness to match."

"I think you've done that." But it didn't escape him that she could just as easily have been describing herself.

A few stalls back, a whispered conversation was being held. Blue ran to the stall where the boys were and sat expectantly, wagging his tail. Ryan was curious about a horse that inspired such affection in two young boys.

Jo waved him off. "The boys have become attached to Tiger. But Prince and Pauper are what you're looking for if you want a pair. Prince is a good head horse and Pauper a good heeler."

Ryan stroked Pauper's neck. "And you have no issue selling to my brother and me? Can I ask what changed your mind?"

"My agreement with my brothers has been terminated." Jo smiled but it didn't quite reach her eyes, indicating there was a story behind her simple statement. "Shall we take them out for a test ride?"

He nodded, feeling anticipation build.

"You bring Pauper down to the tack room. I'll get Prince." Jo handed him a halter and lead rope. "Boys, I'm going to need you to release the cows and time our runs."

"But, Mom, Tiger is lonely and needs us." The playful pitch to the boy's voice gave Ryan the impression that Max was speaking.

"If we help, can we rope later?" And that must be the more serious Dean.

"Work is always rewarded," Jo said crisply from inside Prince's stall. "And don't forget to put the second latch on Tiger's stall or he'll try to get in the house again and scare Grandma to death."

Giggling, two small heads with matching cowboy hats hung over a stall door.

"You don't want to see what's in this stall, Mr. Ryan," one boy said.

"Nope. No horse in here," the other boy said. "Just needs to be mucked out."

A deep chestnut with a black mane poked his head over theirs and looked at Ryan.

"Tiger!" the pair chorused before laughing once more.

They were boys after his own heart, reminding him again of himself and Tate when they'd been placed at the Done Roamin' Ranch, where they'd finally felt safe and loved enough to cut loose like Jo's boys. "You've got some good kids there," Ryan told Jo.

"They're a handful," Jo said warmly. "But they're my kind of handful."

What Ryan would have given to have had a parent like Jo.

A few minutes later, the pair of grays wore roping saddles with coils of rope hanging from the saddle horns. Jo's tack and equipment were first-rate. He had high hopes for the horses. The closer they came to the arena, the antsier Ryan was to climb into the saddle.

Steady now. This could be my future.

Ryan and Jo led Prince and Pauper past the covered arena to the uncovered ring in back, which had a cattle release chute on one end and a cattle catch on the other. Three calves were in a small holding pen, ready to be loaded into the chute. Her boys raced past Ryan with Blue at their heels and scrambled between the arena rails. Pauper barely flicked his tail as the rascals ran by, the sign of a steady mount.

"I prepared three." Jo nodded toward the cows, which she'd fitted with head gear to protect their eyes and ears from the rope. "We can run them each three times."

Ryan nodded. Her suggestion was standard practice for most ropers and rodeo stock.

He led Pauper into the arena after Jo opened the gate. "Nice setup you have here." Her barns and arenas were top-of-the-line and well maintained.

Jo closed the gate and captured his gaze. "Are you trying to butter me up again?"

So touchy.

He held up a hand. "I'm just making polite conversation and honestly admiring what you have."

Jo planted her boots more firmly in the soft soil of the arena. "We didn't talk about payment. I'll need a cashier's check or direct bank transfer by the twentieth."

That gave him fifteen days. He'd gotten truck loans in less time. And yet Ryan's head began to pound because he'd never done anything like this before.

"I haven't even ridden Pauper." Ryan slid the gelding's reins over his head, preparing to mount up. "If I decide to buy, we can talk terms."

Jo reached over and took hold of the reins beneath Pauper's chin. "You *can* afford them, right? You don't want to be wasting my time, Ryan." From the sharp look in Jo's eyes, Ryan had the sinking suspicion that she knew he was in a precarious financial position when it came to this deal.

"If the horses are acceptable, I was going to go to Clementine Savings & Loan tomorrow morning." And talk to his foster brother Dix about a loan.

Jo tsked, gently leading both horses back toward the gate. "I've been down that road before. You should know that banks don't want to make loans for high-priced horses, especially when you've got no property they can seize if you don't pay up."

"Hold on." Ryan lengthened his stride and cut her off at the arena gate. "If I like the horses, I'll find a way to pay."

Jo gave him that look of hers, the one that said if she could, she'd chuck him out of her way.

Max and Dean drifted closer, watching and whispering to each other.

Ryan scratched the back of his neck, gaze still lingering on those boys. "I could…" What could he offer to obtain a ride? What had she said to her kids earlier? Something about work being rewarded? "I could help you around the ranch for a few hours in exchange for a ride. That way, you wouldn't be wasting your time."

"Have him paint the Santapalooza wagon." Max grinned. At least, Ryan assumed it was Max. He was wearing a green coat.

"With candy canes," Dean seconded, thrusting his hands in blue coat pockets.

Jo's expression didn't soften. "Offering to help around here doesn't solve the money problem you face. What you need is less expensive horseflesh. I can point you in the direction of some options." Not that she looked happy about it, reminding Ryan that she needed to make a sale before Christmas.

"Do not say Tiger." Dean jutted his chin.

"If you want to do Mom a favor, ask her out," Max muttered. "All Grandma does is talk about Mom being single."

Jo lowered her hat brim, hiding her expressive eyes.

But not before Ryan saw something in them. *Interest.*

He pounced on the opening. "We could go out to the Buckboard on Saturday night," Ryan offered. That's where Jo and her friends went almost every week. "I've been told I'm a good dancer." And Jo enjoyed the line dances before the live music started. He'd seen her and her friends dancing there on Saturday nights.

He couldn't see Jo's eyes, but her cheeks were a bright red.

"We dance at home all the time." Max put his hands on his hips and began boot-scooting, kicking up dust.

"I'm not going out with you." Jo blew out a breath and lifted her head. "Don't take this personally. I have a policy. No rides if you're not a serious buyer."

"I *am* a serious buyer. *And* I'm willing to take you out."

"Willing?" Her dark eyes flashed. She took a step toward him, sharp chin jutting.

"Uh…" Again, Ryan recalled a younger Jo, marching toward him through the school hallway.

"Like taking me on a date is a hardship?" Jo scoffed. "Have you been talking to my mother?"

Yes, and she warned me you were prickly.

Again, he retreated an inch until he felt an arena rail press into his shoulder blades and his temper press against the back of his throat.

Steady now.

"I meant I'd be *honored* to escort you to the Buckboard or the establishment of your choice, all for the sake of creating a foundation of trust for this sale."

"You're not very good with girls, are you, Mr. Ryan." That was Dean, serious as all get-out as he cast shade on Ryan.

"He's the worst." Max rolled his eyes.

Jo bit back a grin.

And Ryan sensed opportunity once more. "Admittedly, I'm not a ladies' man," he said slowly, easing forward. "But I could arrange a date for you. Maybe with Griff…" Who was a harmless flirt.

Whatever mirth had lifted Jo's expression vanished.

That was a no.

"Or perhaps Chandler." His older foster brother who was recently divorced and a single dad. Surely, they'd have a lot in common and earn Ryan some much-needed trust.

Jo's lips thinned.

"Or Tate." Now he was reaching for straws. His twin was choosy about who he dated, and never dated anyone for long. Except…

Jo's pink lips gently parted, making a small O.

She wants to date Tate? Not me?

A tendril of annoyance threaded itself through Ryan's veins, which was ridiculous. He'd never begrudged his twin anything. And it wasn't as if he was attracted to Jo. She dressed like a throwback cowgirl. And if he had the temper of an annoyed rattler, she had the temper of a territorial mama bear.

"What do you say? I get you a date with Tate and in exchange I can take these horses for a test ride?" He thrust his hand between them.

Jo glanced down at her dirt-streaked blue jeans, which were tucked into those worn cowboy boots. And then up into Ryan's eyes. "I'm not going to shake on something that will never happen."

"Mom." Dean scrambled to Jo's side, tugging her arm. "Think of how happy Grandma would be."

"And quiet." Max flanked her on the other side. "You always tell her you should be able to eat in peace."

Having experienced Lois's determined attempt to bend his will firsthand, Ryan decided it was safe to nod.

"*If* it happens…" Jo squared her shoulders and gestured to herself. "But Tate Oakley takes flashy, gushy women on dates. That's not me. He'll never agree to take me out. He has a type."

She was right. Ryan surveyed Jo's apparel once more, thought about her tomboy style and her take-charge demeanor. He may have overpromised his ability to get her a date with Tate.

Not that a deal had been struck yet.

"*Flashy…*" The twins worked their mouths around the word.

Ryan decided to ease off the accelerator. "If you want a date, Jo, you could ask one of your friends for some advice about—"

Jo scoffed.

"Or I could…um…consult with you to…"

"Careful, cowboy," Jo said crisply.

The twins stared at Ryan as if he'd just spoken a foreign language.

"I mean," Ryan amended quickly, "I know what kind of woman Tate goes for. I don't want to suggest how you should dress…" His gaze landed on her jeans tucked into her boots. "Or how you should do your hair…" It was very nearly as short as his. "Or about makeup." Which he'd never seen her wear.

The boys giggled.

Jo gave herself a little shake. "This conversation is over." She gestured toward the gate.

But not before Ryan noted the disappointment in her eyes.

Jo WAS USED to being the ugly duckling.

What she wasn't used to was having a man so blatantly point it out to her.

Of course, she shouldn't have been surprised that the man doing the pointing was Ryan Oakley, Prince of Tactlessness.

Things he'd said to her that last year in high school came unbidden into her head.

Jo should try out for the football team. No one can knock her down.

Get out of Jo's seat before she throws you out of it, Dix.

Jo, show the rodeo team how bull riding is done.

Ryan had always been quick in school to

point out that Jo acted and appeared unlike the girls she hung out with.

And even though Jo had been angry and using her prickly attitude as an emotional shield, Ryan's comments stung, then and now.

Jo narrowed her eyes as she stared at Ryan, weighing how best to get rid of him. She couldn't raise her voice. They had an audience, after all.

But Ryan solved that problem himself. "Boys, I left doughnuts with your grandmother at the house."

Her sons didn't have to be told twice. Max and Dean raced out of the arena with Blue tagging along behind, leaving Jo and Ryan alone with the horses.

"I'm going to need to apologize to your grandmother for cluing the boys in to those doughnuts." Ryan almost sounded…apologetic.

A chill winter wind blew between them, reminding Jo what kind of guy Ryan really was.

She didn't hesitate to lay down the law. "It's time for you to go."

"You promised me a ride." Ryan shifted his weight from one foot to another, but otherwise stayed where he was. He wore a faded blue sweatshirt beneath a worn black jean jacket. His hat was as black as she'd once thought his heart was. "I didn't mean to hurt your feelings about your date ability. Growing up, my mother always told me I was too much of a straight shooter, usually after I asked her about what happened to the money for groceries that never materialized. She'd spend it on booze and there'd be nothing in the house to eat for days."

For the second time since he'd arrived, Jo's mouth hung open. This time, indelicately. She'd never heard him or Tate say anything about their biological parents. A surge of empathy made her waver. "I'm sorry about your mom."

"My dad wasn't any better." Ryan's gaze dropped. His brow furrowed. "Forget I said that."

"Forgotten." *Never.* And because of that tiny glimpse into his past, her feelings about Ryan began changing again, the same as they'd begun after he'd apologized in the coffee shop yesterday.

Behind her, the horses were getting restless, as were the cattle the boys had loaded into the chute. The animals expected activity. And she did, too. She'd gotten her hopes up about filling her bank account before year's end, paying her father and proving something to her brothers. "Look, I can't afford to let this go any further." Not the horse transaction. And not the different perspective about Ryan. "No money. No ride. I have rules for a reason. That way, I won't get burned again."

"You have rules…" Ryan stared at her, not as if they were at odds, but as if he was just comprehending something life altering.

Men didn't look at Jo and have life-altering epiphanies. What did his expression mean?

Ryan shook his head, as if trying to clear it. "Here's a new rule. We can help each other. Let's ride." He spoke so confidently as he reached for Pauper's reins that she didn't instinctively pull away. His hand touched hers as he claimed the thin strips of leather and she let him because…

She didn't know why.

But something shifted inside of Jo and came to life, something long buried and powerful. Something that said Tate wasn't the only attractive Oakley.

Jo tried to ignore the awareness. "I said no." But she hadn't prevented Ryan from taking the reins.

Why didn't I stop him?

Her fingers felt odd where he'd touched her. "If you've ever been to a luxury car showroom in Vegas, they don't let you handle the merchandise unless you're a serious buyer."

"I *am* a serious buyer. We just haven't come

to terms." Ryan swung into Pauper's saddle and surveyed the arena before returning his gaze to hers. "You need the money. Well, I have needs, too." And with that cryptic comment, he cued Pauper into a quick walk.

Leaving Jo no choice but to mount up and follow him because she did need the money and he seemed confident he could get it. Any other reason for letting this proceed was just too silly to contemplate. "Okay, but this is a simple ride. You won't be roping cattle today. The boys are gone. There's no one to operate the chute."

"They'll be back," Ryan assured her with that same confidence he'd used before.

"How do you know?" The house contained many distractions—TV, tablets, video games—not just doughnuts.

"Because your mother claimed those doughnuts for her Santapalooza meeting and there was a movie on the television." He smiled at her.

And that smile did something to her insides.

Only because he and Tate are identical twins.

And wasn't that annoying? They weren't identical in character. She didn't want to be attracted to this Oakley.

"If Lois is anything like my foster mom," Ryan continued, "she'll shoo those boys back outside in no time."

He was probably right. And that was annoying, too.

"And if they're anything like Tate and me, they'll head straight back here." He grinned. "Where the action is."

He was probably right about that, also.

Jo's thoughts circled around things he'd said while they made a lap around the arena.

We can help each other.

I have needs, too.

Tantalizing statements. She decided the most important thing to focus on was his determination to buy her horses, not any questions she might have about his aid he promised her or his unspoken needs.

"What's the story behind Tiger?" he asked, breaking into her thoughts.

And making her a bit melancholy. "I sold Tiger to a young woman vying for rodeo queen in Nashville. She claimed once she left here that he wouldn't let her ride him." That was the first time she'd heard of anything like that happening with one of her horses. "She demanded her money back."

"You didn't give it to her." Ryan looked appalled.

"Not all of it. I charged her restocking and transportation fees." Jo rolled her eyes. "I did it for Tiger more than her."

"He's not dangerous, is he? You trust him with your kids."

"Tiger always had a soft spot for them." And speaking of soft spots, they were getting too friendly, she and Ryan. And he was making her long for male companionship.

Must be all those romantic Christmas songs I've been listening to.

Ryan cued Pauper into a trot. Jo did the same with Prince, watching the way Ryan handled the gelding. He had a smooth seat, not surprising since he worked the rodeo for a living and did fairly well on the team roping circuit.

Soon, they were loping side by side around the arena. Every so often, Ryan cued Pauper to change the hoof the gelding led with. Again, Jo followed his pace, switching Prince's lead, too. Ryan was an accomplished horseman with a soft touch when it came to cuing a horse. If he had the money, he'd add to her reputation as a horse trainer.

Ryan spared her another smile. "Smooth as butter."

A stiff breeze swept past them again, but Jo wasn't chilled. It was odd, this feeling that they fit. Perhaps it meant he was the right rider for Pauper.

The boys returned to the arena, this time without the dog.

Ryan gave her an I-told-you-so grin.

"Don't rub it in," she told him, tearing her eyes from his lips.

"Do you think they're warm enough to run some cattle?" Ryan brought Pauper to a stop. "The horses, I mean."

She reined in Prince next to him. "Yes, but—"

"Hey, boys," Ryan said, cutting her off. "How about you operate the cattle chute for us?"

The annoyance she associated with Ryan resurfaced. "You're as pushy and irritating as you were in high school."

He nodded briskly. "But I'm efficient. I don't like to waste time—yours or mine. That's why I'll see you Saturday night at the Buckboard. I'll have Tate in tow, and we'll get you that date."

Jo's mouth hung open. "I…I…I didn't ask you to do that."

"I know." Ryan didn't smile and there was no tease in his voice, not even a suggestive waggle of those thick brows. "But I'm going to help you anyway."

And she was afraid to argue lest he realize how big a deal it was to her.

A date with Tate Oakley? A chance to turn her decades-old crush into love?

She almost fell out of the saddle.

CHAPTER EIGHT

"GET OFF, RYAN," Jo commanded after they'd successfully put her pair of well-trained grays through their paces—Jo roping the head and Ryan the heels.

"Why?" Ryan bristled, bringing Pauper to a stop. They were at the far end of the arena. Jo had dismounted to remove their two ropes from the steer they'd just finished running. "What did I do wrong? I roped all three."

As did Jo. They made a good team. Their second run had tied his best time from last season. Now he wanted the horses more than ever. He needed to think about what he'd offer. Jo was in a bind. Would she be open to a lower price? It wouldn't hurt to ask. But not when her mood had turned thorny.

"Calm down. And get down." Jo tossed the end of his rope toward Pauper, then coiled the one she'd thrown while he did the same. She spared him a glance that lacked blazing eyes or fierce frowns, making it hard to read the cause of her stopping his ride. "My arena. My horses. My rules. I've got something to show you and I can't do that when you're on horse-back."

He shouldn't have felt like smiling when she bossed him around. But he did. Everything about Jo was different than he remembered. A surprise. A pleasant surprise. He couldn't remember the last time he'd felt like he was getting more than he was paying for.

She hung her coil of rope on Prince's saddle horn and led the horse over to where Ryan was dismounting.

"Mom, are we done yet?" Max called from the chute, identifiable because his tone was overly dramatic.

"Mom, what do you want done with the cattle?" Dean asked, identifiable because he sounded responsible.

"Put one in the chute and let the rest back in the pasture." She tossed Prince's reins over his head and then over an arena rail, although she didn't tie them.

Ryan dutifully did the same. "What's going on?"

Jo had a good poker face. She stared Ryan down. "Turn around."

"Why?" But he did as she asked, craning his neck to keep his eyes on her.

Her cheeks were flushed with color and her mouth set in a determined line.

Jo put her hands on his hips—*yowzer!*—and then pressed her thumbs into the small of his back—*wowzer!*

Ticklish, Ryan was hard-pressed not to jolt out of reach. "What are you doing?"

Whatever it was…was it supposed to feel good? Because it did and…

Ryan caught himself up short. This was Jo Pierce. He'd made the generous offer to help her around the ranch and maybe even snag a date with his brother. The warm trail her hands made up his back was only an indication that he needed to find himself a date for Saturday night, too.

Unaware of his turmoil, Jo moved her hands upward, thumbs pressing on either side of Ryan's spine, fingers finding the ticklish spot near his lower ribs.

"Hold still," she said when he spasmed, continuing her finger journey up his back.

Ryan had never paid for a massage, but he imagined what Jo was doing was what a masseuse's hands did. As a result of her touch, one of his vertebrae popped. He stood taller, straighter.

"That's better," she murmured.

It might have been better if anyone other

than Jo Pierce had been learning the contours of his back. This was… He felt…mystified.

"Perfect." All too soon, Jo removed her hands. "All right. Let's try it one more time."

"Not before you explain yourself." Ryan turned. His boots sank in the loamy arena soil as he took a stand within touching distance of his former rival. But she wasn't that angry girl of his youth. And she wasn't that plain girl with plain clothes and nothing interesting about her either.

Ryan swallowed back his attraction and waited for her to justify her actions.

"You drive lots of miles for work, Ryan, spending hours behind the wheel or in a cramped seat, same as my brothers. You have a slight tilt to your posture, hardly noticeable. Your right shoulder is a bit higher than your left." She lifted her own shoulder as if to demonstrate.

Ryan wanted to disagree and opened his mouth to protest.

But before a sound crossed his lips, Jo reached around his side and pressed her finger and thumb into his lower back once more—*wowzer!*—silencing him.

All too soon, her hand dropped away. "If you're anything like my brother Eric, you need your spine adjusted regularly to smooth your motion and optimize the timing of your throws."

More like, he needed to check himself because Ryan wanted those small, firm hands to return to his back.

Jo patted his shoulder consolingly, the way he imagined a sister patted a brother. "I can see you're confused."

Honey, you have no idea.

"Tell you what... Do what I do, and you'll see." Jo hinged at her hips, keeping her torso parallel to the ground. When he copied her, feeling foolish, she extended her arms on a similar plane to her upper body. "Do you feel a little crooked?"

He did. "Well, I'll be darned." His right shoulder didn't feel square with his left.

They stood up like regular folk. Smiled at each other.

Again, Ryan looked at Jo in a new light. How had she noticed such a slight misalignment to his posture and movement?

Jo gave him a gentle push toward Pauper. "Come on. Let's have you try one more time and see if it feels different. We're losing the light."

Ryan swung into the saddle and followed Jo back to the release chute, rolling his right shoulder back and trying to self-correct the position of his torso. She backed Prince into the right box while he backed Pauper into the left. He raised his right arm and went through the throwing motion. His shoulder popped with each rotation, but the muscles in his lower back were looser and his arm had a slightly bigger range of motion.

"Okay, boys. Last run and then we'll bring out Tiger." Jo readied her rope for a throw, adjusting her grip. She was skilled at this. Quick and accurate. She'd do well on the circuit. "When Ryan gives you a nod, boys, you hit the release and the timer."

"We know, Mom," Max replied with preteen know-it-all-ness.

"I only remind," Jo said good-naturedly. "I don't belittle, and neither should you."

Another demonstration of her positive parenting ability making Ryan note how lucky her boys were.

He'd learned more about Jo Pierce this afternoon than he had the entire time he'd known her. She was good with horses, with kids and with him, giving Ryan tips to work the run harder without delivering them heavy-handedly. And the pair of horses were well trained, alert and eager to chase down a cow. They were smart and responded to commands with minimal cuing, like true partners who recognized what needed to be done almost before their riders told them.

Ryan nodded to the twins. In a blink, the chute was open and he and Jo were off, riding fast but in slow motion to Ryan's mind.

Jo guided Prince closer to the racing cow. In just a few of Prince's strides, she was in position. Her toss of the rope was a thing of beauty. It landed around the steer's crown perfectly. With economy of movement, she coiled the other end of the rope around the saddle horn, creating tension in the rope while she angled Prince away from the steer, slowing it.

The steer's rear heels came up once, twice. Ryan made his throw in what felt like the smoothest motion of his life. The rope closed around both of the steer's rear hooves. Pauper backed away before Ryan even cued him, such that the rope he was winding around the saddle horn was taut almost immediately.

"Best time today," Dean called out.

The best time of my life!

Ryan beamed at Jo. He'd had high hopes for improved times, but she'd pushed him to a place so much better. He couldn't stop smiling.

I need to swing this deal.

"Thanks, boys. Finish up and get Tiger ready for me." Jo indicated Ryan should join her as she walked Prince around the arena to cool him down. "What do you think?"

"The horses are grand but… Did you study Eastern medicine? That thing you did with my back was…" *Incredible. Miraculous. Sexy.* Ryan sat back in the saddle, considering his words as carefully as he considered Jo. "I don't know how to describe it." Or her. He was drawn to her.

Drawn, not entranced by.

He quickly reframed Jo in his mind. She was no longer ignorable. She was like one of the guys he could talk shop with for hours. And a woman he could see himself enjoying an evening with. A rare find. Like her horses.

"You need to do more than train your horse, Ryan," Jo said in a businesslike voice that helped him fit her in the friend zone. "You need to keep your body in tip-top shape to perform."

"It's just roping." The words dropped out of habit, a habit formed to make it seem as if Ryan and Tate wouldn't be crushed if they never achieved notoriety for their skill.

Jo gasped dramatically, immediately following that quick intake of breath with an amused glance featuring vivacious brown eyes and grinning lips that seemed incredibly kissable. "Anything athletic requires train-

ing. Your brother Wade did well this year on
the bronc riding circuit, making it to several
postseason events. I know he trains hard with
weights and such. You should, too."

It's just roping.

But Ryan didn't voice the thought out loud
this time. He was coming to realize that would
be a cop-out.

"You're good," Jo was saying. "But you
could be better."

"With a better horse." Obviously.

"You rode a better horse, and by loosening
up your back, you shaved nearly a second off
your time, start to finish. That's awesome."
She was serious.

And seriously complimenting him, which
was something he'd never imagined. And
frankly, didn't want. Not from her when she
unsettled him this way. Unlike Tate, Ryan
didn't plan to get married and have a family.
Tate would be ten times better off in every
aspect of his life with a woman like Jo.

"You don't need to buy a different horse,
Ryan. Why not train with Suzie for a few
weeks while you strengthen and stretch your
core? When the circuit begins in the New
Year, you'll see a difference without spending the money."

She's giving me an out?

He didn't want one. "A big enough difference to best your brother Ty?" Who was a heeler and his direct competitor.

Jo kept silent.

"That's what I thought."

"Don't misunderstand me." She tsked. "You can improve. But you and I both know that as a heeler, your time hinges on the talent of the header you rope with. You need a good partner, Ryan, someone with their head one hundred percent in the game."

"And that's not Tate," he muttered, recalling how his twin had slumped in the summer and impacted Ryan's scores. "I admit, something's been bothering him. But all that could change if we buy Prince and Pauper."

Jo made a noncommittal noise.

They'd completed one lap around the arena. Jo kept riding and Ryan stayed with her.

"This isn't my first sale, Ryan. I've had cowboys come to shop for a horse before. They always tell me they can afford my asking price. But when they get here…" Finally, she showed him the closed-off expression he was used to, the one that said she thought the world was against her, but she'd dug in and was ready for whatever calamity came her way. "They try to bargain. The way you planned to." She was onto him. In that respect, at least. And that unrelenting expression dared him to deny it.

He had the good grace to nod. "It must be tough for you in this business."

Jo gave him a surprised look. "I didn't say that."

"You wouldn't." And she wouldn't whine to him, of all people—that's for sure. "But you always were the toughest person I knew."

"*Tougher than anyone else*, was what you used to say." And from her tone, she considered that a slight.

He bit back a curse, remembering what he'd said to her at the coffee shop in much the same terms, words that had sent her storming out the door. "I apologize for that. For all the times in the past, including this morning. As weird as it sounds, I respected your strength in school. You were the person who kept me stoic in the face of so many other disappointments that year." With his mother. And later, with Tate, who blamed Ryan every time their mother disappeared.

I need to stop oversharing.

"We can't choose who our parents are," Jo said wisely, reading his thoughts, at least in part. "But we can forge ahead and build a family we deserve. And we've both done that."

He nodded, although begrudgingly.

The boys returned, riding the bright chestnut—Max grinning mischievously from the saddle, Dean sitting behind the cantle, staring toward the colorful sunset.

The reason for Tiger's name was immediately apparent. His chestnut color was so rich, it was almost orange. There were black stripes on his lower legs, winding delicately around his hocks, reminiscent of tiger stripes. His mane and tail were black, adding another level of contrast.

In a stable full of striking horses, Tiger was a standout.

"Is he a Spanish mustang?" Ryan wondered aloud.

"He looks it, doesn't he?" Jo was back to sounding proud. "But he doesn't have papers and the woman I bought him from had no idea her mare was pregnant with him, much less how she got pregnant. She wasn't a horse trainer. Tiger was two when I bought him and had never been more than halter broke. He thinks he's a dog. Or a boy. Just one of the family."

"What did you train him for?"

"I try all my horses on various disciplines—roping, cutting, barrel racing, regular ranch work. I let them tell me what they want to do." Jo was glowing again. "Tiger loves going fast, which makes him a good barrel racer. But he's a good roper, too. Herding cows… Roping cows… Working cattle is a game to him. Tiger could be anything, as long as he enjoys it. He loves to play."

The chestnut looked their way, ears cocked forward, head held high.

"You should rent him out to Ronnie for one of those photo shoots she does for Cowgirl Pearl."

She stood in the stirrups, eagerly looking Tiger's way. "That's an interesting idea. But I'd worry he'd act up." Her expression fell. She sat back in the saddle. "He's been choosy about that since he returned. Gave the blacksmith a bit of trouble. And no one else but me and the boys can ride him."

"How do you know no one else can ride him?" Ryan was itching to try.

"I had a buyer interested." She gave Ryan a wry smile. "That didn't work out. Then when my brothers heard about it, they gave him a try. Ty was flung to the dirt. Eric never got into the saddle." Jo sized Ryan up with a lingering glance. "I'm not going to ask you to try."

"You don't have to ask. I was going to offer," Ryan said eagerly. "I ride broncs and bulls at home. I can get on Tiger and stay on him, I bet."

"No no no." Max leaned forward and hugged the chestnut's neck. "He's not for sale."

"I didn't say I wanted to buy him," Ryan said carefully. "I want to help your mom fix him."

"To get on my good side?" Jo turned up her nose, returning to her usual barbed self.

"To help out a friend." This time when he said it, he meant it. They did feel like friends. Maybe for the first time ever.

"Thanks, but…" Jo gave herself a little shake. "Tiger is our heart horse. It was hard enough selling him the first time. And if I sell Prince and Pauper to you, we can keep him." And then she smiled at Ryan. She smiled the way she had when she was that perky little cowgirl, the one who didn't think there was any bad in the world.

Ryan decided then and there that he needed to find a way to finance eighty thousand dollars of horseflesh and save Jo's heart horse.

As Tate would say, "No pressure."

CHAPTER NINE

"IT'S TIME TO stop gushing about horses and start talking about Jo Pierce." Mom handed Ryan a bowl of corn-bread muffins that night at dinner. "How did you two get along?"

"Fine." Surprisingly fine. Alarmingly fine. "Her horses are fine, too."

"And we're right back to horses," Mom muttered, tucking her short gray hair behind her ear.

Ryan buttered his corn bread, intent upon not gushing.

"He may say everything went fine," Griff said, grinning. "But you know that come tomorrow Jo Pierce will pull a prank on him. And personally, I can't wait to see what she has up her sleeve."

Ryan scoffed. "You'd lose that bet."

Cheek ticking, Tate excused himself from the dinner table and headed for the door.

"I'll come back and do the dishes," Ryan promised, taking his corn-bread muffin and following his brother. "Hey, wait up."

Tate paused halfway across the ranch yard between the main house and the bunkhouse, right next to those inflatable reindeer. "I'm not interested in a horse."

"Then tell me what's wrong." Ryan fell into step with his brother, ruing the fact that he'd left his jacket at the house. "Something's been stuck in your craw since summer. You know I'm always here for you."

The front lights strobed.

Jingle bells... Jingle bells...

Tate's steps slowed. "I...I've been sending Mom money since July." The statement dropped between them like a thrown horseshoe on pavement—a startling clatter that took a moment to process.

Ryan's knees felt rubbery. The last time their mother had come around was five years ago, and she'd drained Tate's bank account.

"And before you give me grief about financing Mom's drinking problem, she's sober," Tate said in a voice that brooked no argument. He stomped ahead, moving faster. "I saw her one-year sobriety chip."

Ryan charged after him. "She could have gotten that chip anywhere." It wouldn't be the first time she'd lied about something.

"Yeah, but I believe her. She divorced Dad.

And she's working at a diner in Friar's Creek." The next town over.

"Which doesn't explain why she needs your money." Ryan shook his head as they barreled into the bunkhouse, which thankfully was empty of ranch hands. Griff was still in the main house. "You need your money to invest in you and your future."

This was exactly why Tate needed to date Jo. She was down-to-earth, had her priorities straight and was just different than those fancy-dressing cowgirls who chased him.

"Give her a chance." Tate tugged off his boots. "She's renting a ranch and—"

"She needs a ranch hand? A handyman? Or does she need you to front her money for a herd?" Ryan crossed his arms and leaned against the door.

"She's going to raise alpacas and harvest their wool to make yarn. She's opening an on-line yarn shop, too." Tate almost sounded… proud? "She's got it all figured out. She doesn't need my help."

"Then why are you giving her money?" Clearly, their mother had dropped a story on Tate that he'd bitten hook, line and sinker. "We both know that when times get tough, she'll take that money to the bar, not the bank."

"I knew you'd react this way," Tate said sharply, shoving his boots under the bench he sat on. "That's why I didn't want to tell you. But she's changed this time."

"That's what she says every time." Ryan shook his head. "I don't believe it."

"You mean you don't want to. You have this image in your head that she's bad and I'm too naive to protect myself from her." Tate's statement rang with disappointment. It echoed in the empty bunkhouse. It reverberated in Ryan's head, awakening long-buried hopes for their parents to miraculously change and for Tate to learn that people would take advantage if he gave them an inch.

"Sometimes, a promise is broken one time too many." Ryan no longer believed that this time would be different, the way their mother always claimed. "How many times are you going to let her fleece you? She's not going to ask you to come live with her." Or at least, he hoped not.

"It's the season for forgiveness, Ry." Tate moved to the window, gesturing to the holiday display in front of the main house. The faint sound of "Jingle Bells" drifted into the bunkhouse. And then Tate looked at Ryan, his cheek no longer twitching. "Come with me tomorrow morning. I'm having coffee with Mom at Clementine Coffee Grinders."

They're meeting? Here in town?

It was worse than he'd thought. Ryan shook his head, information adding up and resulting in one conclusion. "She's the reason you want to quit."

"Yes." Tate looked grim.

"Because you want to make some happy memories." Because Tate had admitted feeling guilty when they'd been placed in foster care, taking some of the blame for their parents not being able to stay sober. "You want to make sure she stays sober, and to do that, she needs a keeper."

Tate looked out the window toward the main house again. "Buy your horse, Ry. But this is something I have to do."

"Right. Because you're the *nice* Oakley." Ryan marched out the door. "The good son I'll never be."

"Did your Oakley find your horses to his liking?" Ma asked when Jo returned to the house for dinner, long after Ryan had left. "Or should I say, did *you* find your Oakley to your liking?"

"Ma…"

Dinner sat in a casserole dish on the stove.

Something with cheese and chicken. There was no telling what else Ma had put in it. Jo would eat it and be done with it, the same way this deal with Ryan would go if he found financing. Food was fuel and a horse sale made the mortgage payment. She refused to dwell on the tidbits she'd learned about Ryan's past, to go soft, to take less than her horses were worth.

She'd dwelled too much on Ryan while they were together. Gushed about his roping skill. Offered him unsolicited advice. Shared too much about herself. Told him she had a heart horse. This wasn't like her. At least, not the woman she'd become.

"I found your Oakley to be refreshingly charming." Ma sat at the kitchen table, squinting over the rim of her readers as she tried to thread a needle.

"He's a buyer." Jo washed up at the kitchen sink, keeping her face averted and her thoughts carefully locked away.

"You could have both a man *and* a buyer."

"Ma…"

"I know you were always partial to Tate, but it was Ryan you always got in trouble with."

"With?" Jo dried her hands, turning. "I got into trouble on my own." And after hearing

just a bit about Ryan's biological parents, she felt bad about their high school feud. "Please don't say anything about this to the boys."

Who'd earned an hour of television and from the sound of things were planted in front of the screen.

"What do I tell you every time the twins get into trouble?" Her mother stitched fur trim on the cuff of a silver Santa pants leg. "I say that you turned out all right."

And Ryan had turned out all right, too.

Jo hung up the dish towel, hopefully hanging up her attraction to Ryan with it. If Ryan had turned out well, then Tate—who'd always been a sweetheart—would have turned out that much better.

Not that I'm putting any stock in Ryan getting me a date with Tate.

She'd be happy with a dance, though. Being held in Tate's arms…

She allowed herself a dreamy sigh.

"I think you should fly out to Nationals in Las Vegas," Ma said, out of the blue.

"We can't afford it." Like so many other things.

"But you might find a buyer if the Oakleys fall through. Don't put all your eggs in one basket." Ma chuckled. "Or you can make things interesting by inviting your Oakley to go with you."

"That is definitely not happening." She could just see Ryan's lip curl if she asked him to spend a few days with her in Vegas.

And if that finely formed lip didn't curl? Well, he'd still think she was interested in him.

When, in reality, all Jo wanted from Ryan was a chunk of cash and a date with his twin.

CHAPTER TEN

LOIS ENTERED THE Buckboard carrying a finished silver velour Santa costume, a box of doughnuts, and wanting to vent about stubbornly single daughters, vindictive ex-husbands and self-absorbed sons who looked gifted horses their sister trained in the mouth.

That Jo…

Jo had spent most of an afternoon with a fine-looking, single cowboy. And what did she do? Treat him like a customer. Jo bore witness to Lois's single life every day. Did she really want that for herself?

And Herbie…

Was the man going to go to his grave angry at the world? She'd given him up a dozen years ago so that he could be happy. And yet he still made her feel as if she stood in the way of his ray of sunshine.

While those sons of hers…

They were men. But that didn't mean they'd matured. They were still too easily influenced by their father and too caught up in the status that came with winning to be kind to their sister.

Lois approached the set of three tables that had been pushed together for their meeting, agitated and craving a doughnut. At least she was the first committee member to arrive. She needed a few minutes more to compose herself.

Lois set down her things, opened the dough-nut box, breathed in all that sugar and selected a pink-glazed doughnut.

"Can't bring in outside food, Lois." Chet Howell stood behind the bar, wiping the counters clean. No one else was in the Buckboard. "You know the rules." But instead of asking her to remove the doughnut box, he grinned. "I'm paid to remind, not enforce."

Lois set the pink confection back in the box without taking her eyes from Chet's friendly grin.

Normally, Lois paid the older cowboy no more than a passing thought and vice versa. He was at least a decade older than Lois, a jack-of-all-trades who worked mostly for the Done Roamin' Ranch.

From what little she knew of Chet, he wasn't her type at all. There was the mustache, for one. The part-time cowboy, part-time bar-tender had the most famous mustache in town.

It was white and rolled into handlebars. And there was his taste in music, for another. She was more a modern country gal. She'd heard hard rock blaring from his truck once at a gas station.

But there was something about that grin tonight that reminded Lois that she was a woman, not just a divorced grandma trying to keep her family on speaking terms, and not just a woman with enough crafting hobbies to qualify as one of Santa's elves.

"Cat got your tongue?" Chet ditched his rag, his smile for her growing.

"No. I…" The front door opened, disrupting whatever she'd been about to say. Lois gave herself a small shake. She wasn't a woman to fall under the spell of a man. She hadn't been on a date since before her marriage.

Mary Harrison, from the Done Roamin' Ranch, came in the front door along with Rose Youngblood, the local bank president and Santapalooza chairwoman. Rose's little white poodle Brutus trotted ahead of her on his leash. He wore a red-and-green-striped Christmas sweater.

Before Lois had an audience, she wanted to say something to Chet, something a woman would say to a man she had chemistry with.

Anything that made her sound non-grandma-like. "Hey…um…Chet… Can I get an iced tea?"

Lois gave herself a mental head-thunk and told herself the heat she was feeling in her cheeks came from a hot flash, not a silver fox.

"Look at how striking this Santa costume turned out." Mary set down a red suit and picked up the silver one Lois had made. Her tan cowboy hat was set at a jaunty angle over her short gray hair. "Now we just have one problem. Who to choose to wear them."

"I vote for Clementine's most eligible bachelors." Rose took a seat and settled Brutus in her lap. "Make them stand out."

Rose always stood out. She'd been a rodeo queen back in her day, a day long before Lois's youth. Tonight, Rose wore red-and-black cowboy boots, black slacks, a silver-sequined Christmas sweater and a black cowboy hat over her white hair.

"In my experience…" Mary carefully folded the silver suit Lois had made. "Most men don't want to stand out."

Behind the bar, Chet laughed.

Lois glanced at him, unsettled. "Do you have an opinion?"

"Always. It takes a certain type of man to stand out in a crowd." Chet brought Lois her iced tea. "I volunteer." He gave Lois a meaningful look, as if wearing a silver suit wasn't the only thing he was volunteering for.

Oh, my.

Chet singled out Rose next. "You know the rules, Miss Rose. No nonservice dogs allowed." He winked. "But I'm only paid to remind, not enforce. And I find rule-breakers charming." His gaze swiveled to Lois, heating her from the inside out.

That look further confounded Lois. Why the flirtatious signals? She wasn't a rule-breaker, not by any stretch. A box of doughnuts taken into a restaurant didn't count.

The three Santapalooza committee women stared at Chet as he returned to the bar. Mary and Rose seemed as confounded by Chet as Lois was.

Mary was the first to break Chet's spell by whispering, "I'm a happily married woman, but Chet is a *hubba-hubba*."

"I'm too old for romance." Rose smiled softly. "But likewise."

Lois kept carefully silent until Chet disappeared into the back room. Only then did she release a sigh and a soft "*Hubba-hubba* is right."

Lois couldn't remember the last time this had happened—being magnetically drawn to a man who seemed magnetically drawn to her. Her heart was pounding something fierce and all her frustrations with her family were forgotten.

"Before I forget, Lois." Mary touched Lois's arm. "I have some noncommittee business to discuss with you. Ryan was full of praise for Jo's horses at dinner tonight. In fact, he was very complimentary of Jo. *Your* Jo. Are you thinking what I'm thinking?"

"I'm way ahead of you," Lois said, coming back to what she'd been fretting over upon arrival, the issue of her stubbornly single daughter. "Not that I've had much luck encouraging Jo."

"You can lead a horse to water…" Chet said, grinning, having come out of the back room with a bowl of limes. "Rose? Mary? What can I get you to drink?"

While they placed their orders, more Santapalooza committee members entered, distracting Lois from the bartender and stopping more conversation with Mary about getting Ryan and Jo together.

And it wouldn't be revisited until the meeting was called to order and Coronet Blankenship, the committee secretary and owner of the Buffalo Diner, began reading the last meeting's minutes.

Mary leaned in closer to Lois and whispered, "Your Jo is the only female Ryan has ever talked about."

Lois couldn't say the same. Jo had talked sparingly and guardedly about Tate Oakley in high school. How kind he was. How hard he worked at roping. Who he was dating. Since then, Tate had become known in the community for some of the same things—his kindness, cowboy work ethic and who he was dating. He was always dating someone new. Lois didn't understand how Jo would want someone with a history of not settling down.

But on the other hand, Jo had talked a lot about Ryan her last year in high school. How callous he was. How annoying he was. How kids in school gave him a wide berth and called him the cold Oakley twin. Since then, Ryan kept to himself and the crew at the Done Roamin' Ranch. He didn't volunteer for community events like the Fourth of July parade or Santapalooza. No one ever talked bad about him. They just didn't…talk about him.

But he was nice. Good-looking. He'd brought doughnuts and had come to the front door upon arriving at the ranch. And after he left, Jo had seemed preoccupied.

"I want to see my boys settled," Mary continued whispering. "Not live in the bunkhouse forever. That bunkhouse would make an awfully fine She Shed someday."

"Maybe we can help Jo and Ryan date," Lois whispered back, earning a reprimanding look from Rose, who sat at the head of the table.

"They're dating," Cooper Brown whispered from his spot opposite Lois. He'd gone to school with Jo and Ryan. "I saw them having coffee together. They were sitting close and talking as if they were comfortable with each other."

"They had coffee?" Lois blurted, earning a shush from Rose and all pairs of eyes at the table turning her way.

Jo and Ryan had had coffee and Jo hadn't told her? Jo told her everything.

Lois exchanged a look with Mary. A look and a nod.

Interesting…

CHAPTER ELEVEN

"DON'T GO INSIDE." Ryan moved into Jo's path the next morning on the sidewalk a few doors down from Clementine Coffee Grinders. "We need to talk first."

He steered Jo in the opposite direction.

Squinting in the bright sunlight, Jo dragged her feet as Ryan led her toward her truck. She'd skipped her first coffee of the day, having tossed and turned all night, consumed with worry regarding mortgage payments. She'd overslept and barely gotten the boys to school on time. "I should warn you, cowboy, I'm in desperate need of caffeine and you—"

"Need a spy." Instead of stopping by her vehicle, Ryan practically dragged her across the street to his truck and pressed on top of her shoulder until Jo was half crouching behind his truck bed.

If Ryan thought he'd be inconspicuous parked in the middle of downtown Main Street, even crouching down, he was sadly mistaken. Main Street was lined with historic brick buildings featuring large plate-glass windows that allowed everyone working—or drinking coffee—a clear view of all the happenings near and far.

"Have we gone back in time?" Jo swung her face around toward his handsome one—his clean-shaven, chiseled jaw, his sharp brown eyes and thick, expressive brows. She had to blink to remind herself that her attraction was for Tate's face. "Are we hiding from Principal Gordon? Or is this a prank?"

And here she'd had kind thoughts toward him after his visit yesterday.

"I need you to do something." Ryan pointed toward the coffee shop. He wore a black hoodie beneath a jean jacket. His black hair would have been the color of his black felt cowboy hat if it hadn't been sun-faded. "I need you to go inside and say hello to Tate. He's at the table in the back with a woman and—"

"No." Jo stood up, placing a hand on her hat when a gust of cold wind tried to steal it away. "I'm not interrupting his date. And I don't need or want your help to get his attention." That last part didn't sound as convincing as she wanted it to.

Ryan grabbed hold of her hand and tugged her back down next to him.

And Jo would have resisted—*she really*

would have—except his hand felt so right around hers and the warmth of his touch shimmied up her arm, making her heart pound.

Just as she'd always imagined it would with Tate. She set her jaw.

"Tate is in there with my biological mother, who I don't trust. I need you to go inside and smell her."

Without coffee, Jo's brain must not have been fully functioning yet. "I'm sorry. But I thought you just said I need to *smell* your mother?"

He nodded. "I need to know if you smell alcohol."

"At eight in the morning?" At his nod, the meaning of his request sank in, along with his reference the other day to his mother. "Won't Tate be able to tell?"

"Yes, but he wouldn't admit it to me if he did." Ryan bit his bottom lip, clearly worried.

Jo could feel her resistance weakening. "I'm not even going to pretend to understand what's going on with you and your family, but I'll go in there, get us two large coffees and—"

"Say hello to Tate and strike up a conversation with her," he said quickly. "Saying hello to Tate will go a long way in getting you that date you want. And if she's been drinking, you'll smell it on her breath."

Jo refrained from rolling her eyes. Barely. "I'm going in for coffee. I am *not* going to promise anything else." She held a hand up when it seemed he might protest. "That's my final offer. Meet me in my truck. I'll unlock it. If folks see you out here like this, they're going to think you're weirder than you already are."

"Ha ha." Ryan's gaze captured hers and it was like *wham-pow*, just the way it was when Tate looked into her eyes, which was hardly ever. "I can't thank you enough."

Jo nodded numbly, still under the impact of his *wham-pow*.

She crossed the street and entered the coffee shop. Tate sat at a corner table, facing her. He wore a straw cowboy hat and a shearling jacket. His beard was thick and dark and not completely unattractive. But she preferred Ryan's...*Tate's* jaw clean-shaven.

His mother's back was to Jo. Her too-black hair fell past her shoulders. She sat slumped, as if a lifetime of hard times weighed her down. And she wore an outdated tan jacket with faux fur trim. No cowboy hat. No cowboy boots.

Jo had always assumed that Tate and Ryan

came from a ranching family, but that didn't seem the case.

No one was in line, so Jo ordered a very large vanilla latte and a coffee with two sweeteners for Ryan. After placing her order, she turned toward Tate rather than stand with the handful of other customers at the pick-up end of the counter.

"Hey, Tate." She moseyed over on legs that felt like melted butter and a gaze that rested on his Adam's apple, just visible at the bottom of his beard. "I want to invite you for a ride. I think I have a horse you'd really like." Prince.

Only when her boots were planted beside his table did she look at the woman sitting across from him and draw a breath through her nose.

Ryan's mother dipped a candy cane into a lidless cup of hot chocolate.

The smell of peppermint filled Jo's nostrils, masking any alcohol scent that might have been in the air. But it also made her wonder: *Is the candy cane a cover for alcohol on her breath?*

She bit her lip.

I'm as bad as Ryan.

"Thanks for the offer, Jo," Tate said with his usual pleasant demeanor when encountering Jo, smiling at his mother as if he wanted nothing but her affection. "I won't be buying a horse this season."

What? Jo had to stop herself from marching out the door and giving Ryan a piece of her mind. Ryan had lied to her! He didn't need a pair of horses. But he did need a swift boot in the behind!

"I love horses." Ryan's mother preened, like a young child setting up an adult for the next line: *Can I have one?*

It was odd behavior coming from a grown-up, piquing Jo's curiosity and tamping down her annoyance with Ryan.

"I love horses, too," Jo said, giving Mrs. Oakley a belated smile and drawing another deep breath as she remembered her mission.

"I'd love to have horses on my ranch," the woman continued as if Jo hadn't spoken. "But first things first, I suppose. Alpacas. I'm going to make alpaca yarn. Do you knit?" She sent a fleeting glance Jo's way, as if she didn't dare hold eye contact too long for fear of being judged.

I'm reading way too much into this woman's actions.

Jo only had to look at Tate's doting expression to doubt Ryan's suspicions. This Oakley saw nothing amiss. She trusted Tate's opinion over Ryan's, didn't she? Didn't she?

"I don't knit," Jo told her, keeping hold of her doubts. "But my mother does. She's into blanket yarn lately." Which was as thick as Jo's fingers.

"Not as good as alpaca," Ryan's mother said in a knowing tone that raised Jo's eyebrows. "Everyone should knit with alpaca."

"I suppose…" Jo allowed kindly, not wanting to burst the woman's bubble. "If it suits their project."

"Pish." Ryan's mother crunched on her candy cane. "Alpaca is the best and that's what I aim to provide my customers. Only the best." She glanced up at Jo again, not quite meeting her gaze.

Was she shy? Or sly? The only thing Jo knew for certain was that her self-centered, inauthentic attitude and behavior didn't inspire trust.

That said, she couldn't give Ryan the answer he sought. The only things Jo could smell were the shop's fresh-ground-coffee aroma and Mrs. Oakley's candy cane.

"I'm finally getting my life together and I'm doing everything the right way this time. All I need is seed money and there's no chance I can fail." *Crunch, crunch* went the candy cane.

Crunch, crunch went Jo's belief that Ryan's

mother knew what she was getting into. Running a business was a marathon course littered with potholes and detours toward failure.

But Tate was still staring adoringly at his mother. So, Jo tried to be positive. "I'm sure yarn production is like any other business. You've got to find your niche and pick your competitive battles."

"You've done that?" Tate stared up at Jo with a friendly smile, a glad-you're-here smile.

It was one of the rare times he'd shown an interest in Jo. She broke out in a sweat. "I… uh…" *Pull it together!* "Yes. I learned from my mistakes very early." Work long hours and never take a promised sale over a signed contract.

"I won't make mistakes," Ryan's mother said naively.

Tate might have winced. His expression flickered so quickly that Jo couldn't be sure.

"I certainly hope your alpaca business does well," Jo told his mother, thinking that the woman was in for a rocky ride and hoping that wouldn't cause her to drink. "But the reality is that everyone makes mistakes. It's what you learn from them and how you move forward afterward that counts."

Tate blinked up at her, nodding. "Well said."

Praise from her crush? Jo's mouth went dry.

The barista rang a bell. "Jo, your order is ready."

"Okay…um." Jo bowed, like a servant, trying to smell Ryan's mother one last time and feeling like a fool when Tate's thick, dark brows went up. She shuffled the soles of her boots backward. "If you change your mind about a horse before Christmas, Tate, let me know."

In the meantime, Jo was going to chew Ryan out for deceiving her. She said her goodbyes to the Oakleys, collected the coffees and hightailed it to her truck.

"Well?" Ryan asked before she could launch into her tirade.

"I'm not spy material." Jo thrust his coffee toward him. "I couldn't smell anything but your mother's candy cane."

Ryan's jaw dropped. "Classic." He sipped his coffee. "There wasn't an envelope full of cash on the table? She didn't ask for gifts while you were there?"

"Well…" Jo hedged.

"Tell me." Ryan rubbed a hand behind his neck, looking pained. "Give me the worst. I can take it."

"She mentioned wanting horses at her ranch and needing seed money. But rest assured that Tate didn't bite. He even turned down my offer to come ride Prince and..." She narrowed her eyes at him. "Tate doesn't want a horse." She gave Ryan a death glare, trying to squash the attraction she felt when staring into his eyes. "You lied to me."

Ryan made a calm-down gesture with one hand. "He's under our mother's spell. Just wait a week or so. She'll disappoint him. In the worst possible way. And then he'll come around."

"I can't wait a few weeks." The balloon payment loomed in the front of her mind, vivid and demoralizing. "Christmas is almost here."

"It's weeks away." Ryan shook his head. "I should know. It's my least favorite time of year. I hate it."

Jo stared at him, registering something important. Ryan was cold toward his mother, and he hated Christmas. *There's no way I can be attracted to him.* She smiled. "The only people who hate Christmas are the Grinch and Scrooge."

"Exactly."

RYAN EXPECTED Jo to tell him he shouldn't dislike Christmas.

She was wearing another Christmas sweatshirt beneath her puffy vest, after all. But she didn't.

He expected Jo to challenge him to dispute forgiveness and love being the theme of the holiday and therefore discount his opinion.

She didn't.

Instead, Jo sipped her coffee, studying him over the rim of her cup. Then she smiled and said, "I love Christmas. It's the one holiday where I can take off from work and spend time with family and friends guilt free. Everyone's in a good mood. People are kind and giving. The more Christmas, the better, I say. But to each his own." She sounded overjoyed that he was Grinch-ish, as if it was his choice and she didn't care what he felt.

Ryan made a face.

Jo leaned on the truck's center console, smile fading. "I suppose your parents are behind this dislike of Christmas."

He nodded. "You don't really want to hear why."

"And what you mean to say is you don't really want to tell me." Jo didn't sound at all put out by his choice. He was beginning to feel as if she didn't care. "That fits your image as the cold Oakley, although given your dislike of Christmas, maybe they should call you the grumpy Oakley."

Frustration built in his chest. "Why is it that no one calls you the grumpy Pierce?" She was just as touchy as he was.

"Have you met my dad or my brothers?" Jo laughed, long and loud, seemingly with her entire being. "I may have been angry in school, but becoming a parent changed my perspective."

"It didn't change my parents' attitudes." He shifted in his seat to face her. "We never had a Christmas tree. Why waste good drinking money on a dead thing? We didn't have presents. Day-old cookies, maybe. Even if a charity or kind soul delivered some, my parents returned them for cash. There was no Santa. No stockings. And if there were carols, they were liquor induced, slurred in their delivery and off-key. And..."

Jo stared at him with pity growing in her eyes.

He didn't want her pity. And so he pivoted away from telling her the final straw, that his parents disappeared for nearly a week before Christmas and the subsequent, messy fallout. Instead, he said, "There was never snow. Ice, maybe. But snow? Never."

His glib comments had the desired effect. The pity mostly vanished from her expression. "You can't blame Christmas for our weather. This is Oklahoma. If we get snow, it's just a few inches and melts within a day."

He waved her off. "Everyone else has fond memories of Christmas. I don't. I'd rather spend the last few weeks of the year someplace where Christmas isn't celebrated."

"Is there such a place?" Jo wondered aloud.

"No." Sadly.

"Merry Christmas, Ryan." Jo smiled the way she had when she'd pulled off a prank back in the day, like she had his number, and she was going to use it.

"I won't let that get under my skin, Jo." But Ryan was afraid it was too late. Her merry barb didn't sting. It made him want to smile in return.

Bah, humbug.

The last thing he needed was to lose his detachment for the year's biggest commercial event.

"I don't need to rub my Christmas cheer in your face," Jo went on. "I've seen the Done Roamin' Ranch at the holidays. Your mom goes all out, like mine. What do you do when you get home? Close your eyes until you get inside your room?"

"You're a comedian." Ryan sat back in his seat, feeling as grumpy as Scrooge when Bob Cratchit asked for Christmas off.

Jo's cell phone rang. She looked at the display. "Seriously?" She swiped the phone screen. "Ma, what's wrong? And why—"

"I wanted to know what time we're leaving and if we can stop by that store with the cute doodads in Friar's Creek."

"Ma, you called me on video again." Jo showed Ryan her screen, with the now-familiar image of Lois's age-spotted cheek and a side view of her chapped lips.

"Why can't I remember the name of that doodad place?" Lois mused.

"Liberty Finds?" Ryan said.

Jo popped the back of her hand against his abs, a gentle rebuke for speaking.

"Who's that?" Lois moved her phone, filling the screen with her big, curious brown eyes. "Is that your Oakley?"

"Ma, he's not *my* Oakley." Jo moved her screen directly in front of her face. "And you need to stop video calling me. It uses up data on our phone plan."

"Are you parked in your truck?" Lois gasped. "Oh, my. Did I disrupt another secret rendezvous? Put my Oakley back on the phone."

"And now you're my mother's Oakley," Jo muttered, cheeks turning beet red.

Ryan plucked the phone from Jo's hand. "Hey, Lois."

"How do you know the name of my doo-dad store?" Lois demanded.

Jo sank down in her seat and pulled the brim of her wide white hat over her face.

"It's my mom's favorite store." Ryan had a hard time not smiling at Jo's expense.

"Oh, yes. Mary loves it, too. That's right." Lois brightened. "You should buy her something there for Christmas."

"Good idea." Ryan nodded. "I'll pick up a gift card."

"No, you foolish boy." She frowned. "You should find something there that will give Mary joy. Not just a doodad, but a doodad *you* picked out for her. That's what you do at Christmas. You give thoughtful gifts. It shows you care."

Ryan mumbled something that might have been agreement, but he felt cornered into it.

"Ma." Jo snatched her phone back. "We're leaving at nine thirty."

"Okay, but—"

Jo disconnected.

Coronet Blankenship, the elderly cowgirl owner of the Buffalo Diner, walked past on the sidewalk. She stopped at Jo's front fender, smiled and made a heart sign with her hands.

Jo made a no-no gesture, waving both arms back and forth like mad.

But Coronet simply smiled and walked on.

"There goes another one," Jo griped.

"Another what?" Ryan's gaze shifted to the coffee shop door. No one had come in or out in several minutes. He wondered what Tate and his mother were discussing.

"Another person who thinks we've been matched by Ronnie and are dating." Jo waved a few times in front of Ryan's face. "Don't you see? Coronet will text my mother, who'll text your mother. And then the two of them will begin planning our wedding. Merry Christmas, Ryan."

"You're overreacting." He gently moved her hands out of his space, gaze drifting toward the coffee shop door. He hoped his mother hadn't come out while he'd been distracted by Jo. He'd wanted to see her face.

"Did you hear anything I said?" Jo demanded.

Ryan nodded. "It's unfortunate."

"Unfortunate?" Jo sank in her seat again. "I hate to even ask why you think the town believing we're dating is unfortunate."

"Isn't it obvious? Because I'd rather you be considered single so Tate will ask you out." He leaned forward, gaze still trained on the coffee shop door. "Do you mind if we sit here until Tate leaves or the bank opens?" Whichever came first.

"Thirty minutes," Jo mumbled, crossing her arms over her chest. "And then I'll be done with you."

"Thirty minutes? Why's that?" He spared her a glance.

"The bank opens in half an hour and that's when you find out you can't afford my horses." She tsked, scowling. "I mean horse. *Singular.* I'll be charitable and keep you company until then, but I would prefer we don't lie to each other in between."

"I'm not lying per se. Yes, Tate isn't of a mind to make a purchase now. But I'm thinking ahead. I know my mother. And I know Tate. When she burns him, he'll need something positive in his life. And that will be buying Prince."

Movement at the coffee shop door caught his eye. His mother came outside. It was the first time he'd seen her face in years. She'd had her back turned to the windows when he arrived. Her face didn't look gaunt, the way it had the last time he'd seen her. Her cheeks had a healthy pink tone. She shoved a white envelope into her purse—*cash?*—and waved goodbye to Tate. There were no hugs, no lingering goodbyes. She slid behind the wheel of her faded old sedan and looked cheerful.

Satisfaction over a scam well played, I bet.

Ryan looked away and into the bearded face of his twin, who stood at the front bumper of Jo's truck.

"Talk to you later, Jo." Ryan hopped out and joined Tate on the sidewalk.

"Don't say a word," Tate said to him. "Because you didn't come inside."

"I was just going to ask if you'd come with me to the bank when it opens." Ryan turned in that direction and was heartened when Tate fell into step beside him, although that presented a new set of complications. In a few minutes, his twin would know how much the horses cost, which would spark a whole new set of arguments.

"It's been so cold that Mom's heating bill was higher than expected," Tate said simply. "I gave her some money to tide her over."

"I didn't ask." And he wasn't going to voice his disapproval. His brother was important to him.

Also important was this loan. And the closer they came to the bank, the more nervous Ryan became.

No pressure. Just my future and Tate's hanging in the balance.

They arrived at Clementine Savings & Loan just as their foster brother Dix and his grandmother Rose Youngblood arrived to open the doors. Rose held the leash of a small white poodle with Christmas red-and-green bows over his ears.

"You're early for your appointment, Ry," Dix said while turning off the alarm system. He wore blue slacks, a white dress shirt and fancy blue silk tie beneath a heavy black coat. "Good to see you, Tate."

"Come on in." Mrs. Youngblood led the way. She was colorful in her teal cowboy boots, pink jeans and a white Christmas sweater beneath a puffy, teal stadium jacket and matching cowboy hat. "It's cold outside." She unclipped the dog's leash. "You remember Brutus, don't you?"

The delicate little dog pranced over to the lobby area, picked up a Santa squeaker toy and trotted back to them, filling the bank with noise.

"Hey, fella." Ryan tossed Santa the length of the bank, to the little dog's delight.

"I just need to get the tellers set up and then we can talk." Dix disappeared in the back.

A few minutes later, Ryan and Tate sat across from Dix in his office. Brutus was perched in Dix's lap, squeaking Santa happily. If the dog hadn't been there, it would have felt more like the high school principal's office, seeing as how Dix wore that tie and Ryan's nerves were shot.

"What can I do for you today?" Dix asked.

"We need a loan for a pair of horses," Ryan blurted, only to be interrupted by Tate before he could explain why.

"Ry needs a loan." Tate shook his head. "Not me. I'm just here for moral support."

And he was doing a bad job of it with all his negative vibes. "Or…" Ryan cleared his throat. "Tate might be doing his due diligence to see if he really wants a horse or not. It's always smart to invest in your future. Especially when you're supporting more than yourself."

"How much are these horses?" Dix asked, unfazed by their bickering. They'd grown up together, after all. Dix was a Done Roamin' Ranch foster, too.

"Eighty thousand dollars for the pair."

Tate sucked in a breath.

Dix typed something into his computer.

"Half that," Tate said gruffly. "I'm not buying one."

"He's undecided," Ryan said forcefully. "We need to know what it'll take to get a loan for two horses."

Dix ruffled the dog's ears. "Ry, I'm assuming you only own your truck, which isn't near being paid for."

Ryan's heart tumbled to his toes. "Does that mean no?"

"Well…" Dix hedged, smoothing his tie. "We don't normally make loans for livestock."

Tate leaned forward. "I heard you loaned the Burns Ranch money for cattle."

"That's different," Dix said in that steady tone of his, the one he'd used when explaining math problems to Ryan when they were kids, although back then his voice had squeaked like that Santa toy. "Cattle are a good investment. They can be raised and sold. Or used as breeders. They make money."

"These horses will make us money." Ryan had to believe that, or he'd be scared to death about the amount of money being spent.

"You don't have anything to secure the loan," Dix was saying, just as Jo had predicted. "No collateral."

Ryan clenched his jaw. "I know that, but can you loan us the money or not? You know we're good for it."

Tate shook his head.

"Okay, bro," Ryan conceded. "*I'm* good for it."

"Ry…" Dix looked apologetic. "You'll need a cosigner for an unsecured loan."

"I have Tate." Ryan gestured toward Exhibit A.

Dix sighed heavily. "You need a cosigner who owns property or makes significantly more money than you do."

"Oh." Ryan stared at his boots, which was where his hopes and dreams seemed to have dropped and shattered.

"We're done here." Tate stood. "You should have told me the price, Ry. We've just wasted Dix's time." He opened the door and left.

Brutus bolted off Dix's lap and scampered after him, squeaking Santa.

"My mother's got him in her clutches again," Ryan said thickly. "You know how this is going to go. She'll shake as much money out of him as she can and then waste it on alcohol, leaving me to pick him up." Ryan swallowed his pride and asked Dix, "Can you cosign the loan for me? For the pair?"

"As an officer of the bank, I can't." Dix spared him an apologetic glance before tapping a few more computer keys. "But Mom and Dad could."

Their foster parents, Ryan assumed he meant.

"I don't want to ask them, Dix. They've already done so much for us." Putting a roof over their heads, teaching them a way to make a living, providing them with stability and love.

Dix nodded. "Where does that leave you?"

"I suppose I could hit up some livestock auctions and see if any good prospects come on the market." But he wanted Jo's horses. He got to his feet. "I've got seven grand in my account."

"That's not peanuts." Dix came around the desk and gave Ryan a hug. "I'm sorry I couldn't help you."

"Yeah." Ryan glanced out the door, the way Tate had exited. "I'm sorry you couldn't help us both."

CHAPTER TWELVE

"HAVE FAITH IN your Oakley."

"Ma…" Jo walked between holding pens at the livestock auction in Friar's Creek, weaving through milling ranchers and willing sellers.

Jo didn't normally attend the weekly livestock auction in Friar's Creek, mostly because it was managed by her father, but she wanted to scope out the lay of the land—the landscape of sellers and potential buyers of high-end horses, that was.

"Our Oakley is going to come through on that sale." Ma was on the Ryan Oakley train, chugging purposefully down the aisle. "A pair of horses."

"Can we change the subject?" While Jo had talked with horse trainers and breeders who were selling, Ma wouldn't stop talking in between about Ryan. Didn't she realize the news about Ryan was grim? "He lied to me." She'd told her all about her morning coffee run when she picked up Ma for the drive to the auction.

"That's not lying. That's hoping." Ma shoved her hands into her jacket pockets. The exit doors were open, and the large indoor labyrinth of pens was chilly. "Your Oakley is trying to hold his family together, same as I keep holding ours."

"Our Oakley… Your Oakley…" Jo shook her head. "From where I'm sitting, neither you nor *your* Oakley are doing a good job on the family front."

"Keeping everyone talking civilly to each other is a full-time job, as *our* Oakley can attest." Ma nudged Jo with her elbow. "I talked to your brothers on the phone this morning."

"Woke them up with a video call, you mean." Jo chuckled, pausing to check out a pen with some frisky colts.

"Yes, I was their alarm clock," Ma said in a huffy tone. "My point being that they apologized to me for leaving you out of the loop."

"They would." Because it meant Ty and Eric didn't think they had to apologize to Jo. She zipped up her vest jacket as they neared the far end of the building. Jo stopped at a pen with a strawberry roan more because she knew the seller than because she was interested in the horse.

"Not that one," Ma said in an overly loud voice, pointing at the mare. "Cow hocks. Your horses are a cut above what can be found here, Jo."

The seller didn't look kindly on Ma.

Nor did Jo. "Sorry, Dave. Ma hasn't had enough caffeine today," she said, giving up on asking him how his sales were going. She hustled her mother toward the next paddock. "I know how to judge a horse, Ma. You hurt Dave's feelings."

"I don't know what's come over me today. I'm so tense." Ma turned back to Dave and called out an apology. "You know I get flustered when I'm tense. Maybe it's because I expect your father to turn up at any minute." She glanced around.

Jo pulled her mother to a halt and faced her. "Maybe it's because you're worried that I won't make the mortgage."

Ma wouldn't meet Jo's gaze. "We've... *You've* always come through. I just wish I could help financially. If I got a job—"

"You wouldn't keep me and the boys fed. Or the house clean," Jo said sincerely. "Christmas wouldn't get put up until the twenty-fourth, if then." Even if Jo loved the holiday. "And there'd be a hole in town on the committees you volunteer for. You do your part and then some."

Ma hugged her. The good kind of hug with a big squeeze.

"We'll get through this." Jo stepped back, adjusting her hat and then adjusting Ma's.

"Mark my words." Ma raised a finger in the air. "Our Oakley is going to come through."

Jo rolled her eyes and checked out the information sheet on the next pen.

"One white sock?" Ma tsked, pointing at the black horse's hooves. "You know what they say about horses with less than four white socks. 'One white sock, keep him not a day. Two white socks, sell him as you may. Three white socks, give him to a friend. Four white socks, keep him to the end.'"

"That's an old wives' tale." Again, Jo found herself apologizing to the seller and tugging Ma forward. "I should have dropped you at the doodad shop. Now, no more nursery rhymes."

"That wasn't a child's rhyme. Are you going to tell me that old wives' tales have no merit?" Ma marched to the next holding pen. "What about 'a stitch in time saves nine'? Or 'you reap what you sow'?"

"Why don't you go get a coffee?" Jo took her mother by the shoulders and slowly turned her around until she was headed in the direction of the small snack bar on the far side of the building near the entrance. "I should be done soon."

"I think I will." Ma lifted her chin and pasted a smile on her face. "I need a boost before we shop my favorite store."

Jo was just glad her mother hadn't said more about their Oakley.

She hitched her resolve to her forward-moving boots, stepping outside into the strong Oklahoma sunlight and the bracing wind. She needed a boost, too. Just a small nugget of good news to give her hope that a sale was right around the corner.

Dodging vendors leading stock into the auction yard, Jo walked to the next open door, doing exactly what her mother had done, lifting her chin and pasting a smile she didn't feel on her face.

"Fancy meeting you here," a deep, familiar voice said from behind her.

Jo turned to find Ryan ambling up to her. For a moment, her heart leaped, if only because he was her last hope for a mortgage-saving sale. And then she realized why he must be here. Her shoulders slumped. "I guess things went the way I predicted at the bank."

His brow clouded. "I'm coming up with a plan B."

"And this is your contingency." Jo nodded, inordinately demoralized by the loss, even though her gut had told her Ryan couldn't afford to buy Prince and Pauper. Or even just Pauper. She pointed toward the bay gelding in the next pen, walking up and taking hold of the top rail with both hands, propping her foot on the bottom rail. "You could probably pick up this young fella for a song. He's got the same build as Pauper. And he's being sold by a rancher close to Tulsa. He's probably familiar with roping."

"I may not be putting all my eggs in one basket, Jo. But my preference is still to purchase Prince and Pauper." Despite his words, Ryan leaned over the rail and looked at the bay. "Or…do you have any other horses for me to consider?"

"The only competitors ready are Prince and Pauper." She frowned. "I have three pairs in the pipeline for next year, but they're not ready." And she didn't want partially trained horses out there with Regal Robert's lineage and her name as trainer attached. There was too much at risk in case someone less skilled than her brothers would buy them, not do well and taint Jo's reputation.

"What are you selling Tiger for?"

Her boot slipped off the metal rail she'd

been resting it on. "I told you he's not for sale."

"I know, but if I'm looking at my options, he's an option." There was compassion in his gaze, reminding her that they were both in a tough spot. He might be losing his roping partner and she might be losing her ranch. "If you need a sale before Christmas and are unwilling to break up a pair of horses, Tiger could be the solution. From my perspective, you might want substantially less than you do for Pauper, seeing as how Tiger is a utility horse, versed in many things but not specialized as a roper."

Jo didn't know what to say because she felt like she was at a point where she couldn't say no. It was just...*not Tiger*.

"My dad always says that hard times call for hard decisions." Ryan didn't look happy about the situation they were in either. "You implied Tiger is a smart horse and enjoys working cattle. I could use that. And you could use the money. If you can part with him."

She didn't like that he was right. "You'd have to befriend him first, earn his trust, make him feel you're part of the family."

Part of our family? Ma is going to have a field day with this.

A stocky older cowboy walked down the aisle toward them.

She stepped away from Ryan, hope on the horizon. "Merry Christmas, Travis." He was an amateur competitor, but top of the ranks. He'd bought a pair of competition horses from her four years back. It was about time for him to trade up.

"Merry Christmas, Jo." The big cowboy may have stopped to talk, but his eyes roamed the pens. He was looking for a horse, all right. His chin may have been grizzled but his clothes looked brand-new. "I might have expected you to be in Las Vegas if I hadn't heard that your brothers weren't riding your stock."

News travels fast.

Jo held on to her friendliest smile. "You know my brothers, Travis. They change their minds as frequently as the sun rises. Sometimes more so."

Travis tucked his thumbs in his belt loops and guffawed. "Are you buying or selling?"

She silently thanked him for asking. "I'm selling but not here. Got a good pair of competition roping horses, real goers."

"No need to sell me on quality. Tango and Cash have been good for me." That didn't stop Travis from continuing to look elsewhere. "I could swing by after the New Year and take a ride. January always brings a new perspective. You know…*after* the Nationals."

After he found out which horses her brothers had ridden and how they placed in the final postseason competition. He'd have a bargaining chip if they didn't ride Laurel and Hardy. She didn't wish her brothers ill, but if they won on mounts that hadn't been trained by her, she'd have to lower her asking price for Prince and Pauper.

Regardless, January was too late to do her any good with the mortgage.

"Jo, can you give me your opinion on this filly over here?" Ryan called her over to the next holding pen, where he'd been shamelessly listening, no doubt.

And she shamelessly took the out he gave her. "Thanks," she told Ryan after Travis had moved along. "I'm afraid my brothers switching mounts means every negotiation I have will involve a conversation about this year's Nationals."

"You'll ride this out, Jo," Ryan said in a voice that rang with certainty. He had a good heart and a strong pair of shoulders, all indicators that he was a man a woman could lean on through good times and bad. "I know you. You're a survivor, same as me."

Jo swallowed the lump in her throat because increasingly his offer to consider Tiger was looking like the responsible choice. "I can let you ride Tiger, same as we did with Pauper. But you'll have to gain his trust first. I won't have someone break his spirit just because he's not an easy ride."

"Fair." Ryan nodded. "And I'm still going to pursue other financing for Prince and Pauper." He turned, arm resting on the top rail, gaze resting on her the way she'd always imagined Tate would look at her. "But in the meantime, to be clear, you're giving me permission to hang out at your ranch with Tiger."

"When I'm there," she said firmly. "Which is almost always. But let me tell the boys he might be sold. If you tell them, they're going to make things hard on you."

"I've lived through hard."

And the way he said it, she believed him. "Also, Ryan, to be fair, we'll each be looking at other options. You can shop around for another horse. And if I can sell Prince and Pauper, Tiger will *no longer* be for sale."

He extended his hand to shake on the deal, fingers closing around her hand with a firm yet tender hold. A supportive hold.

My Oakley.

Jo didn't want to let go.

She attributed her sudden lack of breath to the hard choices she had ahead, not Ryan Oakley's touch.

CHAPTER THIRTEEN

LOIS STEPPED UP to the snack bar counter at the livestock auction. "One black coffee."

"How about iced tea, no lemon?" The man behind the counter turned. Chet smiled at her, and the tips of his white handlebar mustache quivered like antennae trying to tune to her wavelength. "Or diet soda?"

Hubba-hubba.

Lois tried to clear her head. "I said, one coffee. Black." She took in Chet's weathered hands. His wiry build. And blue eyes that seemed to be twinkling at her. "How many jobs do you have?"

"Several. I'm a hard worker. Feel like a man of thirty." He flexed his muscles.

Hubba-hubba.

Lois's mouth was dry. "All those jobs… That must make it hard at the holidays. You always working, I mean." She might just as well ask in a roundabout way if he was single. "Your family must miss you."

"No family. I never married." He rested

his elbows on the counter and gave her his complete attention, serious for a change as if he was applying for another job. "I work most of the year for the Done Roamin' Ranch, as a cattle rig driver and stock handler. We get most of December off and I don't like to be idle. I like this gig a lot, has good energy, all the hustle and bustle of the auction." He smoothed his mustache, smile returning. "And you...you like your caffeine."

"Doesn't everyone?" Were they flirting? Was she good at it? It had been so long, Lois couldn't tell. "Speaking of which, one coffee. Black."

"Coffee is brewing." He beamed at her. "I offered you iced tea or diet soda."

She liked the way his eyes twinkled. She bet he'd been popular with the ladies all his life. "I'll wait for the coffee."

"I see your daughter is dating Ryan." Chet nodded toward the way she'd come.

Lois turned, spotting Jo talking to her Oakley. "If you ask them, they'd say they *aren't* dating. But I hope that changes."

"He's a good man." Chet was staid with his endorsement. "Hard worker. Nice sense of humor. Skilled roping competitor. Not sure why he gets a bad rap, not that his brother is a bad egg either. It's just that... I don't know."

"Ryan doesn't stand out," Lois decided. "But he shines nonetheless." And she hoped Jo could see it, too. "I think Ryan is a keeper. I like him." She turned back to Chet. *I like you, too.* "Ryan knew the name of my doo-dad store here in Friar's Creek." That had been surprising.

"Liberty Finds?" Chet asked.

"That's the one." She beamed at him. They were definitely flirting, and *he* was doing a fine job of it. "You know it?"

"I do. Sold some of my mother's things there after she passed. Fine china and the like." He cleared his throat, a sentimental look in his eye. "How did your Santapalooza meeting go?"

"Good. The parade should go off without a hitch this year, weather permitting."

Knock on wood.

"Aren't you going to ask me to wear a Santa suit? I'm an eligible bachelor."

Lois chuckled. "A silver one?"

"I wouldn't have any other." He picked up the coffeepot, which had stopped percolating, and poured her a cup. "I'm not your average Santa. I come with my own mustache."

"We don't give out beards without a mustache." She wasn't so bad at this flirting thing. Lois couldn't remember the last time she'd felt so good. "Mary Harrison is handling the sign-ups this year."

"I'll get my name on the list but only if you agree to ride with me." He winked.

Back when Jo was young and had been married to Bobby, Lois had told Jo that winks were outdated and kind of sleazy. Bobby was a winker. He winked at everyone, even the dog. But with Chet, Lois disagreed. His winks made her heart flutter. "What are you up to?"

"Nothing but a harmless flirtation with a pretty lady."

Lois smiled, pleased.

Just then, her ex-husband walked by. "Morning, Chet. I'll need to talk to you about that thing we discussed and…" Herbie's cold gaze landed on Lois. "We'll talk about it later."

Her good mood evaporated like the steam rising off her coffee. She frowned at Chet. "That thing?"

"Work," Chet said gruffly, all traces of a smile gone. "There's a special event being held here between Christmas and New Year's." That sounded like a lie.

And she'd been lied to enough by Herbie.

Lois reached in her pocket for some money, slapped some bills on the counter and took her coffee.

"Did I say something wrong?" Chet asked, mustache still.

Lois started to turn away. And then she thought better of it and faced him. "I wondered why you *suddenly* noticed me. My ex-husband put you up to this, didn't he? The flirting. Trying to get my guard down." And she'd bought it. How that hurt. "He doesn't just want to foreclose on Jo's mortgage and take the roof over my head—he wants to devastate me. Well, he didn't do it when he cheated on me, and he won't do it now!"

Chet's mouth dropped open, but he didn't deny any of it as she walked away.

And as she walked away, Lois couldn't believe she'd spoken up for herself.

So much for keeping the peace.

CHAPTER FOURTEEN

"MA'AM, YOU DROPPED THIS." Ryan bent to retrieve a small, plush bear cast aside by a tiny cowgirl being towed in a wagon by her mama. He brushed off the dirt before handing it to the tyke.

Jo was baffled. Where was the Grinchy, not-nice Oakley?

"Thank you." The toddler's mother gushed. Her Christmas sweater had blinking lights. She smiled at Jo. "You'll probably understand that little dumplings don't sleep if they lose their favorite cuddle bear. You've got a keeper, honey."

"Oh…" Jo held up a hand, ready to deny she and Ryan were a couple, even if they did feel like they were in the same lifeboat.

But the woman had already tipped her hat and moved on, hauling her wagon down the aisle toward the specialty stock pens, leaving Jo alone with Ryan and another wrong impression that they were a thing. They both stood staring straight ahead, not at each other.

Jo cast about for a diverting topic of conversation. Luckily, she immediately found one. "You have me bewildered."

"Me?" Ryan tipped his black hat back and gave her a look that said *There's nothing confusing about me, honey.*

Jo boxed away the thought along with the other ones she attributed to her longtime crush on Tate and Ryan's being his identical twin. "Yes, you."

"I'm just a plain and simple cowboy."

"No. You're supposed to be the not-nice Oakley." She softened her statement with a smile. "And yet I just witnessed you saving a toddler's teddy bear."

"Oh, that." He shifted his feet.

"Yes. *Oh, that.* Explain yourself, cowboy."

His feet shuffled again, like he wanted to dance away from her question. "Isn't it enough that I don't like Christmas?"

"Nope. It occurs to me that you haven't said one deliberately rude thing to me this week. You haven't scowled, muttered, cursed or been curt with anyone else either." She nudged his shoulder, encountering soft flannel and hard muscle. "Fess up."

"Well, I…"

She poked him again, determined not to let him get away with excuses.

Ryan gave a reluctant nod. "I earned that label a long time ago."

"And now you let others use it because it's convenient?" That didn't feel right. She peered up at his face, realizing his features weren't as identical to Tate's as she'd assumed all these years. His resting face was stony. There were fewer laugh lines around his eyes. He wore the grumpy Oakley mantle as if he'd carry it to his grave. And that wasn't right. "I get it now. You truly believe you aren't as nice as Tate."

His head drew back, almost imperceptibly, as if she was the only person to tell him this.

"I'm done, Jo. I cannot keep the peace in this family anymore." Ma stomped up to join them, eyes blazing. "Your father asked Chet to romance me. Or paid him to or something. I don't know. But it's mortifying."

"Chet…" Jo was having trouble shifting gears from Ryan to her mother. "Mustache Chet?"

"One and the same." Ma's head bobbed. She mashed her hat on her head.

"Why would Dad do that?" Jo noted Ryan appeared relieved that the spotlight was no longer on him. She made a mental note to circle back when they were alone again.

"Herbie wants to humiliate me. I bet his plan

was to have Chet reel me in and then toss me out like the trash." Ma was hot. "Tell me if you see him. I want to give him a piece of my mind."

A showdown between her parents never happened and could only end badly under such circumstances.

Jo looped her arm around her mother's waist and gave her a side hug. "Can we talk about this later?"

"Yes, let's get in the truck and leave." The fire drained out of Ma as quickly as it had no doubt sparked. She never ran hot and cold, just lukewarm. "Gosh darn it. I think I lost my appetite for doodad shopping."

"I think that's just what you need to lift your spirits, Lois," Ryan said, proving once again that he could be in the running for the nice Oakley.

A feminine squeal of delight drew Jo's attention. She grabbed Ryan's arm. "Hey, isn't that your mom over there?"

Ryan followed the direction of her gaze, his expression turning back to stone.

RYAN'S MOTHER WAS talking to someone in a pen full of miniature horses, waving what looked like the envelope Tate had given her earlier this morning.

Ryan was moving before he actually thought about it. His lips were moving, too. "She would get distracted by a vendor selling magic beans."

"Miniature horses aren't magic beans." Lois strode on his left.

"They're not alpacas, though." Jo marched on his right.

Before today, if anyone had asked Ryan how he'd feel flanked by two Pierce women, he'd have said he'd feel nothing but annoyance. But the reality was, he felt a strong sense of belonging, as if his place in the world had been solidified with them at his side.

"Are you going to stop her?" Jo asked.

Ryan slowed down, reminding himself that he shouldn't care how his biological mother spent her time or money. "What she does is none of my business, unless…"

"Unless?" Jo stared up at him, looking ready to have his back, if needed.

"Unless she's throwing away Tate's money." Which he presumed she held in that envelope.

Ryan hurried toward his mother, unwilling to allow her to disappoint his brother again.

As he opened the pen's gate, his mother smiled at the middle-aged cowboy and extended the envelope toward him.

"Not so fast." Ryan snatched the envelope

first. "Aren't you supposed to be buying alpacas?" He fixed the cowboy with a hard stare because he was afraid if he looked at his mother, he'd lose his temper. "If you tell me you're selling alpacas, I'll give you this envelope."

The man opened his mouth and then shook his head.

"Ryan. What are you doing here?" His mother looked as if she couldn't decide how to play this scene. As the victim? As an innocent? As the woman annoyed at her plans being foiled?

"I'm protecting Tate's interests, same as always." Ryan curled his fingers around the thick envelope and took a deep breath, smelling hay, horse and peppermint.

Has she been drinking?

He studied her eyes. They weren't bloodshot.

And her stance. She didn't sway or stumble.

And her purse. It wasn't large enough for a flask, much less a tiny bottle of alcohol.

"Ryan, I…" His mother gave herself a little shake, ink-black hair brushing her shoulders. "I saw these darling baby horses and decided to change my plans. I can breed horses, you know. All I have to do is let nature run its course."

"Hey, Grant." Jo stepped forward, addressing the older cowboy. "Are you still trying to sell your mother's hobby horses?"

"Yeah." Grant looked relieved to see Jo. "I sold her miniature carts last summer. I keep hoping someone will want to take on her stock." He gestured to the five miniature horses around him.

"They look a little long in the tooth." Jo gently held a small horse muzzle with one hand, scratching it behind the ears with the other. "Remind me... Your mother stopped breeding them several years back."

Grant nodded. "I was just about to tell this nice lady that they were past their prime when she made me an unexpected offer."

"I love them. They look like babies. My babies." His mother practically cooed.

"You had babies," Ryan said, venting a little. "You don't mother well enough to have more, even if they're the four-legged kind."

Her face went pale.

"Easy now," Lois chastised softly, coming to stand next to Ryan and rubbing a hand back and forth over his back.

Jo's gaze found Ryan's. "Think of Tate and what he'd want you to say."

Something nice and neutral, no doubt.

Frustration balled in his chest, and Ryan

couldn't keep it there, not even if a bull sat on him. "I have always thought of Tate, even when we were left in the car on Christmas Eve while our parents partied in the warm bar until their money ran out. Even when we had nothing to eat in the refrigerator but ketchup. I thought of him when I told Mom and Dad to get up and show up for work and not to drink. I thought of him when I made him laugh every time he wanted to cry because he was scared, and there was no one else to do it."

His mother had stepped back during his tirade, features drawn, hand on the pen rail for support. "It was the alcohol. I'm beating that now."

Lois clasped Ryan's shoulder. Jo took his hand.

He stared deep into Jo's soft brown eyes, knowing what he'd admitted was shocking. "This is why I'm not the nice one." Because he didn't sugarcoat things. Because he stood up against his parents, even if it meant he was the one punished. Because, like Jo, he was the strong one in the family, determined to do what needed to be done so that he and Tate could survive, even if it meant turning in his own parents for neglect.

Jo squeezed his hand before turning to his

mother. "Mrs. Oakley, I think they might have some alpacas farther down the aisle. I don't know much about them, but I do know about raising stock. I can help you gather information." And without waiting for her to consider her offer, Jo took his mother's arm, thanked Grant for his time and herded her away from a bad decision.

What Jo didn't know…what she couldn't know…was that his mother was drawn to bad decisions like bulls to a red cape.

"YOUR OAKLEY NEEDS YOU."

"Ma…" Jo couldn't find it in her heart to argue. Dealing with Mrs. Oakley was like trying to hold water in a child's hands. Good intentions kept slipping through.

They were walking toward the auction exit, slowing their steps by mutual agreement because Ryan had stopped to talk to someone he knew.

"Give me the keys." Ma held out her hand. "I'll wait in the truck. You take as long as you need."

"Thanks, Ma." Jo dug out her key fob, handed it to her mother and turned to wait for Ryan.

From a distance, he looked like any other cowboy. Tall, lean muscles honed by a hard day's work, black hair in need of a trim. He laughed at something the cowboy he was talking to said. And from a distance, someone who didn't know him would have thought he hadn't a care in the world.

But Jo saw and heard something different. Ryan didn't stand square to the man he spoke with. He had one foot back, as if prepared to brace for a blow. His laugh sounded forced. His smile didn't reach his eyes. Jo saw a guarded man, a man who was wary and didn't trust easily.

The cowboy he was talking to may have sensed it, too. He extended his hand to shake but didn't place his opposite hand on Ryan's shoulder the way a more friendly man might have done.

Ryan took a few steps toward Jo and the exit before spotting her. His stride faltered before he gave her a small, weathered smile and quickly covered the remaining steps to her side.

"Ma went ahead. I thought I'd walk you out."

He glanced down at her. "Escorting me to my truck. How gallant."

"That's me. Lady Jo, knight of the two stables." How easy it felt to joke with him.

Ryan didn't laugh. "Thanks for trying to help my mother. You see now what it's like, even when she's sober." He held the exit door open for her. "She's always been this way."

Jo felt compassion for them all. She walked through, passing into and out of Ryan's space with a sense that he needed a hug. That he'd needed many hugs over the years and hadn't been given them. "Ryan, I'm sorry."

"For what?" The guarded look shadowed his eyes better than his hat brim shaded them from the winter sun.

"Growing up, I knew about the Done Roamin' Ranch," Jo said quickly before he could stop her from broaching a subject she doubted he wanted broached. "I knew they took in teenage boys to foster, and that some stayed only a short time and some stayed longer." Through high school graduation and beyond. "But I didn't think about why boys ended up there. I didn't think about how you were brought up differently than I was and why you needed to be in a safer environment."

"I don't want your pity," he said gruffly.

"I'm not giving you my pity, Ryan." She gave in to impulse and looped her arm through his, needing to give him a human touch the way she sometimes gave it to the animals she trained to show them she cared and that they were part of her herd. "If anything, I've gained respect for your strength of character and what you went through as a kid. And like you said, you explained why you were known as the not-nice Oakley."

"Hey, guys!" Tucker Burns walked past, tipping his hat and heading for the auction yard. "I guess the rumors are true. You make a nice couple."

Jo and Ryan jolted apart. They stood, staring at each other in silence.

"That was…" Ryan seemed to be searching for the right word.

"Unfortunate." Jo nodded. She backed slowly away from Ryan, whose soulful expression was nothing like that of his brother, her sunny childhood crush. She was beginning to think she'd wasted too much time daydreaming about Tate. "I better run. Ma will be waiting."

But she didn't run. She turned and walked slowly on unsteady legs.

So much had happened in such a short amount of time, she couldn't seem to control her limbs.

Just like she couldn't seem to control her opinion of her Oakley.

CHAPTER FIFTEEN

"Hurry, Mom." Max led his small brown horse out of the second barn. "Move it, Dean. We're going to be late."

"What's the rush?" Jo checked the girth strap on Max's horse. "You're riding with Piper and Ginny on the Burns Ranch. Same as always." Same as they'd been doing for the past few years after school, on weekends and in the summer.

It was Friday, time to cut loose. But that didn't explain Max's sense of urgency.

"Lila's riding with Piper and Ginny today." Dean climbed into the saddle. "He likes Lila. He's going to buy her a Christmas present and ask her to go steady."

"Who do you like?" Jo knew that Piper had her eye on him.

"I like Button." Dean patted his horse's neck. "Grandma told me I shouldn't start dating until I turn thirty. She says girls are trouble and can make you do crazy things."

She's not wrong.

But trouble from relationships went both ways.

Jo tried to make light of it. "You take your time when it comes to girls, Dean. No rush. Besides, it's Max who gets you into trouble."

"True." Dean urged Button forward just as Max shouted for him to *"Hurry up!"*

Jo watched the boys ride toward the gate that connected the two ranches. Three girls rode to meet them from the Burns Ranch. That was an awkward number for an awkward age.

"They're starting young," Ma said, joining Jo at the barn door. She held a Christmas wreath made of fresh boughs and decorated with red ribbon. Blue sat at her side. "I thought the barn could use some holiday cheer. I put up a wreath in the first barn next to the tack room door."

At Max's shouted greeting to the cowgirls, Blue's ears perked up. And then he ran out of the barn in the direction the boys had gone.

"Knowing you, Ma, you snuck some mistletoe in a doorway as well."

Ma grinned. "I bet you won't complain about that when your Oakley sees you standing under it."

My Oakley.

For a man who'd claimed interest in three of her horses, she hadn't seen him in two days. And that was also two days without any activity on the horse sale front. The bank had turned him down, but she might apply for a home equity loan or a line of credit.

"I need to run into town." Jo headed off. "Can you keep an eye out for the boys? They should be back from their ride in an hour." Long before it got dark.

"Are you having coffee with your Oakley?"

"No," Jo ground out. "I need to go to the bank."

"That doesn't sound like fun."

It wasn't.

When Jo sat down in Dix's office at Clementine Savings & Loan, the news was grim.

"I'm sorry, Jo," Dix said after just a few questions. "Your father holds the paper on the ranch because he financed it personally. You pay him principal and interest on the loan plus the property taxes. But he makes the payments on the original loan we have here. As a lending institution, there is no record of you *owning* the ranch. It's all in your father's name. And therefore, I can't make you a home equity loan. Again, I'm sorry." He spoke sincerely. But that had always been Dix, as nice as a plain white star atop a simply decorated Christmas tree.

"I had to swallow my pride to make the

deal with my father," Jo admitted. "But at the time, I was fresh out of high school with two babies, an ex-husband, and I was self-employed. This bank wouldn't bet on me. No lending institution would."

"It's a sad fact that you have to have an employer and funds or equity to get a loan. It has nothing to do with you personally."

His words didn't make her feel better because they didn't solve her problem. "If I can't get an equity loan, can I get a personal loan?"

Dix typed something into his computer. "Considering you have a loan out for your truck, the bank could probably lend you three thousand."

"I need ten. More, really." To pay the other bills for the next few months. Jo's spirits were lower than they'd ever been. "There must be something I can do. Can I get a cash advance on my credit card?"

"I wouldn't do that. The interest could sink you later if you still experience a sales drought." Dix tapped a line item on her printed inventory list. "Why don't you sell some of your one- and two-year-olds? Or even your younger stock. You've got over twenty colts and fillies."

"My business is a pipeline. Out of twenty, twelve might be competition stock. But I won't discover that until I've given them some training. And out of twelve, five or six—or less—might meet my training standards for a top competition horse. If I sell too much young stock now, I may not have enough to sell later."

"You've been in business with that mortgage ten years, Jo." Dix rested his elbows on his desk and his supportive gaze on her. "And this is the first time you've come in here asking for a loan. It can't be the first time you hit a rough patch."

"No. As you can imagine, I had trouble early on. A young woman trying to train and sell unproven competition horses for a premium price? This was before even my brothers wanted to ride my stock."

Dix nodded.

"I had Regal Robert and put him through his paces at a few exclusive sales, but no one was willing to meet my price." And she'd known that was the one thing she couldn't compromise on or she'd forever be lowering her price. "And then Ford Yardley approached me with an unusual offer."

"Didn't he win the Triple Crown with Regal Robert? Ford was a heeler, right? Like Ryan."

Jo nodded. "Yes. Ford gave me money up front to lease Regal Robert for the year. And then he won all three postseason events. It was a win-win." Jo sat up. "Why didn't I think of that before? Ryan could lease Pauper from me."

"I'm sure he'd like that." Dix gave her a reassuring smile.

"Yes, but…" She inched forward, closer to his desk. And even though his office door was closed, she whispered, "Can I ask you to keep the leasing option a secret from Ryan? Just for another week. There's always a chance that I could get a buyer for Prince and Pauper as a pair, which would tide me over for a couple of months. And I don't want to get Ryan's hopes up…saying I might lease him Pauper and then selling him anyway."

That would just be cruel. And at Christmas!

Dix nodded. "I understand. But won't that be hard on you? I mean…" He laughed self-consciously. "You are dating Ryan, and secrets—"

"We are *not* dating." Jo sat back in her chair.

"Sorry. It's just all around town and—"

"We're *not* dating," Jo repeated, more resolutely this time.

"Okay." Dix still sounded confused. "I won't tell him."

"Thanks, Dix." Jo got to her feet. "And even though things didn't work out the way I wanted them to when I walked through your door, you've reminded me about a lifeline I can use if I need to."

"Glad to help. But…" Dix hesitated. "Go easy on Ry. He's not as tough as he looks, and he rarely dates."

"We're not dating!"

"Lois, WHAT ARE you doing?" Ryan parked his motorcycle at the Pierce Ranch, removed his helmet and took his cowboy hat from the bike's saddle bag. He'd driven it around town with a For Sale sign taped on the gas tank but had no takers yet.

"Isn't it obvious, my darling Oakley?" Jo's mother was in the yard surrounded by three tumbleweeds. She wore scruffy jeans and a paint-splattered jacket. Her brown hair was scrunched beneath a blue knit cap. She appeared to be spray-painting the thorny tumbleweeds white on the brownish-yellow grass on the front lawn. "I'm making a snowman."

"Right." Ryan wasn't on board with her vision.

Lois tossed the can of white spray paint aside and picked up a shovel. "Since we don't get snow here, you have to be creative." She put the shovel in the ground and hopped on it a few times to sink the sharp end in the dirt.

"No inflatable yard decorations for me." She picked up the largest tumbleweed, held the web of its trunk over the shovel handle, then threaded it down to the ground.

"Can't say as I've ever seen a tumbleweed snowman." Couldn't say he fancied it either. "Are you sure that shovel is going to keep your snowman together?"

"It's like staking it to the ground." She slid a second tumbleweed onto the shovel handle to make the snowman's middle.

He threaded the smallest tumbleweed on top. "Folks can't see your house from the highway. You've put a lot of effort into yard decorations no one but you and your family sees." Since he'd been there last, she'd hung lights over bushes and strung them through two trees. There were lights on the eaves and Santa's sleigh on the lawn.

"Ah, your Scrooginess is showing. That's so cute." Lois threw her arms around Ryan and gave him a hug, a quick snuggle that warmed him, followed by a quick release. And then she shook her finger at him. "Holiday decorations aren't for other people. They're for me. To lift my spirits. I want to look out the window and see Frosty, the way my dad used to make him. I want my grandsons to look back on their childhoods and have fun re-creating some of my more unusual holiday traditions. That way, I'll be in their hearts forever."

Having no holiday traditions of his own, Ryan grunted.

Still, he wondered where Jo stood on tumbleweed snowmen.

"Besides, when something annoys me, like my ex-husband, all I have to do is admire my pretty lights or whimsical yard decorations, and I feel better."

Ryan just went for a ride when things got to him, and he was about to say so when Lois continued. "Give him some arms, will you?" She handed Ryan two sticks and then stuffed a carrot in the top tumbleweed for a nose. She picked up a can of black spray paint and painted eyes and buttons. "How jolly. I hardly can remember why I'm upset with Herbie."

"Wasn't that days back?" When they'd been at the auction yard? "Or has he done something else?"

"I've been wrestling with my annoyance since Wednesday," Lois confirmed. "Every time I get stuck in a loop, I decorate for Christmas."

"That explains the snowman." And the oversize ornaments hanging in trees.

Lois might not have heard him. "I don't know why Herbie treats Jo and me like the enemy. He's threatening to foreclose if Jo can't make the Christmas balloon payment on this place." She shook the can of black paint as if she wasn't done painting, a faraway expression on her face. "We loved each other once. He fell out of love. But I've never been vindictive. I've always tried to keep the peace."

"That had to have been hard." Ryan wasn't much for peacemaking, which was something he'd never had success with anyway. He took the paint can from Lois. "I think you need to admire your tumbleweed snowman and take some deep breaths."

"How right you are." But Lois tossed her hands. "Gosh darn you. Can't you act like you're supposed to?"

Ryan pointed at himself. "Me? Are we still taking about your ex?" How was he supposed to react?

"No. I mean him." Lois leaned to one side and pointed.

Something snorted behind Ryan, sniffing his lower back.

Ryan turned slowly around. "Hey, fella." He patted Tiger's neck.

Hopefully, the chestnut's friendliness was a sign that he and Tiger were off on the right foot. Ryan had spent the past few days visiting banks in other towns, exploring loan opportunities. But he'd been turned down at every one.

Tiger nuzzled Ryan's chest, before moseying over to Lois. He tried to nibble her short brown hair.

"Go away, you big flirt." She elbowed the chestnut, to no avail. Tiger continued to crowd her space, like a cat looking for something to rub against. "I swear, he doesn't know he's a horse."

"He seems fond of you." Ryan smiled. "Or maybe he loves Christmas decorations, too."

Lois sighed, finally giving Tiger the attention he wanted. "This horse has given me more than my share of frights. I'll walk into the kitchen and his face fills up the window. Or I'll be tending my vegetable garden and he'll goose my backside."

Tiger blew out a raspberry, as if saying guilty as charged.

"If you have a halter, I can take him back to the barn for you." Ryan welcomed the opportunity to spend some time with his plan B.

"I don't keep horse tack in the house," Lois said crisply. "And he won't follow you. I'll have to walk him over. He's better than Houdini at opening locks. The boys are due back from their ride soon. And I promised Jo I'd keep an eye out for them. She went to the bank."

"I hope she had more luck than I did." Ryan went up to Tiger and stroked his withers. "Hey, buddy."

Tiger pivoted to face Ryan, sniffed him as if he were a dog, not a horse. All the way up. All the way down. And then he turned back to Lois, dismissing Ryan.

Snubbed by a horse. That's a first.

Of course, the horse would be Jo's.

"Come along, Tiger." Lois crossed the front yard, not even bothering to grab hold of his mane.

But then, why would she? The gelding followed her like a well-trained dog.

Ryan walked next to the chestnut. "I hear Tiger is an impossible ride."

"He's quite good at dancing around so no one can get on him. Or bucking if they do. And he has other tricks up his sleeve. When we first got him back, a man from Dallas drove up to give him a ride. Tiger tried to roll with him in the saddle." She chuckled. "He's too clever for most." She eyed Ryan over her shoulder. "Maybe even too clever for you."

Ryan laughed, as he was meant to, he supposed. "I guess Jo told you I might be interested in buying him if I can't get financing for Prince and Pauper."

"Do you own a horse of your own?" Lois asked, still walking ahead.

"I have a ranch horse I mostly ride. I guess that means yes."

"But you haven't bought one yourself and cared for it the way you would an animal only you are responsible for?"

"No, ma'am."

"Then you wouldn't understand what I'm getting at." Lois rounded the house and headed toward the barn. Tiger walked with his head at her shoulder, the same place it would have been had she haltered him. "Have you ever heard about penguins mating for life?"

"In school…maybe."

"Tiger thinks like a penguin. We're his family. And all he wants to do is be a part of the action. When no one else is home, he'll come find me. It's almost like he wants to keep me company."

"I've never heard of a horse acting like that."

"And he knows now that if a stranger comes to ride him, he might be taken away, which is why I think he won't let anyone but Jo and the boys ride him."

That's because Tiger is their heart horse.

A fact that continued to bother Ryan.

They walked through the first barn and into the second. When they reached Tiger's stall, the chestnut ambled right in. Lois closed the door behind him.

He turned and whinnied.

"Oh, he's proud of his independence." Lois may have tried to convey Tiger was a nuisance, but she gave him a good ear rub and kissed his nose.

Ryan examined the locks on the stall door. There was a standard bolt latch near the top and a second halfway down. The stall was an interior one. There was no access to an outdoor paddock. "How does he get out?"

Lois shrugged. "He uses his teeth on the bolts. Or so Jo says."

"You should put a new latch about ankle height. I doubt he could reach it over the stall door."

"Maybe you'll turn out to be clever enough for him after all." Lois laughed. She took Ryan by the arm. "If you're serious about buying him, you'd best take a seat in his stall."

Ryan nodded. "I know the rules. No riding." Just bonding. A concept foreign to Ryan when it came to livestock.

"The boys are out riding on the Burns Ranch. If you hear them coming, I hope you'll get out of Tiger's stall. Sometimes being a working rancher can break your heart. And I don't want them fretting over something that might not come to be."

"I understand." Ryan entered the stall. "Hey, fella."

Tiger turned his back on Ryan.

"You see what I mean." Lois patted Ryan on the back over the stall door. "No one said this would be easy. Good luck."

CHAPTER SIXTEEN

RYAN WAS BORED. Tiger didn't want to play with him.

Ryan leaned over the chestnut's stall door, tapping out a rhythm to an old George Strait song, when a soft muzzle upended his cowboy hat, sending it tumbling to the ground.

Tiger stuck his head over Ryan's shoulder and the stall door, ears cocked forward.

"Is this how we make friends?" Ryan wondered aloud, staring at his hat, which was out of reach on the barn floor. But he was heartened that the horse had stopped ignoring him.

And then he heard a sound. Several sounds, actually. Chattering voices. The whinny of a horse excited to be returning to the barn. The jingle of tack.

Tiger wasn't making a friendly overture to Ryan. Max and Dean were returning from their ride.

Panting, Blue ran into the barn first. He went straight to his water dish, drank his fill and lay down as if done for the day.

"I'm gonna marry Lila one day."

"You need to marry a cowgirl, Max. Lila is a townie."

Ryan slipped out of Tiger's stall, setting both latches on the door before walking out of the barn to greet Jo's boys.

"Lila could become a cowgirl," Max said staunchly. "Look at Mr. Dix. He's gonna marry Piper's mom and live on the Burns Ranch. And he's a *banker*."

"Actually," Ryan said as he stepped out of the barn's shadow into the fading light of the winter day, "Dix was a cowboy, then he became a banker, and now he's a bit of both. And…I used to be a townie." But now cowboying was in his blood.

The boys brought their small horses to a halt and dismounted. The first thing they did was remove their riding helmets. The second thing they did was study Ryan.

"What are you doing here?" Max demanded.

"Mom didn't say you were coming today." Dean frowned.

"I'm trying to buy a horse from your mother. I'll be hanging out here a lot more in the next few weeks."

"'Cause you're dating her?" Max led his horse into the barn, toward the tack room.

"No."

"'Cause you *want to* date her?" Dean led his horse after his brother.

"No. Like I said, I'm in the market for a horse." With a final glance at Tiger, who was staring after his boys, Ryan drifted toward the tack room and took a seat on a nearby bench.

The boys skillfully removed bridles and replaced them with halters, clipping them to lead ropes attached to the wall. And then they removed saddles and brushed down their mounts, followed by cleaning their hooves.

Jo arrived, walking into the breezeway with a look that said all hope was *not* lost. There was a swagger to her step. She was wearing a blue hoodie with the Grinch on the front, which made Ryan want to smile at her.

At least, until she asked him, "Are you just leaving?"

He shook his head, unaccountably disappointed.

"What's this?" Max came out of the tack room holding a straw cowboy hat. "Grandma struck again. Look, Dean." He pointed to the hatband, which was red velour with white furry trim. "Mom, look what Grandma did to my hat."

"It's for Santapalooza, Max." Jo tried to give him a side hug.

Max jerked away. "The Santa ride isn't until Christmas." He stomped in a circle. "She took my regular hatband off and probably hid it somewhere. I gotta wear this to school. You know kids will laugh." Max plopped down on the bench next to Ryan while Dean led his horse back to its stall.

"The only kids who'll tease you are the ones who are jealous that you get to ride in Santapalooza, and they don't," Jo said reasonably, although Ryan could relate more to Max than her argument. He'd been eleven once, too. "Come on now. Put Bobbin away and give her some oats."

Max swung his feet in the air, staying on the bench. "Anybody can ride in Santapalooza. But they don't have to wear Santa gear until Christmas Eve."

Jo gasped in mock horror. "Max, do you have a fever? You used to love everything about Santapalooza, from planning to riding."

"I bet Mr. Ryan doesn't ride in Santapalooza," Max groused.

"Nope. Never have." Ryan was still prickly after being rejected by a horse. A horse. And then Jo—who was wearing a Grinch sweatshirt—was blanking him, too. "Never will."

That didn't ingratiate him with Jo. She frowned at him.

"See!" Max looked as if he was going for the Oakley defense of *If he's not doing it, neither am I!*

"That's because Ryan is the…" Ryan bet Jo had been about to label him the cold Oakley once more. But she pivoted. "He's Grinch Oakley. You don't want to be known as the Grinch, do you? The Grinch doesn't want presents or turkey or pie."

Ryan frowned. "Hey, I enjoy all of that." It was the expense and unnecessary pomp he didn't go for.

"Looks like the Grinch has been redeemed," Dean said solemnly, coming to sit on the other side of Ryan. "That's a spelling word this week. *Redeemed.*"

"You don't have to spell it for them," Max griped in a way that hinted he might not be as good of a speller as his brother.

"I got one hundred percent on my spelling test," Dean said, nose in the air. "You would have, too, if you weren't always dreaming about Lila."

"Say that again." Max clenched his fists.

"Boys." Jo took a step forward. "That's enough."

"Max thinks Lila won't like him if he wears a Santa hatband." Dean wobbled back and forth and fake wailed, *"Oh, no."*

"Girls love Santa," Jo said in a loud voice that Ryan was fairly certain her boys pretended not to hear.

"Lila likes me because I'm cool." Max got to his feet, tossed down his hat and then crossed his arms over his thin chest. "Dean isn't cool."

Dean got to his feet, mirroring his twin's stance. "I don't want to be cool or liked by girls."

"Oh, yeah?"

"Yeah."

"Hey, Jo." Ryan stood, trying to be a distraction. "Do you need help with anything?"

"Thank you for asking," Jo said sweetly, while simultaneously staring down her boys like a hawk. "There's always so much that needs doing around here."

"He *is* dating Mom." Max marched over to Bobbin and unclipped his lead from the wall. "Next thing you know, he'll have one of these Santa hatbands, too."

"We aren't dating," Jo said sharply, her tone rubbing an already irritable Ryan the wrong way. "Thanks for asking, but I don't need help, Ryan. Don't try to butter me up by offering."

Dean sat back down, a rapt audience.

Ryan considered taking a seat next to him. What was going on here? "I'm not trying to..." Oh, what was the use? "Okay. I am trying to play nice. But only because we need to have a hard conversation about…" *Don't talk about horses. Or heart horses.* But what was left? Ah, yes. Tate. "We need to talk about Saturday night."

Jo closed her eyes. "Do not try to set me up with your brother."

"It's too soon for that. You've got to grease the wheels first." Ryan tried not to grimace beneath her resulting hard stare. "I thought you could…you know…smile and say hi."

The twins laughed.

"If I have to act all sweet rather than just be myself to catch a man's interest, that's a deal-breaker." Jo planted her boots and put her hands on her hips.

She had a lot of sweetness in her, despite all the scowls and frowns she'd tossed his way. Ryan couldn't think of a good reason why she wouldn't want to at least try out his strategy and said so. At her continued frown, he asked, "Haven't you ever gone fishing?"

"Yes." She marched to a stall and put a halter on a dainty-looking bay. "It's too slow for my taste."

"I wasn't asking you if you *liked* fishing." He followed her to the stall.

More boyish laughter filled the air.

Ryan unclenched his jaw. "You bait a hook

with something the fish likes. You dangle it in front of him. My brother doesn't always notice women, not until they're right in front of him. Be bold, be outgoing, take the bull by the horns or—"

"Ryan," Jo said in a stubborn tone of voice. "Rest assured that I understand where you're coming from, but I'm not changing up my ways…dangling myself in front of your brother just to show him I'm alive. He knows I'm alive." She led the bay to the tack room, Ryan at her heels. "He's known me for years."

"Mom's Mom. That's it," Max said, trailing after them.

"But if he's known Mom for years and he hasn't asked her out yet…" Dean brought up the rear.

"Everyone is overthinking this. Boys, saddle up Salt and Pepper for some barrel practice. Now. Go." She waited for them to run down a side aisle before clipping the bay to a tie-down and then turning to Ryan.

"Before you flay me alive—" Ryan held up his arms in surrender "—let me point out that you said you'd do anything to make a sale. At some point, my mother is going to make a mistake with Tate. And as much as I don't want him to be hurt, he will be. And when he comes to his senses, I'm not going to rub his nose in it. I want him to feel comfortable buying a horse to better his future. And if you and he were friendly…"

Jo rolled her eyes, moving toward the tack room. "Here we go with your buttering-up strategy again."

"Tate isn't as ornery as I am, but he's stubborn enough that he'd miss out on this opportunity just because he hates it that I'm always right about our parents."

Jo knocked the brim of her hat upward with her knuckles. "You want me to catch Tate's eye. All so you might be able to sway him to buy Prince, even though he probably can't afford to buy him, and you don't have the funds to buy Pauper either?"

"That's right. I have no personal interest in seeing what you're like on a date." That felt like a lie. Ryan swallowed.

"Who's talking about *you* seeing what I'm like on a date?" Jo was in a snit now, practically chafing. And standing in the tack room doorway beneath a sprig of mistletoe. "I wear jeans. Always. The moment I go out in public in a dress, people are going to talk."

"But how can I advise you about Tate if I don't see you two together? Are you worried if folks see you, they'll talk about you?"

Ryan shrugged. "Maybe you need people to talk about you."

"They're already talking. About us. Not me. *Us.*" She stared at him with eyes blazing, hands gesticulating with every syllable and lips moving. The only things that weren't moving were her feet. They didn't budge from beneath that holiday greenery tacked in the doorway. "Everywhere I go, someone comments on the fact that we're dating."

"That's unfortunate." Ryan repeated what he'd said the other morning, moving closer to her and that mistletoe. "You know, Tate might not want to start something with you if he thinks you're mine." And if she was his, he'd have no excuses not to kiss her. If she were his…

Jo pushed past him and went to sit on the bench he'd vacated earlier. "I'm exhausted by your logic."

And she hadn't even heard the stuff he was working through in his head. Ryan sat next to her, unable to tear his gaze from that mistletoe. "I told you I could help. Tell me what you need done around here."

"I'm not physically exhausted," Jo said, although she sounded drained. "It's this idea you have… No, the idea *everyone* seems to have that we're dating. There's no way we could be dating. You don't like anything about me. Or I suppose you would if I flattered you nonstop and kissed you all the time."

For once, Ryan was speechless. And he couldn't even tell himself it wasn't the thought of Jo's kissable lips that had robbed him of the ability to form words. Because it was.

It was. And he had a sinking feeling that wanting to kiss Jo was going to ruin everything.

"Say something, Ryan."

Jo wanted him to speak because she'd just accused him of not liking her unless she paid him compliments and kissed him.

All the time.

She stifled a groan.

Jo didn't dare risk looking at Ryan. How embarrassing. He'd think she wanted to kiss him.

It's Tate I want to kiss.

That had been on her bucket list since she'd gotten her driver's license and considered herself a woman of the world, a woman allowed to dream big.

To be fair, she'd also dreamed about becoming a world-renowned horse trainer that day.

It's Tate I want. Always has been.

But in the past few days, that longing had shifted inside of her.

She glanced at Ryan from beneath her lashes.

He no longer seemed exactly like Tate in appearance. Or at least, not the Tate of her dreams.

When she thought of Ryan, the image that came to mind now wasn't from their youth, wasn't a face with a scowl. No. When she thought about Ryan, she recalled his open, friendly smile. Or the look of determination on his face when he first rode Pauper out of the heeler gate. Or the way he stared at Jo sometimes, as if he didn't know how to feel when he looked at her.

I don't know how to feel when I look at him either.

And that wouldn't do.

Her phone rang. Saved by the bell!

"Ma. You called me on video." Jo held the phone in front of her, sharing the screen with Ryan, but wanting to make sure her mother saw that Ryan was with her so she wouldn't say something that would further embarrass Jo. "I'm in the barn with Ryan and all I see is your nose."

"This darn phone." Ma moved the phone in front of her face. It looked as if she was in the front yard. "Your father just texted asking me when we last updated the kitchen and I'm in need of Christmas cheer. I want to make a family of snowmen on the front lawn. Can you bring me six tumbleweeds?"

"Now?" Jo had a horse to train and a man to figure out.

"I'll put the bay away." Ryan was already moving. Walking to the horse, speaking softly, reassuringly, and then leading it back to a stall. His jeans were worn in the seat and, oddly enough, behind his knees near the outer seams.

"What are you staring at?" Ma demanded. "Did a horse go lame?"

"No." Jo got to her feet, feeling her cheeks heat. "Six tumbleweeds. I'm on my way."

"Six smallish ones. I want the big snowman to be the large-and-in-charge grandma."

"Got it." Jo disconnected and tucked her phone in her pocket.

Somehow, Ryan had put the horse away already and stood in front of her.

They stared at each other.

If I...kissed you all the time.

Jo licked her lips, consumed by nerves because this kind of staring... In the movies, this kind of staring was always the moment before the hero and heroine came together in a passionate first kiss.

Do I want to kiss Ryan?

By the way her boots were frozen in place, she'd hazard to guess the answer was yes.

Do I remember how to kiss?

Wow, that was another thing entirely. She hadn't kissed anyone since she'd been married to Bobby, because no one had so much as asked her out since then.

Is kissing Ryan wise?

That was a big whopper of a no.

Jo drew a deep, shaky breath at the same time that Ryan did.

They both took a small step back.

"Tumbleweeds?" he asked.

"They're in a paddock outside." Miraculously, Jo's feet moved in that direction. "Ma finds them alongside the road at the end of summer and tosses them in there. If she doesn't use them at Christmas, she makes Easter bunnies out of them come spring. And if there are any left, we stake them in the firepit and burn them at the beginning of summer."

"Sounds like you have a handle on your tumbleweed supply chain."

"If only I had a handle on everything." Jo

had to take hold of her feelings for Tate and not let them drift in Ryan's direction.

It was Tate she'd always wanted a chance with.

She had to keep telling herself that because she didn't have room in her life for a man as complicated and non-Christmas-loving as Ryan.

CHAPTER SEVENTEEN

"YOUR HAIR IS DRY." Ronnie Pickett gave Jo a good once-over as they entered the Buckboard together on Saturday night. Ronnie wore an ankle-length black dress and her favorite red boots. "You've got lipstick on. And you're wearing your good hat. What's going on? Who's the lucky fella?"

Jo scoffed, cheeks turning pink. "You always see hearts and romance where there are none."

"And that's why I'm such a good matchmaker." Ronnie fluffed her long dark hair. "I've heard rumors about you and Ryan Oakley."

"You've heard?" Jo nudged her friend's shoulder. "Or did you spread some of those rumors yourself? Because Ginny told me that you told her—"

"I told her what Ryan told me. That he had coffee with you." Ronnie wasn't a good liar. She walked faster.

Jo let her lead. "Ryan wants to buy a horse

from me. It's as simple as that." Except things between them weren't that simple.

Ryan was becoming her backup plan to meet the mortgage. And although she didn't want to extend the leasing offer just yet in case a sale came through, she'd tossed and turned last night, feeling bad for holding the offer back. Ryan had stayed late at the ranch last night helping Ma make snowmen and helping Jo and the boys put horses through their paces. Too often, she'd found herself staring in the direction of his lips. She'd become obsessed with them.

Jo and Ronnie headed toward their usual booth near the dance floor. Jo's gaze roamed the sparse crowd. It was early. Not even the Oakley brothers were here.

Ronnie and Jo shed their jackets.

"If it's not Ryan, are you going to tell me who it is?" Ronnie settled into their booth and called to the waitress to bring their usual pre-dancing order of beer and popcorn. "If you've got your eye on someone, I can help."

Meddle, she meant, good-natured though the meddling would be.

"You're reading more into my appearance than you should," Jo assured her. Lied, really. And Jo felt bad about that. But as the group's ugly duckling, she wasn't going to open the door to Ronnie's persistent, almost heavy-handed approach to romance. "I finished work early today and had time to dry my hair. And my ranch hat looks like a starling's landing pad right now." She forced out a laugh. "You can't show up to the Buckboard on Saturday night with a hat like that."

Ronnie didn't look like she believed her.

"Hey, I was wondering…" Jo took out her phone and pulled up a photo of Tiger. She turned the screen Ronnie's way. "Do you think Cowgirl Pearl would like to use my horse in a photo shoot with you?" Ronnie was a former barrel racing champion and modeled for Cowgirl Pearl Western fashions, one of her sponsors.

Ronnie leaned forward. "I always forget how gorgeous he is. I can ask." She sat back, smiling a little. "But he might upstage me and the clothing. I'm only half joking about that."

The waitress arrived, and soon after, Jo's mother called. On video chat. Again.

"Ma. Turn off the video."

"Won't that hang up on you?" Her mother held the phone in front of her nose. "I can't see the button thingy."

"Because you're not wearing your glasses."

"I put them in my knitting bag so I wouldn't forget to bring them to my knitting circle."

Her mother walked through the house. "I just wanted to let you know that Henry Jack's mother picked up the boys. Meryl said she'd have them back tomorrow before dinner."

"You could have texted me."

"And have autocorrect massacre my message again? Ha! The last time I sent you a message it read, Meryl just plucked the bodies. You wanted to call the sheriff. I'm not texting." Her mother set the phone down on the table by the front door, such that Jo had a good picture of the ceiling. "I'm a caller. Always have been. Always will be."

Jo sighed. If only she could wean Ma off the video chat. "Okay, Ma. Have fun with your knitters."

"I will. And if you see your handsome Oakley—"

Across the table from Jo, Ronnie's head whipped around, and she mouthed, *"Your handsome Oakley?"*

Jo waved Ronnie off.

"—you can thank him for helping me decorate the front lawn for Christmas yesterday. He makes a great tumbleweed snowman. Check out Mr. Snowman's arms when you get home." Jo's mother picked the phone up again, although the visual was of her shoulder this time.

Jo had nothing to say. She couldn't recall anything special about the snowman's stick arms. Now, if they were talking about Ryan's arms…

Stop.

"You should sell your Oakley those horses," Ma said as if her word was gospel. "You know how vindictive your father is. If you miss that balloon payment, he'll most likely cause trouble simply because I'm living in the house with you."

That was true, not that she wanted Ma to worry.

"Have fun knitting tonight," Jo said instead before hanging up.

Ronnie shook with laughter.

"Don't get any ideas," Jo told her. "Ryan has visited the ranch *and my horses* a few times. You know how my mother is. The last time Mike Barkley came over to fix a burst pipe, she was calling him *'your Mike.'*" Mike had been in the midst of a messy divorce and had wanted nothing to do with Jo. Not that she'd been interested in him at all either.

"Yes, but…" Ronnie's brows rose suggestively. "Ryan helped your mother decorate for Christmas. That doesn't seem like nothing."

"Look at me." Jo held out her arms, bumping her elbows on the table. "Do I act and

sound like the women who come in here looking to catch a man's eye? I'm not batting my
eyes or wearing a dress or standing directly in
some guy's way trying to hook his attention."
And suddenly, she was afraid that was exactly
what she wanted to do. But with Ryan.

Gosh darn it.

"A clean hat, dry hair and lipstick" was
all Ronnie said, smiling like it was already
Christmas.

Jo shook her head. "Nothing I do is going
to convince you that I'm not interested in
Ryan, is it?"

"Nope."

Izzy and Bess joined them.

"I finished my Christmas shopping," Izzy
said triumphantly. She'd woven her white-
blond hair into a side braid and wore a floor-
length denim skirt topped with a gold sweater.
"Even my Secret Santa gift for our group."

"Izzy, I love you," Bess said crisply, tossing
her long red hair over one shoulder. She shooed
Jo over to make room for her in the booth.
She wore a short green dress with black boots.
"But, Izzy, if you give us hints about who you
drew for Secret Santa again this year…"

Izzy was suitably chastised. Her smile
dimmed. "I was just excited. It's adorable
and so hard to find."

"What's hard to find?" Allison joined them next, also wearing a dress, making Jo look like the odd man out. "Nothing can be as hard as peaches were to find last summer." She waved at Evie Grace, her peach-hoarding former nemesis.

They all laughed, even Evie.

Try as she might, Jo couldn't shake the tension in her shoulders. Would Ryan show up as promised with Tate? Would Tate really see her? The way he had in the coffee shop the other morning? Would he ask her out?

Girl, you're dreaming.

Jo rubbed her palms over her jean-clad thighs. What was the use of dreaming? In her experience, dreams were hard to come by and harder to keep.

Not to mention, she didn't know how to fish.

"Line dancing is about to begin."

The announcement sent the five friends toward the dance floor.

They started with the Electric Slide.

It was easy to get lost in the steps, the same way Jo got lost in training horses. While she was busy, she didn't think about things like debt or the empty half of her bed that was only filled with stacks of clean, folded laundry.

A group of familiar cowboys entered the

Buckboard. The men associated with the Done Roamin' Ranch had arrived. There was Wade, Ronnie's fiancé. And Dix, Allison's fiancé. And Ryan, whose stare made Jo miss a step. Or more likely, it was because Tate was right behind him, smiling broadly at everyone, including a table of boisterous cowgirls Jo didn't recognize. Cowgirls exuding style and confidence, and already smiling and waving at cowboys.

Doesn't anyone realize the music's playing?

"What's wrong?" Ronnie elbowed her.

"Nothing." Jo twirled and picked up the steps to "Cotton-Eyed Joe."

When the line dancing was done, the band began to play. The five friends returned to their booth. An order of nachos was made. While they were waiting, Ronnie and Allison went to greet their significant others.

Jo glanced casually around. Not surprisingly, a chatty cowgirl with a big voice asked Tate for a dance. Jo followed their progress to the dance floor with a heavy sigh.

What's the use in dreaming?

Ryan gestured to her from the bar, making her heart pound.

"Did Ryan Oakley just call you over?" Bess grinned to beat the band. "And here I thought the rumors weren't true."

Jo recited what was now becoming rote. "We're not dating. He's interested in buying a horse." *And helping me catch his brother's attention.* Not that she'd asked for his help. And not that she was succeeding in taking it. "I'll be right back."

Carrying her beer, Jo joined Ryan at the bar.

But before she could say anything, Ryan began chastising her. "I thought we agreed that you'd be different tonight."

"I am different." She turned her back to the mirror behind the colorful liquor bottles and propped her elbows on the bar top. "Not that it should matter how I act or how I look or how I do my hair. I'll still be Jo Pierce, hard-working horse trainer."

"You're not making this easy," Ryan grumbled, leaning close until his warm breath wafted over her cheek. "Look. I told you that Tate goes for women who catch his eye, who make him stop and take notice."

"I think you're wrong. I think Tate values a woman who exudes a quiet strength." From their booth, Ronnie winked at Jo. She shooed the gesture away. "Someone who isn't in his face all the time plying a smile for a kind word or asking for a dance."

"You never dance to the live band," Ryan said in sudden wonder. He sat up. "Why not?"

Jo considered not answering, but what was the use? "Because no one asks me. Wallflowers are wallflowers for a reason."

She bit her lip.

Tate danced past, laughing at whatever the woman in the dress said to him.

"If you want to project a quiet strength and *wait to be discovered...*" Ryan grumbled, doom and gloom in his dark eyes. "Then you're not getting a date with my brother."

They each sipped their beer. Tate twirled his partner around the dance floor. And Jo began to doubt styling her hair and putting on makeup would ever capture his attention.

"Okay," Ryan said gruffly. "I admit that it could feel wrong to throw yourself in someone's path to get noticed. If I wanted to get noticed I'd..." His gaze landed on her mouth.

Womp-pow!

"Actually, never mind what I'd do. How many times do I have to say it?" He dragged his gaze away from her mouth. "Tate goes through life with blinders on. You need to be bold, outrageous even."

"Actually, you don't need to keep going on about this." She willed her pulse to steady. "I never told you I wanted a date with Tate," Jo said, too late to be believed. "I don't need a man. I need money before Christmas. I need a horse sale. A big horse sale."

Ryan tipped his hat back. "I'm just trying to help you get what I think you want and what you think you want. And what I think is that you need to plant your boots in front of Tate."

He heaved a sigh, his exasperation with her evident for all to see.

"I've never liked you." Jo sniffed, pushing away from the bar.

"That's not true." Ryan's gaze snagged hers, lowering to her lips before rising back up to her eyes.

Womp-pow!

Jo swallowed thickly. Ryan was making her pulse race. Ryan, not Tate.

But Tate no longer looked like the man of her dreams, not with that full beard. And she had the sneaking suspicion that she shouldn't be crushing on Tate. He never dated anyone seriously.

It was just that she'd been crushing on Tate for over a decade.

But she had to face facts. The only way an ugly duckling could attract Tate's attention was if she transformed into a swan—a loud, look-at-me one who just went right up and asked for what she wanted. "You're so confident in business and on a horse. You shine everywhere but in here," Ryan told her, sounding as if he'd been talking while her mind wandered. "In here, your light dims and you shrink."

He was right.

"Trust me on this." Ryan stared at her intently, so intently Jo started to feel another *womp-pow* coming on. "I'm putting you on call tomorrow. Tate's probably going to run errands. And when I know where he's going, I want you to be there, standing in front of him and radiating who you are. I promise you that he won't be able to overlook you."

Jo gave herself a little shake.

"Sorry. I just remembered something I forgot to tell Ronnie."

Ryan hooked his arm around her and whispered in her ear, "At some point, you have to go after what you want. *Jo—*"

"I guess the rumor is true." Griff stopped in front of them, raising his beer bottle. "Cheers! You're dating."

Jo and Ryan exchanged a glance and then, as one, extended their arms and pushed Griff away.

"HAVE YOU SEEN Jo Pierce tonight?" Ryan nodded in the direction of the booth where Jo was sitting with her friends when Tate returned from dancing. "She dances really well, doesn't she?"

Tate didn't look. "Are you being nice to her so that she'll sell you a horse at a discount? You can leave me out of your schemes."

"This is no scheme." Ryan had seen the hurt in Jo's eyes when she'd watched Tate dancing. He didn't want her hurting. She was a good person, and if only she wouldn't shrink when Tate was near, his brother might see her, too. His brother needed someone like her in his corner. Jo had been great with their mother. She was caring, funny, a hard worker with her eyes on the future, and she'd expect Tate to be the same.

"I still don't believe Jo let you take a horse for a test ride," Tate was saying. "What deal did you make with the devil to achieve such a thing?"

"There's no deal. I like her." At Tate's quick glance, Ryan hurried to clarify. "I don't *like her* like her. I have a lot of respect for what she does. I've learned a lot of great tips about competing just by hanging out with her. And you should see her with her twin boys. It reminds me of when we were kids."

"I thought you didn't want to remember some of those times." Tate noticed a woman smiling at his reflection and dutifully gave her a friendly smile and nod.

"Look, I think it would help our cause if you'd ask Jo to dance. Would it kill you to do something nice for a wallflower?"

"A…a what?" Tate frowned.

"A wallflower," Ryan grumbled. "I heard someone say it earlier."

Sophie Jean wormed her way between the brothers. The redhead wore a red sweater-dress and smelled of roses and alcohol. "Tate Oakley. I love you."

"I know, Sophie Jean. You told me last summer." Tate leaned away from her and caught Ryan's eye in the bar mirror with an expression of *help*. "And last Easter. And last Christmas."

"You're forgetting New Year's." Sophie Jean batted her eyelashes at Tate. "It's just that when I drink whiskey sours, I have the need to tell you how I feel. I love you, Tate. And I love your beard. It gives you this…lumberjack vibe." She giggled.

"I appreciate the share." Tate pried her hand from his neck. "Have you met my brother Ryan?"

Sophie Jean glanced at Ryan over her shoulder. "He's not you, Tate. No one is as kind and friendly as you, Tate. And that's why I love you."

"Sorry, Sophie Jean." Ryan tried to carefully pry her off his twin. "But Tate has promised this dance to another."

"I have?" Tate's eyes widened. "That's right. I have. Jo Pierce."

"Noooo," Sophie Jean wailed. "It's my turn, Tate. I love you."

"Sophie Jean, it's time to go home." Her sister Babs appeared at the bar. She took Sophie Jean by the arm. "Hey, Tate. It wouldn't be the holiday season without a profession of love, now, would it?"

"Nope." Tate grinned, recovering some of his good-naturedness now that he was free of Sophie Jean. "Merry Christmas, Babs."

Ryan rolled his eyes. "Why can't you just swat down Sophie Jean so that she never makes a fool of herself again?"

"Because I don't want to hurt her." Tate sipped his beer.

"Then date her."

"I don't want to date her." Tate finished his drink. "And I don't want to ask Jo Pierce to dance. That's your mess. You clean it up." He started a conversation with Daniel Corbin, one of the Done Roamin' Ranch's fosters. Or at least, he tried to.

Kiera Edwards approached, flaunting her wide smile and putting sass in her step. She asked Tate to dance and off they went to the dance floor.

Ryan sighed, listening to Babs and Sophie Jean wish folks a merry Christmas as they headed toward the door. He caught the bartender's eye. "Hey, Chet. Could I get another beer? I'm parched. I've been doing too much talking."

Chet laughed, mustache twitching.

Ryan laughed along with him. He liked Chet. He was a good worker during rodeo season at the Done Roamin' Ranch. But he was reminded of the way Lois had been upset with Chet at the stock auction. "Hey, Chet. Can I ask you something?"

"I've had this mustache since I could legally drink." Chet twisted one waxed end of his magnificent handlebar mustache. He paused for a beat. "That's what you were going to ask me, wasn't it? That's what most people ask me."

"No, Chet. I was wondering about you and Lois. She mentioned something about her ex and you and—"

"She's got the wrong idea." Chet snapped his bar towel at a phantom fly. "I tried to tell her but she wasn't interested."

"That's too bad that happened." Ryan inched back on his bar stool in case his next words drew more towel snaps. "I thought you two make sense, you know?"

"Really? I sure do like her." Chet wiped down the bar on either side of Ryan. "You don't think I'm too old for her?"

"Naw."

"I may just try to clear things up with her again. You know, she's on the Santapalooza committee. They're going to give out special silver Santa suits this year to guys who qualify, and I told her I qualify."

"What are the qualifications?" Ryan leaned forward, intrigued despite being Scrooge.

But someone farther down the bar called for Chet before he could answer. The old cowboy strutted away to take an order like he was the cock of the walk.

"Chet?" Ryan called half-heartedly.

Ryan nursed his beer until the song the band was playing ended and Tate returned to his seat.

"What's with you tonight?" Tate rested his forearms on the bar. "You're wound up tighter than a fresh rope on a hot day. And it's like you're giving Ronnie a run for her match-making money, trying to set me up with Jo."

"It's this horse deal." And getting to know

Jo. She was nothing like what he remembered or what he expected. She was smart, loyal, interesting, sexy and… But he couldn't tell his twin any of that. Tate would think *he* was interested in her.

"Horse deal," Tate muttered.

"Don't knock the horse deal. I'm not ready to be an alpaca farmer." Ryan added under his breath, *"Or a miniature horse keeper."*

"Alpaca," Tate muttered.

"How is she going to harvest their wool?" Ryan wondered aloud, more than happy to shoot holes in his mother's farcical plan. "Do you have to shear the alpaca the way they do sheep? And when I say you, I mean *you*, brother dear."

"Sheep," Tate muttered.

"I can see you're in a bad mood. Why don't you find a partner and do-si-do on the dance floor. There are plenty of women in the Buckboard tonight. Why, take Jo Pierce, for example." He gestured her way. "If you were with a good woman, you probably wouldn't fund so many of our mother's doomed-to-fail plans."

"I'm done." Tate set his empty beer bottle on the bar. "Heading home. Are you coming?"

"After one beer?" This was unusual. "And before nine o'clock?"

"I'm not in the mood for…" Tate glanced around the bar. "Can you catch a ride home with Wade or Griff?"

"Sure."

But right now, he needed to talk to Jo and finalize plans for the morning.

CHAPTER EIGHTEEN

Tate's eating breakfast at the Buffalo Diner.

Jo IGNORED RYAN'S text message. She was busy mucking out stalls.

Tate's headed toward the feed store.

Jo ignored Ryan's text message. She was busy exercising a horse on a lunge line.

Jo's phone rang as she was cleaning a horse's hooves. She answered. "Ryan, I'm not going to chase your brother down. I'm busy."

Silence.

"Ryan?"

"Yeah. It's me," he said. "I just called to ask if you'd go with me to see a horse that's for sale in Friar's Creek. Lydia Hartley is calling it quits."

Lydia Hartley had started training horses around the time Jo had. They were the same age.

"She's...'going under'...selling off stock?"

"Yeah. From what I hear, she only has a few

horses left for sale. She's moving to Washington or Oregon or something."

"Wow." That was demoralizing. And sad. Not just for Lydia, who was a great horse trainer and a nice person, but for Jo. It made her own situation seem more dire.

"Will you come with me? I'd like your opinion."

"Sure."

HALF AN HOUR LATER, Jo opened the passenger door to Ryan's truck.

"Morning," Ryan said in a chipper voice that matched the crisp, sunny day.

"You don't need to gush." Jo was still in a somber mood from Lydia's news.

"Maybe I'm a gusher. How would you know?" He tapped the second cup of coffee in his console. "I got you a vanilla latte."

"Your caffeine bribe won't distract me from this topic. You've never been a gusher." Jo buckled her seat belt. "You're a sourpuss. You always have been."

He gasped dramatically, as if comfortable with her ribbing. But his eyes told a different story. She'd struck a nerve.

"And I've been a sourpuss, too, I suppose." It was only fair to admit it. Jo took a sip of her latte.

"I'm not comfortable with the title *sourpuss*." Ryan made a face as he pulled out on the highway. "I prefer the term *grumpy*."

"Cowboys can be grumpy. But they call grumpy cowgirls something else."

"What is it that makes you grumpy?" Ryan flashed her a smile that was as warm as her coffee.

Whatever their differences in the past, talking to Ryan was easy.

"What *doesn't* make me grumpy nowadays?" Jo scoffed. "Bills. Slow internet. Boys who delay going to bed on time. Mothers who are convinced I won't be happy if I'm not in a relationship."

"Maybe that's because your mother would like to be in a relationship. Chet swears your father has nothing to do with his sudden interest in your mom, by the way. I encouraged him not to be discouraged."

Jo opened her mouth to argue, but then shut it. Ryan might be right about Ma wanting male companionship.

Ryan pulled up to a stop sign and lifted his hat from his head and readjusted it. Twice. Was he fretting about something? "I've thought about this a lot," he went on as if he had an important announcement to make. "You just need a couple of really good jokes to be less bland."

Jo dissolved into laughter. It was either that or be a grumpy sourpuss. "Do you know how silly *you* sound? I'm not going to be a comedian for anyone."

"I've got several you could use. Knock-knock?"

"You're skating on thin ice, Oakley."

"You tried it your way last night. Next time, it's my turn." Again with that encouraging smile. Too many of those and Jo might melt.

"Making your brother laugh isn't going to win me a date with Tate."

"Trust me."

She rolled her eyes. "And since we're on the topic of your family, I will no longer be your official smell tester. You can smell your mother yourself. She smelled of mints at the livestock auction, by the way."

He laughed. "Fair enough. I'll do all the smelling from here on out."

They made small talk the rest of the way to Friar's Creek and Lydia's tidy ranch.

"Jo, I'm so happy I got to see you before I left." Lydia had shoulder-length brown hair, a worn-out smile and an empty moving van in her ranch yard. "I'm reinventing myself. I'm becoming a hazelnut farmer in Oregon.

Did you know there's a worldwide hazelnut shortage?"

"No." Jo hugged her friend. "I guess selling hazelnuts will be less competitive than selling competition horses."

"Exactly." Lydia turned her attention to Ryan, who stood next to Jo looking nervous. He had his hands in his jacket pockets and his black hat brim pulled low. "I'm hoping Banana is right for you. He's a good roper and... Well, I'll let you decide."

"What are you going to do with him if you can't sell him?" Or the rest of her stock.

"I was hoping to sell off all my stock before the move. And my trailer, too." Lydia sounded wistful. "It's just down to Banana and Cheesecake. It's been a hard few weeks for me, letting them go for less than I think they're worth."

It was on the tip of Jo's tongue to offer to buy the horses and help Lydia out, but she didn't know the nature of the horses, not to mention she didn't have the funds and wouldn't until she'd made a sale of her own. "I'm sorry Banana didn't work out for you," Jo told Ryan on the drive home.

"Me, too." Ryan sighed. Banana wasn't near as good as Pauper and he was nearly the same price. "I would have made an offer and then asked you for help training him, but you didn't seem enthused."

"He didn't love roping," Jo said in a careful voice. "He just did what you asked him, nothing more. He'd make a good ranch horse."

"I don't need another ranch horse." His cell phone rang. Ryan answered it using the speaker function in the dashboard. "Hey, Tate. What's up?"

"I'm going to meet Mom at the coffee shop. Want to come?"

Jo gestured yes.

Ryan shook his head no.

"Ry?"

"The coffee shop?" Ryan pointed at Jo and mouthed, *"You should go."*

"Yeah."

Jo shook her head and swept a hand over herself as if to say, *I'm covered in horse hair and dirt.*

"So?" Ryan pressed. Out loud.

"So…I'm meeting Mom at the coffee shop. Do you want to come or not?" Tate asked.

"Yes. Sorry. I'm driving. See you later." Ryan disconnected. "This is it. Your chance to stand in front of Tate and let him see you as the competent horsewoman you are."

Jo sniffed her T-shirt and screwed up her nose in disgust. "No. I'm not going to show up looking and smelling like I've been mucking stalls all day."

"Fine. We'll stop off at your house first." Which he thought was a grand idea, until he was left in the truck waiting for her to clean up.

His eye caught on the tall roof of the barn where he knew mistletoe hung. Where he'd almost kissed Jo. And when he looked the other way, there was an array of tumbleweed snow-people, reminding him of how Jo and her mother playfully sparred with each other. The same way he and Jo playfully sparred with each other—because they enjoyed each other's company. And when he tried to focus on the truck's interior, his gaze landed on the two coffee cups in the center console.

Jo ran out the front door and flung the passenger door of his truck open and tossed a small handbag to the floorboard.

"Oh." Ryan leaned back against his door. "You…uh…changed."

Indeed, she had.

"I didn't have any clean jeans to wear." Jo climbed up carefully. She wore an understated, pretty blue dress, her cowboy hat and a pair of incredibly high heels. She flopped into the seat. Her lips… Her lips were a bright red that nearly matched the color in her cheeks. "This is the dress I wear to weddings and funerals.

It's literally the only clean thing I have to wear and I..." She pressed her hands to her cheeks. "I'm dying of embarrassment that it's come to this. Me walking around town. In a dress."

"Don't be embarrassed," Ryan said gruffly, resisting the urge to reach over and take a hand off her cheek. "You look great."

And she did. She looked beautiful. Even if she was presenting herself in a way he'd never seen before. Or maybe *because* she was presenting herself in a way she hadn't before.

"Thank you." Jo squared her shoulders. "You'd better drive before I lose my nerve." She buckled her seat belt. "Let's get this over with."

"ARE YOU LOOKING at my legs?" Jo tugged the hem of her dress toward her knees. She removed her hat and draped it over her thighs.

"I wasn't looking at your legs..." Ryan drew a breath, clenching the steering wheel. "Okay, I was looking at your legs, but only because I can't remember seeing them before." He made the turn toward the small ribbon of highway that led to town.

Jo had never been one for half measures. And so when she'd gone inside to clean up and hadn't had a decent pair of jeans to wear, she'd ransacked her closet, found a dress that she didn't hate and a pair of shoes she'd had for her wedding and never worn again. And then she'd gotten out the makeup that she'd bought years ago and never used. And now… she was having regrets. Starting with the length of her skirt. "I have knobby knees."

"Your knees are fine. Pretty, in fact." There was a trace of something in his voice she struggled to identify. Something akin to annoyance but with a note of another, unidentifiable emotion.

Jo gave up trying to decipher his mood and scoffed. "Knees can't be pretty."

"That's like saying a horse's hoof can't be pretty. Can't you gracefully accept a compliment?"

Jo plucked at her hat. "I'm not used to compliments like that, is all."

"Didn't Bobby give you any? You married him, after all."

"We eloped. On a whim." Hers. She still felt guilty about that. "And we were still kids when we had the twins. Do you know how often teenage boys compliment anyone? That would be hardly ever."

"Is that why the marriage didn't work? Did he take you for granted?" Ryan cast her a concerned look.

"It didn't work because we didn't love each

other." She was in a prickly mood. If she'd been her mother, she'd be thinking of ways to decorate the house for Christmas to channel her emotions in a positive direction. But she wasn't her mother. And something needed to be said. "It's your fault that I married him."

Ryan burst out laughing.

"It is." Anger built in Jo. She'd never imagined having this conversation, let alone with this Oakley.

"How is your marriage my fault? You're the one who put my motorcycle in a tree." Ryan grinned like he'd won the lottery. "Don't blame me for being expelled and then eloping."

"I'm not talking about that." Jo sat back in her seat and crossed her arms. "I'm talking about the week before Christmas our senior year. I was Tate's Secret Santa, and you threw away every gift I put in his locker."

"That was you?" Ryan slowed the truck and spared her a glance. "I thought it was his ex, trying to get back together with him. Nia Plevins was a train wreck."

Silently, Jo agreed. "I was his Secret Santa, trying to prove how well I knew him and work up the courage to ask him out for the annual Holiday Dance. But I couldn't even tell him I was his Secret Santa because as far as he was concerned, he didn't get any gifts that year."

"Hang on. It's all starting to make sense." Ryan sobered. "You resented me for ruining your plan to ask Tate out?"

"Yes."

"But you could have asked him out anyway."

Jo executed an eye roll that gummed up her false eyelashes. It took her a moment to unstick them. "Tate wouldn't have accepted because he probably didn't know my name back then. And that's because you completely ruined Secret Santa."

"Which doesn't explain why you married Bobby," Ryan pointed out.

"I wanted out of the house. My dad was… Whatever. Bobby was leaving anyway and said I should go with him." It sounded so stupid now. Back then, it had been a dream come true.

"You can't settle when it comes to love, Jo," Ryan said gruffly. "Even I know that."

"You *shouldn't* settle. But I did. And when I realized my mistake, I did the right thing for everyone involved and got a divorce. You'd do the same if it happened to you. You'd pick yourself up and move on."

"WHY ARE YOU so quiet?" Jo asked. "Did I say something wrong?"

"No." Ryan squeezed the steering wheel,

thinking that he'd picked himself and Tate up after every time his parents had let them down. But Tate was right. Ryan hadn't moved on from that part of his past. And he wasn't sure he was capable of doing so. Not when Tate was still so vulnerable.

"I take it from the pensive wrinkle between your brows that you're about to issue me an apology for ruining my one chance with your brother." Jo sounded so certain.

Ryan laughed. "That's a good one." He laughed again. "Can't you see that it's on you? You could have asked him out anytime." Tate hardly ever turned a woman down. "You lacked confidence, then and now."

Jo sat up taller. "I run a very successful business, making dozens of decisions every day. I do *not* lack confidence."

"You do." Ryan saw it now, clearer than his memory when it came to the past. "You're passive when it comes to your business. Why else would you have submitted to your brothers banning you from selling to their competitors?"

"It's called keeping the peace in the family," she said doggedly. "Peace is very important to my mother."

"Yeah, well. I wouldn't have done it," Ryan

said ruthlessly. "And neither would your brothers if your positions had been reversed."

She tightened her arms over her chest.

"You stay quiet because it's easier to try to be invisible than to risk having your heart broken. Being passive isn't something confident people do. They're bold, assertive even."

She stared out the window as they neared Clementine, humming what sounded like "Jingle Bells."

He'd crossed a line. That seemed hard to believe. He and Jo had talked about almost everything and anything this past week.

She's afraid.

The thought rattled around in his head. Meanwhile, her humming was getting louder and the miles to Clementine were diminishing.

"I'm sorry," he told her. "That might have been my grumpy side coming out."

"Hmm." She didn't look away from the window. "Jingle Bells" continued to fill the cab the rest of the way to town.

Ryan parked across the street from Clementine Coffee Grinders and turned off his truck. "I see Tate inside. All you need to do is walk in and take a beat to read the room, the same way you took your time evaluating Banana when Lydia first showed him to us.

Then walk up to him with a big smile and a big wave, and say something about someone you both know—not me!"

He forced out a laugh, trying to deflate the tension they were both feeling. "Use your mom voice to get his attention if you have to. What I mean is," he added when she rolled her eyes, "talk to him the way you do to me. Tate won't frown at you or tell you to go away." Ryan knew his twin well enough to predict that. Tate never wanted to hurt anyone's feelings, especially if they made an effort to be friendly.

Jo stared at Ryan with big brown eyes. "This isn't going to work. He's in there mooning at your mother. I'll be *that* woman. The one who is insensitive about his personal life."

"Of course it's going to work. I know my brother. And I know you. If you get nervous, keep moving. Walk past him a few times."

He held up two fingers, kept one still, and motioned the other one back and forth in front of it. "He'll engage in your conversation. I promise."

Jo gripped his arm. "When I flounder… because I will…" Her wide eyes betrayed her fear. "You need to be like a lifeguard racing to my rescue."

That wouldn't help either one of them. He

covered her hand with one of his. "How can you possibly flounder?"

"I could fall flat on my face." She drew back and removed the wide-brimmed cowboy hat from her legs. She set it on the floorboards. "I could order a red velvet cupcake and it could stain my teeth."

He almost laughed. "Don't do that."

Jo shrugged. "It's my panic comfort food."

"You're not going in there to eat or to panic. You're grabbing a cup of coffee after… I don't know. Lunch with friends? And then you're leaving. If too much talk unnerves you, don't linger after you get your coffee."

"Thanks. That helps." Jo squared her shoulders and then carefully climbed down to the pavement. She tottered on those heels the first few steps away from his door before slowing down.

He watched her progress in his side-view mirror. Jo made each step with deliberate grace, the way a giraffe did. Not exactly a sexy cat-walk.

Ryan smiled. She may not have been good at walking with full-blown confidence, but she had game.

Jo entered the coffee shop and paused at the door, possibly panicking.

"Don't be scared," Ryan whispered, even though she couldn't hear him.

Jo half glanced over her shoulder toward him before gathering herself and moving forward.

"That's it," Ryan whispered. "Go get him."

Jo continued her giraffe walk toward the cash register, not Tate.

Ryan forgot that wasn't the plan. She really did have nice legs. The hem of her blue dress floated around her knees, which weren't knobby.

Tate did a double take as she passed his table.

Jo kept walking. Instead of greeting Tate, she gave a little wave to whoever was standing behind the cash register, perhaps placing an order.

Ryan's shoulders tensed. "Come on. Say something to him."

Tate half turned, following Jo's progress. He said something. Ryan could almost hear his twin's tone of voice, one of friendly surprise.

Jo, good to see you.

Jo, how are your boys? Growing fast, I bet.

Jo, nice dress. Why don't you wear that on Saturday night? I'll pick you up at eight.

Ryan washed a hand over his face, frowning.

Jo turned at the cash register, cheeks a bright red once more, and said something back to

Tate. And then the barista waved to get her attention.

Jo patted her hips, as if she wore a jacket and needed to know which pocket she'd put her wallet into.

"Oh, no." Ryan scrambled to grab her purse, searching for her wallet. But when he had it in hand, he froze. He couldn't exactly run it in there and say, *Hey, you left your wallet in my truck.*

Thankfully, Tate got out of his chair and reached in his back pocket. He withdrew some bills and walked them over to the cashier.

Jo looked like she was refusing his offer to pay, hands fluttering as she backed away.

"Be gracious, Jo," Ryan murmured, heaving a sigh of relief when she seemed to let Tate pay.

His brother said something else to her and the barista. Jo pressed her palms briefly to her cheeks, an indication that she was flustered and blushing. And then Tate returned to the table and their mother.

All Jo needed to do was collect her coffee, give Tate a nod as she walked by and make it back to Ryan's truck, safe and sound.

She picked up two coffee cups, which was odd.

"Did she order two coffees instead of one coffee and a red velvet cupcake?" Ryan's neck was kinking from trying to watch what was happening in his side-view mirror.

Jo moseyed toward the door, balancing on those heels and holding on to two cups of coffee as if it was the hardest thing she'd ever done in her life. She approached Tate's table, glanced up and said something to his mother. And as she passed, her ankle twisted, and she fell into Tate's lap.

It looked as if she screamed. Her eyes were huge, her legs wheeling.

Tate's eyes were huge.

Reflexively, Ryan reached for the door handle, ready to ruin everything by running to her rescue.

But Jo stumbled off Tate's lap and onto her feet, her face flaming.

"What the…?" A muffled, feminine voice carried from in front of his truck.

Ronnie stood at Ryan's front bumper. She'd been staring across the street at the spectacle in the coffee shop, but her gaze recentered on Ryan when he jolted around at her exclamation.

And then Jo trotted across the street, running on the balls of her feet, like she'd stolen something and had to sprint to the getaway vehicle.

"Jo?" Ronnie called to her. "Did you just fall on Tate's lap?"

"Can you just forget you saw me? Er...saw that?" Jo wobbled to Ryan's door, still carrying two coffee cups. "It's freezing in this dress."

Ryan leaned across and opened the door for Jo. And then he started his truck and set the heater to full blast.

Jo handed him one of the coffee cups. "Here. Tate ordered you a cup of coffee with two sweeteners." She set her coffee in the center console and began the treacherous climb into the front seat.

Meanwhile, Ronnie hopped into the back seat behind Ryan. "Jo, I want a full debrief on what just happened, including why we're all sitting in Ryan's truck."

Jo groaned and sank into her seat. "Would you believe me if I told you that I just accidentally jumped into Ryan's truck because I locked my keys in my truck?"

"No. Your truck isn't here." Ronnie glanced around, as if to double-check. "And that's your cowboy hat on the floor, Jo. You two have been acting suspicious lately. Talking in bars and at coffee shops. Spill all the tea."

"There's nothing to say. About us, that is," Ryan said defensively.

"I'm not buying it, Ryan." Ronnie leaned

forward and shook his shoulder. "Just look at the pair of you, huddling in this truck as if you're planning to rob a bank or something."

"Everyone needs to take a breath." Jo slid out of her high heels and flexed her pretty little toes into Ryan's carpet beneath the dashboard heating vent. "I'm the one who should be upset and mortified."

Ryan and Ronnie reluctantly agreed.

But Ryan couldn't let that stand. "I don't think it went as bad as you think."

"Which part?" Jo plopped her cowboy hat on her head. "My cringeworthy hello? How I paraded myself in front of your brother and fell in his lap? Or how it felt when he told me he saw me get out of your truck?"

"Okay." Ryan nodded. "When you put it like that, it sounds bad."

"Mortifying," Jo repeated. "I'm a businesswoman, a mother of two. I know who I am and what I do well. If only I'd had a clean pair of jeans…"

"And now you're going to have to let me take the reins on this runaway," Ronnie said crisply. "Grab your stuff, Jo. You're coming with me."

"No, thank you." Jo sipped her coffee. "I need to go home and do laundry."

Ryan reached for Jo's hand and gave it a squeeze.

Jo stared at their joined hands in silence.

In the back seat, Ronnie heaved a sigh. "Jo, I'm not going to make you over. You just fell in a handsome cowboy's lap. You need a girlfriend right now. Someone who's experienced similar mortification and someone who can help you transition to laughing about this humbling experience."

After a moment of consideration, Ryan said, "Ronnie's right." He conceded the task of comforting Jo to Ronnie and withdrew his hand.

After a moment, Jo nodded. She set her cowboy hat on her head just so and got out of his truck.

Ryan gripped the steering wheel because his hand, his truck and his life suddenly felt overwhelmingly empty.

CHAPTER NINETEEN

"I DON'T KNOW why you're trying to reinvent yourself just to get a date with Ryan," Ronnie told Jo when she sat on a dressing table stool in Ronnie's bedroom in downtown Clementine. "I see you two together all the time. Up until today, I would have said I wouldn't pair you together, but somehow it works. And now..."

"I'm not dating Ryan," Jo said miserably. "I never was. He said he could get me a date with Tate. I admit, I let things get out of hand back there."

Ronnie looked deep into Jo's eyes. "Tate? Still? Is a date with him on your bucket list? You can't be in love with him. That man doesn't even know what he's looking for."

"Maybe he's looking for me." And he just couldn't see her.

Ronnie very wisely kept her thoughts to herself. She wiped the makeup from Jo's face with a gentle touch and a compassionate expression. "This reminds me of when I was thirteen and I tried on my mother's makeup."

"I remember. You made a statement at school that day."

"I was too proud to ask my mother how to use makeup and too proud to remove it after my first class at school." She paused to look Jo in the eyes. "Thank you for standing by me."

"Thank you for standing by me today." Ronnie had taken no pictures to share with their friends and hadn't rubbed in all Jo's fashion faux pas. "I should get back to the ranch."

"Not so fast." Ronnie slid a tray filled with makeup forward on her dressing table. "First, let's talk makeup."

Jo hesitated. The Pierce women didn't wear makeup. Usually.

"I've always envied how comfortable you are in your own skin. But if you've ever been curious about makeup, you can ask me."

Ronnie was being so gracious and gentle that Jo nodded. "I'm curious."

Ronnie spent the next fifteen minutes talking about foundation, eye accents, blush and lipstick. And then she helped Jo apply a little makeup. Only a little.

"I still look like me," Jo said when they were done, immensely relieved.

"Now, let's find you something a little less out of your comfort zone to wear. We'll start with boots, because that's what I believe is the foundation of every cowgirl's wardrobe." Ronnie bent next to Jo's leg and picked up her foot as if she were a horse who needed their hoof examined. "What's your shoe size? Eight? I have boots you can borrow that you can actually walk in. Well, actually, they're Bess's boots. But she left them here years ago and I'm sure she won't mind."

"Have I told you lately that you are the gem of friends?" Jo followed Ronnie to her guest bedroom, where she opened the closet door to reveal cubbies filled with boots of every shape and color.

A few hours later, Jo looked more like a slightly polished version of herself. She felt it, too. "Are you sure you don't mind me borrowing a couple of dresses?"

"I think I have enough to wear," Ronnie assured her. She was something of a fashion plate, having landed that clothing endorsement from Cowboy Pearl. "I won't miss a thing."

AFTER JO LEFT in Ronnie's car, Ryan decided to take the bull by the horns.

He set the brim of his hat to eyebrow height and walked into Clementine Coffee Grinders carrying the coffee Tate had bought for him.

"Just wanted to thank you for the hot beverage, bro. It's mighty cold outside."

"Sitting in your truck and watching us." Tate sounded irate, but he pulled out a chair for Ryan to sit down on. And then he made an awkward gesture toward their mother. "You remember…"

"Our mother? Donna Oakley? It's been a long time, but yes, I do remember her. In fact, I saw her the other day at the auction yard." He looked into his mother's clear brown eyes. Or he tried to.

She was unwrapping a round, red-and-white mint.

Because she'd been drinking?

Ryan's gaze slashed to Tate, who was staring into his coffee cup.

"Didn't she tell you about shopping for a trio of alpacas last Wednesday?" Ryan sat back from the table, his chair closer to Tate than to his mother. "You did buy them after I left, didn't you? And not the miniature horses?" He was betting the tiny horses had a new home.

"Miniature horses? Mom? Ry?" Steam rose from Tate. He concentrated most of that heat on Ryan. "You didn't tell me you ran into each other."

"I haven't seen you much. I've been trying to land financing for that venture of ours and spending time over at the Pierce Ranch. Plus, you've been working long hours at her spread." Ryan sipped his coffee, trying not to use the word *Mom* when referring to her. "Did the alpaca deal fall through?"

"I didn't buy anything." His mother smacked the mint about her mouth. She had a frosty, pink drink in front of her that was half-drunk. Pun intended. "I want to start with the best. And they didn't seem like the best to me."

They'd been healthy animals. Young, with years of breeding ahead of them. But they hadn't been as cute as the miniature horses.

Ryan breathed through a wave of frustration.

"After you and Jo left, that alpaca breeder told me he went to Chile to study with an alpaca whisperer." His mother traced a knot in the wooden tabletop with one finger. "That's the way to do it. Go to the source and learn from the best."

Ryan clung to the back of his jeans with one hand. Was she trying to get Tate to pay for that pilgrimage?

"Can't you learn from the guy at the auction yard?" Ryan set his coffee down on the edge of her finger doodles, crowding her on purpose. "He could pass on the information he learned to you. Save you all that travel to South America."

Tate rubbed a hand behind his neck. He didn't like conflict.

"It wouldn't be the same." She drew her hand back and crunched the mint in her mouth.

Ryan waited for an explanation. Beneath the table, Tate slid his pointed boot into the side of Ryan's foot, a sign they used to tell each other to ease off. Ryan gave him a dark look.

"What if that fella heard wrong?" Their mother started talking again in that distracted way of hers. "They speak Spanish down there, don't they? He could have gotten all mixed up. How could I trust anything he says about those alpacas?"

"Do *you* speak Spanish?" Ryan asked casually.

"Ry," Tate whispered, eyes shooting daggers.

Their mother seemed oblivious to the tension between her two sons. "Well, I'd understand Spanish if I was down there. You absorb the language when you live in a place."

"So, your plan is," Ryan began carefully, evenly, although he felt like shouting at high speed, "that you'll travel to Chile to study alpacas before buying any stock? What about the ranch you've been renting in Friar's Creek?" The one Tate had been working on.

"I'm proud of you boys." Her gaze brushed over Ryan and then away. "And especially you, Ryan. You always were sharp, understanding what needed to be done."

"He's so sharp, he cuts like a knife," Tate muttered.

"That's a great girl you're dating, Ryan." His mother gestured toward Tate and, presumably, his lap. She smiled for the first time, although not for long.

"I'm not dating Jo." As if Ryan could be that lucky. She wanted Tate. "I'm trying to buy a horse from her. Actually, I think Tate should—"

"Not date her," Tate finished for him.

"I was going to say buy a horse from her, too." Ryan spun his coffee cup on the table. "Of course, he probably can't help you every day with the alpacas and get his money's worth out of a horse."

"I'm retiring." Tate was a barrel of laughs today.

"And if he's retiring, I think he should settle down, don't you?" Ryan directed his question at their mother. "Get a ranch of his own. Of course, he'd still need a good horse or two. And if he dated Jo, he'd have a direct line to good stock. Plus, she has twin boys." Despite the tension, he smiled, thinking of those two pistols.

"Troublemakers, are they?" Their mother shook her head. "That's too bad. We could hardly trust you two alone in the house without wondering if it was going to burn down."

"And that was when we were six," Ryan muttered, earning another boot from Tate. "Well, it's been a nice visit. Thanks again for the coffee, bro. See you back at the ranch."

"Not if I see you first," Tate muttered.

"Mom, what are you doing?" Ryan entered the Done Roamin' Ranch's bunkhouse after a disastrous Sunday. He hung up his hat and coat in the foyer, gaze catching on a picture of himself and Tate as kids, arms slung around each other with cheek-splitting grins on their faces. "You know I don't celebrate the holidays the way you do." Lavishly.

"It's just a wreath in the window." His foster mother stepped back to survey her work. She wore a fuzzy sweater with a Christmas tree on the front. "I can see this wreath from our living room. It makes me feel happy to think I've given you boys and the bunkhouse some Christmas cheer. I hope you don't mind."

Christmas cheer? Images flitted through Ryan's mind. Jo wearing a sweatshirt with the Grinch on it. Jo standing beneath the mistletoe.

Ryan sat down on the bench and removed his boots.

"Are you sure you want to put that wreath there?" Ryan shook his head. "The only guys left here are me, Tate and Griff. Tate's never here. And Griff said he might fly to Las Vegas for Christmas."

"Bite your tongue." Mom tidied up the bunkhouse, gathering books and magazines and putting them in a neat pile. "Christmas is a time for family."

Ryan was too demoralized to argue. He was no closer to buying a horse than he'd been this morning. And Jo…

"What's wrong?" Mom stared at him, coming closer. "Bad day?"

He sighed. "It's a long story." He gave her a weary smile. "You think I need that wreath, don't you?"

"My dear, darling son." Mom sat down next to him. "You know, life and the years change us. When you first arrived here, you watched out for Tate like a hawk. If anyone picked on him or even looked at him wrong, you had no problem getting right up in their face."

"He didn't see the danger, even when someone was pushing his buttons. He'd just smile." Tate was still naive, in need of Ryan's protection, whether he wanted it or not.

"Tate has always needed people to like him, even if it meant they might take advantage."

"That hasn't changed," Ryan said, thinking of their biological mother.

Mom laughed. "It makes it hard for him to be in a lasting relationship."

Ryan scoffed. "He just doesn't want to be tied down."

"No," Mom said carefully. "Sometimes children of absentee parents grow up wanting to please everyone who shows them interest. That makes it hard for someone like Tate to stay in a relationship. Not because the grass is greener but because he doesn't want to be rejected. By anyone. So, he doesn't reject anyone who shows interest in him."

"Oh." What if Jo asked Tate out?

Ryan felt gut punched.

Oblivious to his turmoil, Mom continued, laying her head on his shoulder, "On the other hand, your defensive instinct is to push people and anything smacking of commitment away, because you don't want to be hurt again. Your friend network outside of the ranch is practically nil."

She wasn't wrong.

"That attitude of yours was fine when you were with your biological parents, fending for yourself and your brother much of the time. When you first got here, you used to tell me you'd never get married, have kids or celebrate Christmas. You were going to grow up and make a lot of money."

"Still working on making a name and bank account for myself." Still rejecting the idea of family and Christmas, even if tumbleweed snowmen were growing on him.

"You're doing just fine." Mom sandwiched his hand in both of hers, patting it with her top hand. "Plenty of cowboys can't afford a new truck, much less a new horse. You have a family here who love and support you, including having your back."

"You make me sound like a success." If that was true, why was he having a hard time filling his lungs with air?

"A man who's a success can afford to breathe easy and give back to his community."

"Is this…a reference to Santapalooza?"

"How'd you guess? I'm recruiting riders." She patted his leg. "Plus, you seemed to be holding your breath."

He drew a deep breath, expelled it, then drew another.

"You need to let Tate make his own decisions, even if it means he'll fail. We learn from our mistakes, you know."

A lump formed in Ryan's throat.

"And while you're letting go, you might also let go of the idea that you weren't meant to have the things you didn't have when you were young. Like the love of a good woman, a passel of children filling a house you own and a spectacularly big Christmas with all the traditions and trimmings."

"I should have known this was going to come back to holiday decorations."

Mom smiled softly. "If you had your way, it'd come back to horses."

"Horses I can't afford."

"You'll find a way to get that horse." She kissed his cheek. "I love you, Ryan. And I'm proud of you and how far you've come from that angry, defensive boy who was dropped off here almost two decades ago. But that doesn't mean you can't come a little farther into the light of a glowing Christmas tree and into the arms of someone who could love you the way you deserve to be loved."

Ryan gently eased away from his mother. "I'm not dating Jo. I have things I want to do." None of which included a woman, a family or Christmas.

So, it made no sense that after his mother left, humming "Jingle Bells," his mind immediately turned to Jo.

CHAPTER TWENTY

LOIS WAS SPENDING her Sunday afternoon in peace.

Max and Dean were at a friend's house until dinnertime.

Jo had left on a *not*-date with Ryan, something Lois was extremely curious about.

Blue was curled beneath the Christmas tree, his collar adorned with red velvet and white faux fur.

Tiger had been returned to his stall, not once but twice.

Lois had a Christmas romance movie marathon playing on the television while she attached fur trim to Santa costumes and hats. With a turn of her head, she could see Christmas decorations inside and out. No one texted. No one called. It was all very…grandma-like.

"All I need is a rocking chair," she told Blue, peering over the rim of her glasses at him. "And then I will truly be all but forgotten."

The cute young couple on-screen was talking through their feelings on their way to a chaste kiss and their promise of happily-ever-after.

"I don't even remember Herbie proposing to me," Lois told Blue. There was just a vague memory of excitement. And then her life had been one big treadmill.

Marriage. *Check.*

Babies. *Check.*

Run the household and help on the ranch. *Check-check.*

Try to make everyone happy or at least even-keeled so that Herbie wouldn't explode. That had been her daily check those last few years. Avoid setting off Hurricane Herbie.

Avoid shouting. Avoid unkind words. Avoid, avoid, avoid.

Until her world became smaller than the stitches holding fake fur trim on a cheap Santa suit.

Is that how life is supposed to be?

She hadn't wanted to say the words out loud, not even to Blue, in case that might be true.

Tires crunched over gravel, the sounds of an approaching vehicle.

Blue lifted his head, then got up and trotted to the door.

What if it's Herbie?

Lois set the Santa suit aside. She didn't want it to be her blustery ex-husband. She didn't want to keep the peace. She didn't want to feel small, not anymore.

She got to her feet and went to the front door, heart pounding.

"Thanks for the ride, Ronnie." Jo waved to her friend and then came up the front walk, arms full of clothing. She wore a dress, but that wasn't the only thing about her that looked different. She seemed more confident. Lighter. Happier.

"Bigger stitches," Lois murmured.

"Hi, Ma." Jo came in. She wore a pretty green dress and silver cowboy boots. Her hair was cut differently, long enough on one side to begin to curl around her cheek, shorter on the other. She set her things down on the couch, greeted Blue and then removed her cowboy hat.

"You're wearing makeup," Lois said. "And you…you did…"

"Pretty much everything." Unexpectedly, Jo hugged her. She smelled like lemons and hair product. "Ronnie took me to a salon for a haircut. She did my makeup, too. And the dress… Well…what do you think?"

"You look beautiful." Lois held her at arm's length. "But you always look beautiful to me."

"I'm not going to look like this every day," Jo said, blushing a little. "Maybe on weekends."

"Or when our Oakley takes you out." Lois glanced out the window toward the dust made by Ronnie's disappearing green Volkswagen. "What happened to Ryan?"

Jo's expression shuttered. "I should change and see to the horses."

"Wait…" Lois reached out and touched Jo's arm. "Can you help me with something? I've been feeling…stuck."

Jo paused midflight, returning to face her. "Ma, you know I'd help you with anything. You've always been there for me. What do you need?"

"I know this sounds funny, but…" Lois fingered a lock of Jo's hair. "I need a little confidence."

HOURS LATER, Lois walked into the Buckboard.

She'd taken a page from Jo's transformation, and with a little help from her daughter, including a dig into the dusty end of her closet, Lois was ready to expand her world.

There was a small dinner crowd sitting at tables. The stage and dance floor were empty. A few patrons sat perched at the bar, watching a football game on the big-screen television.

Chet was talking to a young cowboy while pouring him a shot of whiskey. He glanced up, eyes finding hers. His mustache barely twitched. His eyes didn't sparkle. And yet she still felt that *hubba-hubba* attraction.

While helping her apply makeup, Jo had told Lois that Chet wasn't a pawn in some game Herbie was playing. Not that it mattered. Lois had already been set on coming here and taking a chance.

She drew a deep breath and walked across the room toward an empty bar stool. And when she was settled, purse strap hooked over her knee, she curled her finger toward Chet in a come-hither motion.

His mustache twitched as he slowly approached.

"I'd like a drink," Lois said while he placed a small, square napkin in front of her.

"Coffee, black, or iced tea?" Still no twinkle. Still no grin highlighted by a handlebar mustache twitch.

But there was a flutter in her stomach and a feeling that even if things didn't work out with her and Chet, from now on she was going to try things that might upset her carefully crafted sense of peace.

Lois placed her elbows on the bar and leaned

forward. "I'd like a drink that says a lady is interested in the man behind the bar."

Chet's lips curled in a smile and the ends of his white mustache quivered.

CHAPTER TWENTY-ONE

"WHY ARE YOU sitting in a horse stall, son?"

"Testing out a theory," Ryan told his dad from the floor of Suzie's stall. It was Monday morning, and he was trying to get his head on straight.

Suzie had been nuzzling his hat, as if worried about him. But when Ryan's father leaned on the stall door, she ambled over to greet him.

"That's interesting." Frank Harrison wore a hat the same style as Jo's—a wide-brimmed white hat that shaded his face and neck from the sun. He wore a tan jacket over a black-and-white-checked shirt. And he wore an expression that said he was here to talk business. "You've never struck me as the theoretical type."

Ryan stood and came to stand next to Suzie, slinging an arm over her back. "Jo thinks I can make Suzie a better competitor if she bonds with me."

"Things are always better with strong relationships." Dad cleared his throat. "Which is why I've come. I want you to go somewhere with me."

"Sure." Ryan came out of the stall, latching it behind him. "Where are we going?"

"To Friar's Creek." Dad set a swift pace toward the door. "Your brother is in need of assistance."

Ryan dragged his feet. "Not at my mother's place."

"Exactly that." Dad gestured for Ryan to hurry without looking back. "I didn't raise you to second-guess someone's request for help."

"He didn't ask me," Ryan said mulishly.

"That's because you boys are out of sorts with each other. Your mother asked me to step in. And now I'm asking you."

Ryan was quiet for most of the drive to Friar's Creek. He didn't know what to expect. Tension knotted his shoulders and his insides. "You want me to be nice to her after everything she did to us."

"I want you to take what she's offering, which might never be much," Dad said. "Don't let her mistakes ruin other aspects of your life, like your relationship with Tate."

They pulled into a small property with barbed wire fencing and a small house that didn't look sturdier than an old miner's shack in an abandoned field. It needed paint, probably a new roof and a good deal of weeding.

Tate was just visible around the back, working on the roof of a dilapidated sheep shed. He glanced over when they parked and then went back to work, nailing a board into place.

"Her car isn't here," Ryan said with more than a bit of relief.

"But your brother is." Dad pocketed his truck keys and gave Ryan a searching look. "When your mother and I are gone…when your foster brothers are scattered to the corners of the earth…then you'll need to know how to mend a fence with Tate." Dad picked his hat from where it rested on the dashboard and settled it on his head. "And today, we're going to practice that skill."

Knowing he was right, Ryan followed him.

"Reinforcements have arrived," Dad announced as they walked toward the back.

The pasture had clumps of overgrown brown grass, leaning fence posts and an air of neglect. The good news was that there were no animals in the pasture. No miniature horses. No alpaca. Not so much as a stray cat.

Dad's phone rang. He moved to the back patio to take the call on speaker because he had trouble hearing when he held it to his ear.

Could be worse. He could be answering on video.

Ryan chuckled, coming to stand near the sheep shed. "So, this is an alpaca ranch."

"Soon to be." Tate glanced around. "Doesn't appeal to me in the slightest."

"That's a relief to hear." Ryan smiled. "What needs to be done?"

"Well…a lot." Tate whacked his hammer one last time against the nail. "Truth be told, the inside is worse than the outside. It's why her rent is so cheap."

Like that's a surprise.

Ryan tightened his arms over his chest.

"I now pronounce the pasture safe for animals." Tate tossed his hammer into a red metal tool chest and then stood, turning toward the house. "The first thing I did was make sure her doors locked solid."

"Smart."

"I patched the roof." Tate pointed upward. "The windows are drafty and need caulking. The faucets leak. There's a spot in the kitchen floor that might collapse and another in front of the bathtub. I called the landlord and told him I'd sue if Mom fell through. He's supposed to do something about it next week. Finally."

"Nice."

"And it's been fumigated, along with the vermin being gone." Tate rapped his knuckles on the sheep shed. "Knock on wood."

"That's quite a lot." And Ryan suspected there was more his brother had done. "Where is she?"

"About that…" Tate seemed to withdraw a little. "Mom left this morning with that alpaca breeder she met at the livestock auction. Marcus Caldwell."

"You mean they…eloped?" Or went on a bender? Ryan's neck twinged.

"It's nothing like that. She and Marcus…" Tate shrugged. "They made an agreement to partner together on this alpaca business. Marcus will do most of the breeding and shearing, and she'll make the yarn. But first, he's taking her on a tour of different alpaca operations."

"In Chile?" Ryan's shoulders sagged and his hands fell to his sides. "Did you pay for her ticket?" Because he imagined that was extremely pricey.

"They didn't go to Chile." Tate shifted his feet and his gaze. At the edge of his beard, his cheek twitched. "Apparently, Marcus has friends in Colorado who raise alpaca and make yarn. They went out there to spend a few days so Mom could learn the ropes."

"Did you give her money?"

"No. I refused." Tate sighed. "It was the first time I said no to her without…without you by my side."

This was huge. A weight felt like it had been lifted from Ryan's shoulders. "That must have been hard for you."

Tate smiled a little. "It was. But it was time. She's always been a dreamer and she'll always need someone to help her make positive moves toward those dreams or…"

He didn't need to finish that sentence. Ryan knew what he meant. Their mother needed support, plain and simple. "What made you change your mind?"

"You. How determined you've been to move forward, not to quit, even when the price of a horse should deter you."

That warmed Ryan's heart. "I'm going to make it happen for both of us."

"I know you will." Tate turned to look at the small house. "Looking at this place… I don't want that to be my life. I want a decent place to live when I move out of the bunkhouse. And if that means shifting my main focus to myself rather than to Mom, then that's what I've got to do. She understands. I think."

"I love you, man." Ryan came forward and hugged his brother. "And I'm proud of you."

Tate stepped back first. "Yeah, well. There's still the question of how we're going to find the money to buy these horses."

They nodded at each other.

"Sorry about the phone call." Dad walked back toward them. "What did I miss?"

"Nothing," both Oakleys said, grinning.

"So." Ryan drew a breath and faced his twin. "What needs to be done next?"

"WHAT'S GOING ON HERE?" Ryan entered the covered arena at the Pierce Ranch in disbelief, having stopped by to tell Jo that Tate was on board with a horse purchase.

Three pairs of eyes swiveled his way.

Jo was nowhere in sight.

Max, Dean and Tiger stared at him from the center of the arena. Dean sat on Tiger without a bridle or saddle. Tiger held a big red ball the size of a beach ball in his mouth. Max hung from it.

Ryan strode toward them.

Correction: there was a handle on the ball and Tiger had that handle in his mouth. It was one of those weighted horse exercise balls made of hard plastic with a handle on it for people—or horses—to grab on to.

Max put his boots on the ground and let go of the ball, turning slightly to face Ryan.

Tiger shook his head, swinging the ball into Max's backside.

"Hey!" Max stumbled forward.

Dean laughed so hard he almost fell off Tiger's back.

"Ow." Max danced out of the way. And then he put his hands on his hips, staring at an approaching Ryan. "Are you dating Mom?"

"No." Ryan bypassed Max and checked to make sure Tiger was okay. "What does that have to do with anything?"

"Sw-weet!" Max cried. "You're *not* dating her, so you can just look the other way right now."

The chestnut eyed Ryan like a linebacker eyed an opposing quarterback. And then he shook the ball again, whacking Ryan on the shoulder and very nearly knocking him down.

"What is going on?" Ryan rubbed his shoulder. "Someone explain, please."

Clucking and using his legs, Dean cued Tiger to back up and away from Ryan. "We're playing Bareback Folly Ball."

Ryan rolled his shoulder, eyeing the big red ball Tiger had grasped in his teeth. "I've heard of Folly Ball. Isn't that something a horse plays in the pasture?" Horses with a penchant for trouble were given those big plastic balls to keep themselves occupied.

"Folly Ball isn't unsupervised." Max ran toward Tiger, jumped and hugged the ball with both arms.

Tiger shook the ball—and Max—like a dog playing tug with a rope.

Dean clung to Tiger, fingers buried in his mane.

Both boys were shrieking with delight, so loud that they couldn't hear Ryan yell, "Hey! Hey! Somebody's gonna get hurt." He ran up to Tiger, only to have the chestnut trot off with Max still clinging to the Folly Ball.

That only made the boys laugh harder.

And from the way Tiger trotted—ears up and tail in the air—the gelding was probably having a good time, too.

Ryan stopped and allowed himself to laugh as well. This was the kind of mischief he and Tate used to get into. "Okay. All right. What are the rules here?"

Max let the ball go and moved to Tiger's side, giving him a good hard pat as if he truly was an oversize dog that didn't need to be treated with a fragile touch. "The rules to Bareback Folly Ball are simple. Hang on."

"Hang on to the ball or stay on Tiger's back." Dean nodded. He hopped off. "It's my turn on the ball."

Ryan came over to pat Tiger and give the

Folly Ball a good squeeze. It wasn't inflated. It was solid. "Seems hard to hold."

"Life is hard," Max said, taking hold of Tiger's mane and hopping onto his back.

"So, we gotta be tough," Dean said, gently pushing Ryan aside. "I don't want to hurt you, Mr. Ryan. Grandma says old people don't bounce. They break."

"I'm not old." Ryan scoffed.

"Yeah, right." Max gave Tiger a couple more hearty pats.

The horse snorted, more like a challenge than an expelling of breath.

Ryan gave the boys space to play.

"This is not going to end well." But Ryan was laughing at the sheer joy of it.

And it seemed no more dangerous than tackle football. Although Tiger was big, he was also relatively gentle with them. When he shook Dean off and into the dirt, he stood stock-still until Dean got back to his feet, as if he didn't want to accidentally step on him. And when Max lost his balance on his back, lying like a sack of potatoes sideways on him, Tiger again stood still until Max regained his seat.

"Okay, guys." Ryan approached them after they'd both had a round of turns and Tiger had set the ball down in the dirt. "I want to give it a try."

Max scoffed. "You're too big."

"I've never heard of an adult playing Folly Ball." Dean looked Ryan up and down. "Not even Mom."

"Plus, you're old and breakable." Grinning, Max high-fived Dean.

It was a good thing that Ryan had thick skin. "Let's let Tiger decide." He picked up the ball, extending the slobbery handle toward the horse.

Tiger chuffed, shifting slightly sideways. He extended his nose toward Ryan and then drew it back.

This was a playground face-off. And Ryan had experienced plenty of those. You had to prove to the home team that the new kid had game.

"Ha. You're giving it to me?" Ryan drew the bulky ball under his arm. "Thanks." He backed up quickly, zigging to the right, zagging to the left.

"Hey, that's our ball." Max trotted forward.

Dean and Tiger followed suit.

"Okay." Ryan backed up another few feet before making a stand. "Take it, then." He held out the ball with the handle toward Tiger.

Tiger and the boys came to a halt. The gelding stretched his nose forward, slowly.

Ryan tucked it back under his arm. "You can't take it, Tiger."

"He can," Dean cried.

"Get the ball, Tiger." Max pointed at the ball, as if telling Blue to retrieve it.

Ryan held it out again.

This time, Tiger extended his neck, opened his mouth and took the handle, moving his jaw until he seemed to have it in a comfortable position, like where a bit usually fit when he wore a bridle.

"Knock him down, Tiger," Max said.

"Just don't break him," Dean cautioned.

Tiger chuffed. And then the fun began.

CHAPTER TWENTY-TWO

"WHAT IN THE WORLD…?" Jo entered the covered arena after having taken the bay she'd been training out for a long ride.

Four pairs of eyes swiveled her way.

The twins looked mutinously guilty, if there was such a thing. Tiger had a spark of enthusiasm in his eye, his muzzle locked onto the Folly Ball.

And then there was Ryan.

Ryan looked as if he'd been dragged across the arena in the dirt and back again. But his grin… She'd never seen him smile with such pure, unadulterated joy.

Normally, when she caught the boys doing something they weren't supposed to be doing, she marched right up to them and read them the riot act. Give them an inch and they'd take a mile.

But this…

This was different. While she'd been riding in the big pasture, something had been going on that felt game-changing.

Ryan let go of the Folly Ball. It landed in the dirt at his feet. The boys moved next to Ryan, flanking Tiger.

She gave her boys a close inspection as she crossed the length of the arena. Their hats and boots had the grimy, working-ranch-hand look, as always. But their jeans and jackets were streaked with dirt. Thankfully, no blood was visible.

Tiger stood tall and alert. He was the cleanest of the lot.

The trio of males—a foursome, if you counted Tiger—closed ranks. They looked like a team of coconspirators. Some might even say…*a family*.

Jo's heart melted.

Don't think like that.

She was the ugly duckling. And Ryan wasn't what she had in mind for a life partner. He was Scrooge. Or the Grinch. Or any number of characters who didn't like Christmas.

"We made up a new game." Max hooked his thumbs through his belt loops.

Dean followed suit, rocking back on his heels. "It was Mr. Ryan's idea."

Ryan remained carefully silent, although he took in the boys' stances and hooked his thumbs through his own belt loops. He had dirt streaked across one cheek. His black hat and jacket were filthy, his knuckles scraped.

"And what is this game called?" Jo asked when she'd almost reached them and no more information was forthcoming.

"Keep Away from Tiger," Ryan said, looking adorably sheepish. "And can I just say that no boys were hurt in this game?"

"Do I want to know what the rules of this game are?" Or should she just ban it from ever being played again?

"Well, Mr. Ryan almost got broken," Dean said, always the one Jo relied on to spill the beans. "Once or twice."

"It's just a scratch." Ryan twitched as if a muscle cramped. "Or two."

"Old people are tougher than they look." Max nodded, wiping his nose with his jacket sleeve. "Mr. Ryan mostly bounced when he fell."

"I doubt that." Jo reached them. She gave each of the boys another once-over. Ryan took a step to one side, as if giving her room to examine her crew. "I'll deal with you in a minute. Don't go anywhere," she told him.

"Is Mr. Ryan going to get in trouble?" Dean slid his hand into Jo's. "I didn't mean to fall on him."

"And I didn't mean to crush his hand with my boot heel," Max admitted, adding quickly, "but he said it didn't hurt. Much."

"Boys, the first rule of Keep Away from Tiger is not to tell anyone about Keep Away from Tiger," Ryan deadpanned.

Jo knew if she looked at Ryan at that moment that she'd do something foolish, like blush or giggle, or both. So, she didn't look at him.

"Everybody be quiet for a minute." Jo moved to Tiger's side and ran her hand from his withers to his flank, coming around behind him and inspecting his other side. She did the same with each leg. She checked his eyes, his nose, his teeth, and received a shoulder nudge for her troubles. The gelding was fine, if warm and in need of a cooldown.

"Boys, you need to walk Tiger around the arena until he's cooled down." She caught the twins' attention. "Ten laps to start. Then check him. When he's cool, make sure he has water and some oats before you do anything else."

"Yes, ma'am," they chorused, moving to flank the gelding and escort him around the arena.

Only then did Jo face Ryan. He stood waiting expectantly with a half smile on his dirt-streaked face. His clothes were filthy. The fingers on his left hand were scraped and swelling. It didn't matter. She looked into his eyes and wanted to smile.

Pride and sucking in her bottom lip kept her from doing so. "Reliving your youth, cowboy?"

"My glory days?" The half smile blossomed into a mischievous grin. "This came awfully close." He rolled his shoulder, groaning. "I'm feeling my age."

"Uh-huh." Jo took Ryan's arm with one hand and picked up the Folly Ball with the other. "Come along, cowboy. You've earned a seat in the medical tent." She set a brisk pace across the arena.

"There's chocolate in the cabinet, Mr. Ryan." Dean had his hat tipped back and a smile on his face. "That always makes owies feel better."

"If Mr. Ryan gets a candy cane, can we get one, too?" That was Max, kicking up dirt as he walked.

"Cool down Tiger and then we'll talk." Jo released Ryan to open the arena gate. She closed it behind him and headed for the first barn and the ranch office. "How on earth did Scrooge charm my boys and my heart horse?"

"We bonded over good, clean ranch fun." There was a lightness in Ryan's words that she wasn't used to hearing from him. He couldn't be seriously injured, although he might be stiff tomorrow.

She led him into the ranch office, where she kept her medical kit, and had him sit down in the old chair that was next to the storage cabinet. "I don't think I'm going to let them give a horse the Folly Ball again."

"Oh, I don't know. We all had a jolly good time." He grinned at her.

She liked that grin. She liked it too much. "Take off your jacket. Let me see what we're dealing with." Jo turned on the radio. It was set to a Christmas station.

"Here Comes Santa Claus" filled the office.

Ryan rolled his eyes.

"Scrooge will just have to deal with the sounds of Christmas present." Jo opened the medical kit and rummaged around until she found the disinfectant wipes. "Give me the hand Max stepped on."

"I'm fine." He sat with his hands on the sides of his knees.

"If you were fine, you wouldn't have followed me in here. Gimme." She held out her hand.

He placed his hand in hers.

Her heart *ka-thumped*. Reflexively, her fingers curled around his. A distraction was required. "Why do you grab on to your blue jeans at the knees? I noticed the other day they were worn on the sides."

"I…uh… It's just something I do…when I get nervous." He drew in a breath as she dabbed his scraped knuckles. "It helps me sit still."

"Hmm." Jo processed the meaning behind his words while she continued to thoroughly clean his fingers. "That's a skill you have. Sitting still. I think it adds to the mystique of the *cold* Oakley. What did you say to me the other day? I measure my words like you measure out oats? Is that the pot calling the kettle black?"

"What can I say? You were the motor-mouth and I was the tall, dark, handsome, silent type."

Oh, it was hard not to laugh at that. "Motor-mouth? That's about as bad as calling me a grumpy sourpuss." She disposed of the wipe and performed a gentle evaluation of his swollen fingers. "Does this hurt?"

"No," he said thickly. "I'm fine."

"You need bandages on your fingers." She rummaged in the first aid kit.

"No bandages necessary." Ryan crossed his arms over his chest, hiding his injured hand from view. "If I show up at the ranch with bandages on my fingers without stitches or serious gashes beneath them, I'll be laughed right out of the bunkhouse."

Jo laughed. "And here I thought you didn't care what anyone thought of you."

"I don't." He started to rise.

She pressed Ryan back down with her hands on his shoulders. It felt good to boss him around a little. "Show me where Dean fell on you, tough guy."

"I'm fine." He lowered his hat brim, wincing.

Jo snatched his hat, tossing it onto the counter. As she suspected, there was a lump forming on his temple. "How on earth did he fall on your head? Please tell me his noggin didn't bounce off your noggin."

"Naw. It was his knee." Ryan grinned. "Missed my face, though."

She got him a small ice pack from the refrigerator. "No more Folly Ball. Are you sure those are all your wounds?"

"Yes, ma'am." He pressed the ice to his temple. "I've been meaning to tell you. Tate is interested in giving Prince a go."

"Does that mean your mother disappointed him?" Jo gasped. "The poor guy. Is he all right?"

Ryan frowned. "He didn't get knocked about

or stomped on. He's fine emotionally. He wants to buy a horse. You should be happy."

A sale? A sale!

Jo tried not to jump up and down with joy. There were still hurdles to be overcome. "And his financial situation is…"

"No better than mine, I'm afraid." Ryan leaned forward, dark eyes bright. "But together, he and I can do this. We can make this sale happen."

Having years of sales experience under her belt, Jo wasn't so sure.

"Jo? Say something."

"What if I offered you another option?" Jo said carefully. "Not to buy, but to lease?"

"Monthly payments?" Ryan perked up.

"I can't keep the place running on monthly payments." Jo took a step back from Ryan. And hope. "There's the balloon payment and the feed bill and…"

"You don't have to explain." Ryan tossed the ice pack on the counter.

"I need ten thousand for each horse. That's a quarter of my sales price. Most cowboys change horses about every four years, so I think that's fair." If only it was also doable for the Oakleys.

If it wasn't, perhaps she could find someone on the circuit willing to lease them.

Jo took the ice pack, tossing it from hand to hand. "Why don't you talk it over with Tate? And Dix? Meanwhile, let me clean up your face."

Ryan leaped to his feet as if he couldn't bear her to touch him. "I'll do it." He crossed the room to the small sink and set about washing his face. He dried his face with a paper towel and turned toward her, setting his cowboy hat back on his head. "You haven't had any calls of interest for Prince and Pauper, have you?"

"No." She held out a small candy cane to him.

"What's this?" He eyed her offering with suspicion.

"It's sugar. And according to Max, it makes any owie feel better, even the emotional hurts." And if Ryan took it, she'd allow herself a little hope where he was concerned, hope her heart wanted to entertain. That he wasn't completely opposed to Christmas, and that if she did find someone to buy or lease Prince and Pauper, he wouldn't hold it against her.

"I'm more like Dean," Ryan said, disappointing her. "Where do you keep your chocolate?"

"YOU REALLY ARE SCROOGE." Jo handed Ryan a small heart-shaped piece of chocolate wrapped in bright red foil. "You won't even eat a candy cane."

"I prefer chocolate. It has redeeming qualities, you know." Ryan unwrapped the candy and put it in his mouth.

Jo had him off his game. Touching him. Looking him in the eyes as if she wanted to know what he was thinking. Playing nurse. Offering to lease him horses and not throwing him out when he admitted they couldn't even afford that.

"What was the last straw for you?" Jo asked softly. She'd unwrapped the candy cane and was eating it, leaning against the door frame under which there was another sprig of mistletoe. "About Christmas, I mean. You were going to tell me the other day. And then you started talking about the lack of snow in Oklahoma."

It should have unnerved him how well Jo read him. Back in the day, when he was young and vulnerable, he'd have denied her statement in a cold, hard voice. But he was discovering something different about himself with Jo. She'd managed to worm her way past his defenses. He wanted to tell her things, share bits of his life, feel as if she understood him.

"Scrooge wouldn't tell me." Jo bit off a piece

of candy cane. "The cold Oakley from high school wouldn't tell me either." She pointed at him with what was left of her candy cane, leaning a bit so she was under that distracting mistletoe. "But somehow, I think you will."

He pulled out the chair behind her desk, needing to sit down and collect his thoughts. "Why did you talk to me?"

"Today or…when?"

"The day we met. Fun Day. When we were in the seventh grade." He leaned forward, resting his elbows on his knees. "After I competed, you sat with me in the stands. Why did you do that?"

"I don't know. That was a long time ago." She stared at the ceiling. "You were good. You moved as if you'd been born to ride and rope. Ma always told me it's important to tell someone when they've done a good job because good jobs don't always get praise." She took another bite of her candy cane. It made sense that she'd eat it bite by bite rather than suck on it. She had too much energy and not enough patience.

But back to her reasoning… Ryan shook his head. "But we were so young, and it was my first time competing."

"You don't want to believe you were good right off the bat. Okay… Um… I didn't tell

Griff he did a good job riding that young bull.
He was awful." Jo laughed. "And Bess ran the
barrels. She had the worst time of all competitors that day. I didn't praise her and she's
my friend."

"So, you just picked me out during the
rodeo? A complete stranger?"

Jo shrugged. "I knew who you were. Everybody knew who you were. Anytime anyone
new landed at the Done Roamin' Ranch,
the whole town knew. It's not as if we're a
large metropolis." She shoved the rest of the
candy cane in her mouth, pausing to chew,
making him wait. "My dad wouldn't let me
compete. Not even in barrels. So, I watched
everybody. I watched the horses. I watched
the rough stock. And when I saw something
good, I made sure to tell whoever it was." She
blinked. "I told your dad he had a doozy of a
bucking horse. What was his name? Jester?"

"Jouster." Ryan realized he'd been looking
for some kind of sign from Jo as to why she'd
talked to him, as if the clouds had parted and
the sun had shone down on him and him
alone.

He scoffed. There was no such thing as
signs.

"Do you know what else impressed me that
day?" Jo pushed away from the doorjamb,

stuck her hands in her back pockets and stood directly beneath that troublesome mistletoe. "You watched out for Tate. You made sure he was settled in the saddle, that he had the right grip on the rope, that he wasn't too far forward in the starting box. It's why I never had a problem talking to you about anything. Because I knew that a boy as caring as that wasn't going to say something mean. And you didn't."

The clouds had parted. She'd seen something no one else had. A sign. A ray of sunshine that told him someone had seen through his defenses to his true character.

"Was I never the cold Oakley to you?"

"Not until senior year." Jo fidgeted. "And even then, you weren't cold so much as an annoyance. And in hindsight, that back-and-forth we had released a lot of the anger my home life created. I suppose I should thank you." She went to get another small candy cane from the cupboard. "But all that goodwill is headed out the window if you don't tell me why you have it out for Christmas."

Ryan supposed he did owe her. And so he told Jo about Tate's fever, about his parents taking a bus trip to a casino the week before Christmas without telling their children where they were off to or making arrangements for someone to watch them. He told her about having no food and eating ketchup. He told her about coming to school and telling their teacher about their situation, something his parents had warned him never to do, something Tate hadn't wanted him to do, something Tate held against him for months afterward.

And when he was done, he was surprised to find that Jo was sitting on the desk in front of him, gently holding his hands.

Was it a sign? He hoped not, because increasingly, he thought Jo would be perfect for Tate. She'd watch his back and keep him on the right path.

If only his heart didn't ache at the thought.

CHAPTER TWENTY-THREE

"Didn't you hear the dinner bell?" Ma joined Jo at the Santapalooza wagon, along with Blue. "I rang it three times."

"I heard." Jo leaned against the wagon, arms wrapped tight around her body because it felt like she needed something to hold her life together. "What do you think about candy canes this year? We could save money by painting the sides of some hay bales instead of wood. I could ask the feed store to donate some."

"That's not my style." Ma surveyed the wagon. "What if we bought sheets of plywood? I'm good with a jigsaw."

"Wood costs more than gasoline right now."

Ma stared at her for a good long time. "Is it that bad? Bad enough that we can't donate a little to a community event?"

Jo nodded. "I've been lucky for ten years, making ends meet, making enough to pay cash to build the new barn and the arena. I didn't plan for this."

"What about our Oakley? I was so hopeful he'd be able to buy Prince and Pauper."

Jo told her about Ryan and Tate being unable to lease the horses, about calls that went unanswered or were politely cut off. "We might make it. I still haven't been paid for training the bay. I've got to deliver her in a few days and collect. I can take some one- and two-year-olds to the local livestock auction next week. Maybe if we sold Great-Aunt Dorothy's ring." It was a big diamond and not of good quality. But it was an antique and was kept in a box where no one ever enjoyed it. "I can try the bank again. They said I could get three thousand dollars and there's still my credit card." Although Dix hadn't recommended it, Jo was at the end of her rope. She'd worry about the interest later.

"I can try to sell some of my knitting," Ma said slowly. "And ask the Santapalooza committee to pay for wagon-decorating supplies. Maybe Betty's Bakery needs some seasonal help. I do frost a wickedly good-looking Santa sugar cookie."

"But you wouldn't get paid until after Christmas," Jo pointed out.

"You and I both know there will be bills rolling in after Christmas." Ma sniffed, trying to look brave. "You can take the Christmas presents you bought for me and the boys back."

Jo blinked back tears, the limit to hard decisions and bravery having been reached. "I can't ruin their Christmas."

Ma pulled her into a tender embrace. "Our Christmas will be ruined if we lose this place."

They held each other, crying a little.

The clip-clop of approaching horse hooves made them both look up.

Tiger ambled over, nuzzling them, rubbing against them and finally making them laugh.

"We're going to sell whatever we can," Jo said. "But we're never selling you, Tiger."

She had to draw the line somewhere. If Christmas had to go, her heart horse had to stay.

"You put Tiger to bed." Ma marched toward the house, back stiff. "I need to decorate something."

"I HAVE SOMETHING to discuss." Ryan pushed his chair back at the dinner table that night.

The dinner table at the Done Roamin' Ranch went quiet. Mom had been buttering a slice of bread. Dad had been helping himself to another serving of steamed vegetables. Griff had been cutting his steak. And Tate? He'd been picking at his mashed potatoes. He and Ryan had talked about the lease earlier.

Ryan sucked down half a glass of water,

putting off the inquisitive stares of his family for as long as he could.

Tate nudged his foot beneath the table.

"Okay." Ryan set down his water glass. "Jo Pierce made us an offer today to lease her horses for one year. Ten thousand dollars apiece."

Griff whistled.

"Together, we have close to nine thousand dollars." That was tough to admit. Ryan pressed on. "I think we can sell some stuff and maybe collect a couple of thousand more. I'm going to sell my truck and ride the motorcycle."

"We'd still be short," Tate chimed in. "Which is where you come in."

Griff pushed away from the table, holding up his hands.

"Mom and Dad," Tate said to Griff. "Not you, Griff. Everybody knows you never have any money."

"Because I'm saving it so I can buy a ranch of my own someday." Griff scooted back to the table, returning his attention to his steak. "Can't a man live a frugal lifestyle without being called a cheapskate?"

"No one called you that, honey," Mom said consolingly.

Ryan cleared his throat. "We'd like an advance on our pay," he said evenly. "You know we aren't going anywhere. And you know it about kills us to ask you for charity."

"It's not charity," Dad said in a gruff voice.

Mom took his hand in hers. "We believe in you."

Dad cleared his throat. "There's something we haven't done for you boys and maybe we should have before this."

"You've done more than anyone could ask for," Ryan said.

Dad exchanged a glance with Mom, waiting for her nod before saying more. "We could sponsor you, enough to make up the difference in exchange for you wearing a Done Roamin' Ranch Rodeo Stock Company patch on your shirt during competition."

"You'd do that?" Ryan was floored.

"For you." Dad nodded. "And Tate. And Wade, if he wants. I know it's not much of a sponsorship but—"

"But it's enough." Ryan couldn't believe it. He was going to get a high-quality horse to compete with. He snagged Tate's gaze. "What do you think? Are you still in?"

Tate nodded slowly. "Mom seems on the right track. She's got Marcus to help her."

"And us, if she needs us," Ryan reassured him.

Tate smiled.

"Do you know what we need?" Mom got to her feet, tugging Dad along with her.

"Cinnamon rolls for dessert?" Griff said hopefully.

"No." Mom got Griff to stand. "We need a group hug."

She held her arms out until all the men there had filled them.

And when they were done, Ryan pulled out his cell phone. "I'm going to call Jo and tell her the good news."

CHAPTER TWENTY-FOUR

THERE WAS AN audience for the morning test ride of Prince and Pauper.

It wasn't entirely unusual for rodeo competitors to bring their team along when they rode. It was a big purchase and that made some folks nervous.

But Jo hadn't expected Frank and Mary Harrison to show up with the Oakleys, or Griff. She offered her visitors bottles of water and candy canes, of course. She was glad she had a small set of bleachers in between the two arenas. With Ryan and Tate's help, she swiveled them around to face the arena where they roped cattle. Ma came out with Blue to help entertain the crowd, although she'd brought her knitting, so how much entertaining she'd do was up for grabs.

"How are you feeling this morning?" Jo asked Ryan. His call last night had been an answer to her prayers. All that seemed left to seal the deal was this ride and the agreement of Tate to lease Prince.

"I'm good." Ryan tightened Pauper's girth strap before nodding to his brother. "Tate's nervous. The fingers on his throwing hand are just starting to heal. Maybe you can talk to him."

"I can, but I know he performs better after you talk to him."

Ryan shrugged. "Give it a shot, would you?"

"Sure." Jo walked over to Tate and Prince. Out of habit, she did a quick inspection of the horse's bridle, girth and stirrups, which Tate had extended for his long legs. "Prince starts fast, so be ready," Jo told Tate, a part of her in awe that she was giving her teenage dream advice. "But don't overthink it. He likes to close in on cows and give you a good shot. Just…" She had much more advice she could give him, but she could tell by the slant to his thick, dark brows that Tate was beginning to get spooked by so much advice. "Just have fun."

He thanked her and rode next to Ryan around the ring.

Identical twins on a matched pair of grays. Jo dreamy-sighed. It was a little slice of cowgirl heaven.

She retreated back to the cattle chute, where she had three cows waiting to be released. She'd put aside horse training for the morning and ridden Tiger into the back pasture to cut the trio of cows from the thirty-odd Corrientes herd she kept. She'd done everything to prepare for this showing. It was up to the horses now.

And the riders.

Jo worried a little about Tate. He was a good roper, but his fastest times were when his horse came quick and smooth out of the starting box. If anything went wrong, he started overthinking, adding precious seconds to his time.

And speaking of which... "I need someone to time the runs," Jo called to the audience.

"Me." Griff stood, scaled the arena fence and jogged over to join Jo. "I prefer to be up close and personal to my brothers at a time like this."

She handed Griff a stopwatch. "For moral support?"

"I'll let you think that." Griff played with the watch. Clicking, clicking, clicking. And then he glanced up. "And who might this fine fellow be?"

Tiger trotted up to the arena gate and whinnied, as if asking to be let in.

"That escape artist is not for sale." Jo hurried over to the gate and slipped out. "Come on, you big stinker. I don't have time for your antics right now." She marched off toward the back door of the second barn, only to realize after a few steps that the gelding wasn't following her.

Tiger still stood at the gate, prancing a little as Ryan and Tate loped past.

"Oh, no." He'd bonded with Ryan. *Same as me.* "Can you moon over him another day?" She grabbed hold of Tiger's mane and swung onto his back, giving him leg and hand cues to head back to the barn.

Tiger obeyed, although he walked slowly, the way Max and Dean did when they didn't want to go to bed.

"Honestly, I thought you'd grow out of escaping your stall. You leave me no choice but to increase your door locks." She rode him into the barn and into his stall, hopped off and locked him in. And then she shut both exterior barn doors before returning to the arena where Tate and Ryan were backing Prince and Pauper into either side of the cattle chute.

"Sorry about the interruption." She joined Griff at the cattle gate. "Are you two ready for a test run?"

"I'm ready." Tate looked fiercely determined. Mouth set in a hard line. Thick brows drawn low. "No pressure."

Ryan looked more at ease. "Steady now. On my nod."

"My hands are on the release." Jo stared at Ryan, waiting for his signal.

And with a brisk nod, he gave it.

Jo opened the latch, the cow darted forward and the horses leaped after it almost as one. The Oakleys' ropes were swinging. Tate released his quickly, dropping a near-perfect noose around the cow's horns. Prince had begun adjusting his stride when the lasso sailed over his head. He danced sideways as Tate wound the rope around the saddle horn.

And in the meantime, Ryan had made a toss that caught the cow's back feet, drawing his rope around his saddle horn in one smooth movement.

"You don't hear me say this very often," Griff said after shutting off the stopwatch. "But that was a thing of beauty."

Jo couldn't have agreed more.

"WHAT DO YOU THINK?" Ryan asked Tate when they'd run through the trio of cows three times.

"Riding this horse is like butter." Tate was in awe. He gave Prince a hearty shoulder pat. "It's like that time we took that Lexus SUV for a test-drive in Dallas. Such a smooth ride."

Ryan agreed. "Let's do this, then."

"Let's do this." But Tate reached across to grab hold of Ryan's arm. "Thank you."

"For what?"

"For not giving up on me. You could have said I was too much trouble when we were younger. You could have gone your own way, competing without me long ago. But you didn't. And this... If we can swing this deal, you're right. It's a game changer. I can't tell you how much more confident I feel riding Prince."

"I could tell. After that first run, I didn't have to encourage you to steady yourself."

"That's right." Tate grinned.

"You can make other changes, too, you know." Ryan nodded toward Jo dutifully. "She's the kind of woman who'll be your rock when I can't be there for you."

Tate did a double take. "Are you going somewhere?"

"No. I'm just saying that you should think about settling down and surrounding yourself with people who love and support you."

Tate grinned. "And now you're pressing your luck."

"Hey, it took me over a week to convince you to buy a new horse. You need to be open to other changes, too."

Tate glanced over at Jo, looking thoughtful.

"Hey." Ryan found Jo standing in front of that old wagon in between the two barns. "Everybody's left. Everybody's happy." He bent a little to catch a better look at her face. "Except you. You don't have to worry. We're going to get you the money by the twentieth. That's enough time for you to make the mortgage, right?"

"Yes. Thanks to you." Her smile could best be called *attempted*. "I'm just having a what-if moment. You know…" She took a few steps to the side, hand fluttering in the air between them. "What if you hadn't moved so quickly to try and make the lease happen? What if you couldn't pull it together?" She knocked the side of the wagon the way one did for luck. "I would have been scrambling, and Christmas… Well, Christmas might have been different this year."

The space between the two barns was sheltered from the wind. And it was quiet without the twins around.

"But everything's okay?" Ryan phrased it as a question because for some reason he wasn't sure. And if he didn't ask, he might do something stupid, like hug her.

She nodded, giving him a brave smile. "Every cowgirl just needs a moment after the storm. Business saved. Crisis averted."

"You had this all the time. No worries." Ryan tipped his hat. "Okay. I'm going to head out. I have things to list for sale. I'll be back tomorrow with Tate for another ride."

"Sure." But Jo lunged forward to catch his arm before he was out of reach. "I've been wondering…"

He glanced down at her hand, resisting the urge to take it in his. A joke was called for. "You had time to wonder when you were under all this stress?"

Jo smiled up at him. It was a watery smile that he didn't quite understand. "If you could wipe your Christmas slate clean, what would you wish for?"

"You mean my ideal Christmas? That's asking a lot of Scrooge, isn't it?" But he wanted to tell her because deep inside, where he kept his most private secrets, he'd thought about it.

"If you'd never been a child deprived of Christmas…if you'd never been the cold Oakley…what would your ideal Christmas look like?" Her hand slipped from his arm.

He found it, cradling it gently in his. "You're not going to let me off the hook on this, are you?"

"Nope." She shook her head, eyes taking him in warmly. "Tell me."

"First off, there'd be a nice tree with sparkling white lights and strings of popcorn." He wanted to stop talking. Or at least, not tell her something so dear to him without having her in his arms. But Jo deserved everything she wanted in life. And everything included a heart horse and the heart of his brother. And apparently, his deepest holiday secret. "There'd be a big wreath in the front window and another on the door." Mom would be happy that he mentioned that. "There'd be stockings hung, those big fuzzy red ones with the white trim. And… This is going to sound silly, but I always wanted lights strung around my bed or on the wall above my bed." He hadn't always had a bed. "A red tablecloth on the dinner table with those kitschy salt and pepper shakers in the middle. You know, like they have at the Buffalo Diner every year. Santa and Frosty."

Jo still stared up at him with what he thought of as stars in her eyes.

But she'd stared at him like that when they were younger. When she was the motormouth and he was the cold Oakley. It wasn't like she was attracted to him or anything.

And as if to prove it, Jo took a step back. "You've thought a lot about this."

"Well, you know," he said, voice thick with

unexpected emotion, "I had a lot of time to think about it."

"I hope you get that Christmas someday, Ryan," Jo said softly. "I hope you get everything you want out of life. The wins. The accolades. And the Christmas."

"Thanks." He backed away. "Now, if you ever repeat what I just said to anyone, I'm going to have to think of a retaliation prank."

"I'd expect nothing less."

Ryan took another step back. He didn't want to leave if she was going to continue to look at him like that. But he didn't want to linger and get caught mooning over her.

"See you tomorrow, Ryan." She waved and turned toward the second barn.

He turned to leave. But he walked slowly out to where he'd parked his motorcycle, hoping that she'd run after him and tell him they could have that Christmas.

Together.

CHAPTER TWENTY-FIVE

LOIS CAME EARLY for her Santapalooza meeting.

She'd written a list of questions she had for Chet, plus a list of supplies she and Jo needed to prepare the Santapalooza wagon. Lois was taking nothing for granted. Not a potential beau's background or a potential horse leasing deal falling through.

"There's the face I've been waiting to see." Chet was behind the bar when Lois arrived at the Buckboard, which was blessedly empty on a weekday at this hour.

Lois hurried to the last bar stool nearest the tables where the Santapalooza committee would be meeting. She hooked the strap of her purse on her knee and reached across the bar to take Chet's hands. "I've missed you."

Granted, it had only been a few days since they'd seen each other, and it wasn't as if they'd gone on a date. She'd sat at the bar, and he'd come over to talk to her in between serving customers.

Chet's whiskers danced upward, lifted by his welcoming smile. "You could have called. Or texted. As I recall, I gave you my number."

"I have a confession to make."

His white handlebars lowered.

"No, no. It's nothing to worry about. It's just that I don't do well with texts and my phone seems dead set on making video chat instead of a regular call. And I didn't want to make a fool of myself when we'd already agreed to meet here tonight." She stared at him with wide eyes, fully expecting him to laugh at her foolishness.

"Lois..." Chet drew his hands back and reached into a pants pocket. He held up an ancient flip phone. "I couldn't receive a video call if I tried. And when it comes to texting, I'm slow and I always seem to misspell things."

"Oh." Lois wanted to faint with relief.

"I'm glad you didn't text me. But you can call. Anytime." Chet's mustache smile reappeared. "Day or night. I'm a light sleeper and I'd be more than happy to help if you can't get your car started or your oven doesn't preheat properly." He winked. "I'm also very handy around the house."

"Oh." Lois thought that was the most romantic thing any man had ever said to her.

CHAPTER TWENTY-SIX

"DID YOU SEE?" Jo's father barged into the first barn in the morning, rushing in like a stormy winter wind. "Ty and Eric placed third on those new mounts."

"I saw," Jo said. She couldn't bring herself to watch them compete live on television, but she'd refreshed the results page on the internet all evening long. Jo had been installing a new bolt on the bottom of Tiger's stall, having let him out so the drill wouldn't bother him. She leaned into the drill as she put the last screw in place. "Congratulations, Dad."

"I told them they needed a change." Her father paced around the breezeway restlessly but without his usually crushing bootsteps.

Jo closed up the metal toolbox and carried it, along with the drill, back to the supply room. "Did you want something, Dad?" Other than to gloat.

He came to stand in the doorway. "You should call your brothers and congratulate them. This is huge. Third in Nationals."

"I'll make sure to get in touch after the work is done." After she'd had time to grieve over this setback. Unlike the previous few years, there'd been no calls about horses available while or after her brothers competed.

"Call them," Dad commanded. "Call them now."

"Dad, I'm busy." She brushed past him, looking out the back breezeway for Tiger and not seeing anything. "Daylight's burning. I'll call them tonight. Right now I—"

"What? No." The wind and his mood shifted. Dad scowled. "You should have called them last night after the competition. They deserve your praise."

"Settle down, you old coot." Ma marched into the breezeway with Blue at her side. Ever since Sunday when she'd paid a visit to the Buckboard, there'd been a change to Jo's mother, a confidence in the set to her shoulders, a different tone to her voice. "Your daughter has work to do."

"But the boys—"

"Our boys did well," Ma allowed, giving Blue a pat. And then she straightened. "But your daughter does well, too. And I don't see you shouting her praises the way you do those two sons of ours. Jo trained the horses that got them to qualify for the postseason. And she's coached Ty and Eric whenever they've asked her to. Who's to say they wouldn't have placed third—*or even first*—on her horses this year?"

Dad stomped his feet, moving closer. "I told them—"

"*You* didn't win anything, Herbie," Ma said in a way Jo had never heard her talk to her father before. She'd fully come into her own. "The boys did all the work, just like this ranch was worth much less than you bought the land for when you sold it to Jo. But she's built it up with hard work into something that she and our grandsons can be proud of, that you and I can be proud of. But because they give trophies to your sons and not to your daughter, you seem to think less of her. And I'm tired of it."

"No." Dad blustered about in a small circle. "I...I...I'm proud of Jo."

"She's an afterthought to you, unless you're coveting this property," Ma said plainly. "Don't lie."

Dad's face was a deep, deep red.

It was time to make peace while Ma was ahead. Jo took a step forward. "Ma—"

She waved Jo off. "I've spent too many years trying to keep the peace and letting this man bully us around. And I'm done with it.

Herbie, you should be crowing like a proud rooster about all three of your kids. And since you can't, I'm telling you to leave."

Way to go, Ma.

"Leave?" Dad drew a deep breath, but his cheeks were already puffing in and out like fire bellows.

But that fire was rapidly dying, no matter how much hot air her father expelled, Jo realized.

She took a stand next to Ma. "Yes, Dad. *Leave.* You have no right to be here. I've never been late on a payment and I'm not going to be late on this one either. Ma's right. You stomp around here, shouting and trying to put us down. But my horses made Eric's and Ty's careers. They never had a postseason until they rode them. If you've got nothing nice to say, you'd best be on your way."

"You…you…" He shook his finger at them, marching toward them. "You can't disrespect me like this."

Blue stood in between them, hair raised and growling. And Tiger trotted up to their side, pawing the ground and tossing his head as if considering trampling Dad.

Jo laid a hand on the gelding's neck. "Easy, boy."

"Respect goes both ways, Herbie." Ma

pointed toward his truck. "And if you value that reputation of yours, such as it is, you'll get out of here before we call the sheriff."

Jo and Ma watched him leave. They watched him drive away, spinning his wheels and spitting gravel. They watched his tailgate disappear in a cloud of road dust.

And then they hugged each other, because they knew this was a turning point. Ma had finally stood up for herself and Jo.

But that didn't mean things were going to be easier with Dad from now on. It might even make it more difficult.

"HAVE WE SOLD anything yet?"

"Nothing." Ryan glanced up from his phone. He was sitting on the couch in the bunkhouse waiting for something to happen. "But Griff told me most people buy from that online site on the weekends." Still, Ryan was nervous. He'd promised Jo they'd have the money. And the more money they raised, the less money they'd be accepting from Mom and Dad. "I was going to head over to Jo's to get a ride in before lunch. Want to come?"

"I need to run errands for Mom and Dad first." Tate poured himself half a cup of coffee. "Mom needs me to pick up stuff to decorate the Santapalooza wagon that's over at

Jo's. Paint, wood, hay bales. And Dad needs me to pick up some metal fence posts and barbed wire." He took a sip, staring at Ryan. His cheek twitched.

"What's wrong?" Ryan stood. "You changed your mind about the horses, didn't you?"

"No. I…I've just been thinking about asking Jo out."

Time slowed. Ryan sat back down.

This is good. This is what I want.

But time continued to move slowly, as if the universe was trying to tell Ryan to pay attention.

Tate came over to sit in a nearby chair. He rubbed his beard. He sipped his coffee. His cheek twitched. And then time came back online. "I couldn't sleep last night. I kept thinking how my life would be different if I just had listened to you more often. About horses, about roping, about Mom and money. And I thought…maybe I should ask Jo out. Except it feels weird because you two have been hanging out."

"It was always just about her horses." Until it wasn't. Ryan sucked in air, wondering why it had become so hard to breathe. He wanted this. Jo was what was best for Tate. "I've been saying for a long time that you need to date someone who's grounded. Well, that's Jo. Her business is established. She knows about our past. She understands rodeo. And like the rest of the female population of Clementine, she's had a crush on you forever." And didn't that hurt to admit?

Tate looked relieved. No longer twitchy. He drank the last of his coffee and went to rinse out his mug in the sink. Back turned to Ryan, he said, "It feels weird, though. Asking someone out. I can't remember the last time I did it."

Ryan recognized that tone of voice. Tate thought he'd be rejected. Next thing he'd do was talk himself out of it.

Ryan didn't waste time arguing or thinking how hard it would be to see Jo with his brother. "I'm going to head out and run some errands. We'll go ride at Jo's after lunch." He gathered his truck keys and his courage and headed out the door.

"Hey, Ryan," Jo called to him when he arrived at the Pierce Ranch.

She was in the breezeway of the second barn, brushing down the delicate bay mare. Same old Jo. Wide-brimmed white hat, Christmas green hoodie beneath her puffy maroon vest. Faded blue jeans tucked into her boots. Same old Jo.

But Ryan didn't feel like the same old anything.

He walked toward her, through the first barn,
past the wagon that was apparently going to be
used in Santapalooza once it was remodeled,
into the second barn.

"I'm going to miss this girl." Jo took a hoof
pick to the mare's rear hoof. "I've got to deliver her day after tomorrow." She set down
the bay's hoof and straightened, turning to
look at Ryan. "Is something wrong? Why
aren't you saying anything?"

Ryan stopped about ten feet away from her
and took stock.

Why wasn't he saying anything?

Because he'd spent the drive over thinking about Jo, thinking about family and pro-
cessing the hurts of his past. He'd changed
over this past week. He viewed himself and
horses differently because of her. He viewed
his mother and her relationship with Tate differently, partly because of her. He was the last
person to claim he knew what love was. But
what he thought he felt for Jo had to be love.
She was his first thought in the morning and
his last thought at night. He went over the
things they'd said to each other all the time,
the looks they'd exchanged, the longing he
had to hold her in his arms and kiss her.

But that didn't mean that he couldn't love her just as well as her brother-in-law, as a friend, as a client of hers. Everyone said attraction faded with time. And Tate needed someone like Jo more than Ryan did. And he always put what Tate needed first.

That's why he'd rushed over here. To make sure Tate had what he needed. *Who* he needed.

"Ryan?" Jo peered at him.

Ryan cleared his throat. "I…uh…just came by to say that Tate is headed over to the feed store. You got his attention this past week. And I…I think you should ask him out. Now. Today."

Jo stared at Ryan equally as long and silently as he'd just stared at her. And then she said, "What's this about? Is your mother at the feed store, too? Do you suspect her of drinking?"

"No. We should hurry." Because who knew how busy the feed store was or if they'd prepared the order from the Done Roamin' Ranch in advance.

Jo walked slowly toward him. As usual, horses poked their heads out of stalls to see her, as eager for her attention as Ryan was. "You think he needs someone like me as a wedge between him and your mother." She inched closer, gaze never leaving his face. "Because you're giving up on protecting him?"

"Yes. No." It was an effort to keep his hands at his sides when Jo was within reach. "I thought you wanted to date him."

"This was supposed to be my year," Jo said slowly. "My horse inventory is optimized. I have plenty of two- and three-year-old colts from Regal Robert in the pipeline. I've traded most of his fillies for prime breeding mares with cutting and roping experience and credentials. My brothers were supposed to win the Nationals on Laurel and Hardy. I planned out my sales, so I'd have a pad in my bank account if one sale fell through. And then the unthinkable happened. Three sales fell through, and my brothers didn't ride my horses in Nationals. And yet they came in third. Now a lot of people are going to be questioning my product. Instead of this being my year, I'm on the precipice of failure."

Jo had every reason to crumple. But Jo had never been the fold-under-pressure kind of person. Her shoulders were square and her head high. Ryan had to follow her lead.

"So, if I had a dream once about dating your brother, of course, it would also go wrong this year, along with everything else. And it did go wrong. Spectacularly." She turned back to the bay. "I'm not going to the feed store. Find someone else to babysit your brother."

"The year isn't a total bust," Ryan told her, moving quickly to her side, taking her arm. "Since I asked to buy a horse from you, you've changed. I've seen it. You've pushed yourself outside of your comfort zone, and instead of hiding away in mortification, you've come through the fire a stronger person. And if we hurry, you can test that newfound confidence and ask Tate out." Much as it killed him to say.

Another round of silent stares ensued.

"If I do this, it's not for you or to save Tate from your mother's clutches forevermore." Jo sighed. "If I do this, it's for me. And for every wallflower who's ever risked social suicide by asking the most popular boy out."

"Yes." He'd agree to anything as long as she'd get moving. "But it would have to be now."

She rolled her eyes. "It can't be now. I have to change and pull myself together."

"Or you could go as you are." With a Frosty the Snowman sweatshirt and a streak of dirt on her cheek. "If Tate can't appreciate you like this…" Then his brother didn't deserve her.

Jo stared at him suspiciously. "I need ten minutes, Ryan."

He'd been hoping she'd ask him to complete his sentence. Instead, he said, "I'll put away the bay."

"To be clear, I'm going in there to get a bag of dog food." Jo hopped out of Ryan's truck when he parked alongside the feed store. She wore a long blue dress, silver cowboy boots and an understated long wool coat. She still felt like herself, a different facet of herself, to be sure. But she wasn't self-conscious.

Thank you, Ronnie.

"Dog food?" Ryan looked pained, coming to stand by her at the front of his truck. "Can't you buy something more feminine? Like a mane brush? Or sparkly hoof paint?"

"Or a ribbon for my hair?" Jo gave Ryan a half-hearted shove. "Have you been watching Jane Austen movies?"

"Jane who?" He looked handsome in his black hoodie and black flannel shirt. Good enough to ask out on a date.

Not that he wants one from me.

"Jane Austen? The patron saint of romance?" She fiddled with the collar of her jacket. "Never mind, cowboy. Wish me luck."

"Break a leg," he said in an odd tone of voice.

She marched around the corner as if she

was going for a root canal and just wanted to get it over with.

Jo spotted Tate as soon as she got inside. He was at the sales counter.

"Be with you in a minute, Jo," Izzy called, while ringing up his purchase. Tate didn't even turn around. "Ludlow will have your order ready for pickup in ten or fifteen minutes, Tate. If you have any other errands in town..."

"I'll grab a coffee," Tate told her.

Jo was about to go to the dog food aisle. She paused at the horse aisle, staring at the display of currycombs and brushes, hoof paint and fly masks. Ryan was wrong. Those items weren't feminine. She pivoted and went to the aisle filled with miscellaneous items from local vendors, gaze quickly scanning her options.

Not a goat-milk candle.

Not a quilted pot holder.

Not a jar of canned peaches. Wait. Did Evie Grace can those peaches?

"What were you looking for, Jo?" Izzy called over the sound of footsteps.

Was Tate coming her way?

"Dog food and..." Jo reached for the first thing that caught her eye.

"Hey, Jo." Tate stood at the opening of the

aisle, apparently on his way out the door. "What's that you've got there?"

"It's a…" Jo glanced down. "A baby name book?"

"Is there something Ryan needs to know?" Tate deadpanned.

"We're not dating." Jo's cheeks were flaming hot. "I'm expecting a new crop of as-yet-unnamed foals come spring." She put the book back on the shelf. And then pivoted, trying to look casual, but feeling as if she was riding the wave of an earthquake, a real shaker that was about to roll her to the ground. Because her longtime crush was staring at her and all her thoughts about him being the wrong cowboy for her were somehow not top of mind anymore.

Quit fan-girling and ask him already!

She cleared her throat. "Are you riding in Santapalooza this year?" *Not that.*

"Yeah." Tate shifted his feet, eyeing the door. "You?"

"Yep. That's me. Always a Santa, never an elf." Jo wished the ground would open up and swallow her. Asking Tate out had become something of a personal challenge now, proof that she could do hard things. Except she was choking. "First, though, I need to paint the wagon. You know, the wagon non-riders ride on."

"Yep." He stared at her oddly and then took a step away from her.

"Listen, Tate," she blurted, lunging for her courage and leaving decorum behind. "Cooper's brewery is once again trying out a new menu and I thought it'd be nice to try it out…with someone…like you?"

"You're asking me out?" Tate appeared perplexed. "But what about Ryan?"

Her heart broke a little.

She wanted to say, *Your brother wants a horse, not me. And he always puts you first, instead of himself.*

But all she said was "He's a friend of mine. Always had been. Oddly. What do you say?"

"Yeah." Tate gave her a lopsided smile that a month ago would have had her swooning. But somewhere along the way, Ryan's more straightforward smile had become more to her liking. "Yeah. Let's go out. Saturday night? Six o'clock? I'll pick you up."

Izzy lingered behind Tate in the clothing section, pretending to straighten the merchandise. She gave Jo two thumbs up.

"Great," Jo said hollowly, wishing he'd have turned her down. "We'll have drinks at the Buckboard first."

"Sure. See you then." With one last smile, Tate left.

Izzy ran up to her, flinging her arms around her. "You give hope that romance can be found anywhere, even your local feed store. You've got to be ecstatic."

"Right." Jo put her hands on her knees and took several deep breaths. "That was something, wasn't it? Me asking the nice Oakley out."

Izzy drew her up and spun her around. "Jo, it's your dream. And my dream. This is huge!"

"You're right. It is huge." Jo was having trouble breathing. She felt like she might pass out.

"You need to celebrate this."

"You're right. I rock. I need to celebrate." Jo thrust both fists in the air as if she'd made a touchdown and then darted out of the store, ran around to the side parking lot where Ryan was leaning against his truck's fender.

"I did it! I did it!" The impossible was beginning to sink in. She threw her arms around Ryan, whose face was the mirror image of Tate's before he'd grown that beard. This was the appearance of the man she'd dreamed of sitting across a restaurant table from, the face she'd fancied would smile at her, the lips she'd imagined kissing her. And now it was all going to happen.

Caught up in the moment, Jo wrapped her arms around Ryan and kissed him on the lips.

If she'd ever imagined kissing Ryan, she would have also imagined him leaping back as if scalded, scowling at her and asking her what in the world she'd been thinking.

Ryan drew her closer and kissed her slowly, deeply, completely.

Just the way she'd always dreamed Tate would.

"Oh." Jo wiggled free. "Oh." She stepped back. "For a minute there, I thought you were…" *The man of my dreams.*

But he was. She looked into those dark eyes and thought about all he'd been through, all they'd both been through, separately and together. And she'd run to him to celebrate a personal victory because…

I love him.

Jo started to reach for him again.

Ryan inched back. "Sorry. For a minute there, I thought…" He cleared his throat. "Well, it doesn't matter what I thought because, clearly, I wasn't thinking." He pressed his key fob into her hand. "Here. Take my truck back. I'll see you later this afternoon with Tate when we come riding."

Forget the thrill of victory.

As Ryan walked away from Jo, she felt the agony of defeat.

CHAPTER TWENTY-SEVEN

Jo's DAY WAS completely thrown off.

She had to call her neighbor and friend Allison Burns to cover her after-school car pool. After Jo got home, she changed into her usual clothes and sat in front of her desk, trying to work on the accounts.

Because she was hiding from the Oakleys and didn't know when they'd show up to ride.

"Mom, why are you inside?" Dean asked when he arrived home. "Are we going somewhere?"

"Did someone die?" Max asked, staring into her face. "You look sad."

"That's because nothing that's happened to me today has turned out the way I imagined." A confrontation with her dad? A date with Tate? A kiss from Ryan?

A kiss he apologized for.

"You should ask our Oakley to stay for dinner after his ride." Ma's gaze was piercing. She'd gone to lunch with Chet and had arrived about the time the boys did. "Sometimes you have to say what you want."

"I want this conversation to be over," Jo muttered and rearranged the papers in front of her. A few minutes later, she realized she was still looking at the same numbers.

"Did you fight with our Oakley?" Ma demanded, sitting by the living room window and stitching faux fur trim on another silver Santa hat.

"When you gave Dad a piece of your mind this morning, did it feel the way you'd always imagined?" Jo took an elf-shaped peanut butter cookie from the cookie jar and leaned against the counter, in desperate need of reassurance that she'd done the right thing by accepting a date with her childhood crush.

"You know me." Ma set down her needle. "I don't want to make waves. But sometimes you have to cannonball into the water in order to shake up someone else and make them see whatever it is they've been missing."

Jo wasn't sure if she'd shaken up Ryan, Tate or both today. She was shaken. She was still hiding in the house.

Ma continued to stare at Jo. "What's bothering you?"

"I think I made a date with the wrong cowboy." Jo explained what had happened earlier, including kissing Ryan. "And Ryan apologized afterward. *Apologized.*"

"Everyone over the age of twenty knows you don't apologize after a kiss, especially the good ones." Ma smiled. "All you have to do to make this right is cancel your date with Tate and tell Ryan the truth. That you have feelings for him."

Jo shook her head. "Ryan thinks I'm just what Tate needs. Ryan is Tate's protector. And… Well…" She blinked back tears. "What if my feelings for Ryan are misplaced? He looks like Tate." More so since Tate had grown a beard. "And then there's Christmas. I know Ryan never had a good Christmas growing up, but he's so against it. And I…"

"You have a small Christmas tree in your bedroom." Ma nodded. "But all those things are just excuses. What does your heart tell you?"

"That I might love Ryan. That Tate isn't for me."

"Then we should do something about it."

CHAPTER TWENTY-EIGHT

"Hi, Mary. Jo has a favor to ask of you." Ma had called Ryan's foster mother via video chat.

Mary Harrison wasn't much better at the video phone function than Ma was. Her phone was aimed toward the ceiling. "I knew this question was coming. She wants to wear one of the silver Santa costumes in the parade, doesn't she?"

"No, Mary." Ma chuckled. "Can you pick up your phone? I can't see you."

"I have it on speaker." Mary picked up the phone and held it beneath her chin. "Can you hear me?"

"Yes, but now I owe Jo an apology." Ma smiled at Jo, chuckling. "I can't see your pretty face, Mary."

"I can see you."

Jo sighed. This was going nowhere fast. "Hi, Mary. This is Jo. I just have a quick favor to ask you."

"She wants to decorate the bunkhouse for Christmas," Ma said, spilling the beans.

"Oh, we don't do that." Mary held up her phone in front of her face, tilting her head from side to side as if looking at her reflection in a compact mirror. "Ryan isn't really a Christmas fan."

"I know he says he isn't," Jo said carefully. "But I think he wants to be. He helped my mother with her Christmas decorations. He might have shared something that led me to believe he'd like this." She'd been sworn to secrecy, but that wasn't spilling the beans. "And I want to thank him for leasing Pauper."

"I think it's a good idea," Ma said quickly. "Who knows? Ryan might even be so full of holiday cheer that he signs up for the Santa-palooza ride."

"That might be a stretch," Mary said. "But if you really want to do this, he's helping out with a bull riding class all day Friday at the Burns Ranch, along with Tate and Griff. Could you decorate the bunkhouse then?"

Jo assured her she could.

"I'VE GOT TO SAY, of all the favors you ever asked of me, Jo, this is the one I'll remember for years." Bess set down a large box of Christmas lights in the bunkhouse at the Done Roamin' Ranch on Friday morning.

"Can I flour Griff's bedsheets while we're in here?"

"No," Jo said firmly, wrestling a Christmas tree in the door and leaving a trail of pine needles. "Can't you take a page from Ryan and me getting over our high school rivalry and make peace with Griff?"

"No," Bess said just as firmly, tossing her red hair over her shoulder.

"I think it's sweet of you to do this, Jo." Ronnie set down a large plastic container filled with ornaments on a small kitchen table. "A true sign of friendship."

Jo didn't clarify her motivations. Instead, she looked around the bunkhouse. "I've always wondered what this place looked like inside." She'd heard that the ranch fosters had to earn the right to live in the bunkhouse, not the main house.

It was essentially a large dorm room. There was a small kitchenette on the far wall, flanked by what looked like two bathrooms. There were five bunk beds and ten dressers along the walls. A large dining table sat near the kitchenette with a carousel of poker chips in the middle next to a set of salt and pepper shakers. And there was a television surrounded by two couches and two comfy chairs. There was a wreath in one window, something Mary had confessed to hanging.

"Which bunk is Ryan's?" Ronnie asked, glancing around. "They all look the same. You wanted to put lights on his."

Jo walked through the room and finally stopped in front of a bottom bunk near the corner. "This one. His bed is made. And there's the shirt he bought when we went to Friar's Creek." What a fun day that had been, even though it had been filled with highs and lows. Best change the subject. Jo turned and pointed to a spot next to the television. "Let's put the tree over there."

"If you're putting lights on Ryan's bunk, can I drape garland over Griff's?" Bess stood frowning at a particularly messy bed with a hat that looked like one of Griff's on the pillow. "And maybe put some tinsel—"

"This is about goodwill and holiday spirit, Bess." Jo opened the box with Christmas lights. "Save your vendettas for a later date."

"Ho ho ho," Bess said morosely. But she helped Jo untangle the lights.

They strung lights on the tree, around window frames and on Ryan's bunk. They hung ornaments on the tree and stockings on kitchen cabinet knobs. They put a bright red tablecloth on the table, as well as a pair of Santa and

Frosty salt and pepper shakers, which Jo had borrowed from Coronet at the Buffalo Diner.

When they finished, Jo went to get Mary from the main house. "What do you think?"

"I've been wanting to do this for years. It's lovely." Mary hugged Jo. "I just hope Ryan takes this in the spirit it was offered."

Jo hoped so, too.

RYAN, TATE AND Griff arrived back at the Done Roamin' Ranch after dark. They were grimy and dusty after helping Tucker Burns run a daylong bull riding clinic for high schoolers.

Griff headed into the bunkhouse, intent on using up all the hot water on a long shower, as was his habit. But instead of rushing inside, he leaned back out and shouted, "Santa's elves paid us a visit. Christmas is here!" He grinned. "I've been waiting years for this."

"There's a wreath on the door," Tate said. "That's nice."

"On the door?" Ryan pushed past Tate to get inside. "Who did this?"

But he knew. The tree had white lights and popcorn garland. His bunk was strung with a canopy of lights. The red tablecloth. The kitschy salt and pepper shakers.

"Look! Stockings." Griff chucked off his

boots and ran across the room to the kitchenette like the young boy he'd been when he first arrived at the ranch. "Oh, this had to be Mom."

Nope.

Ryan smiled as he shed his boots, hat and jacket. He padded inside, grinning as he took it all in.

"Is it okay?" Tate asked him. "I can take it down."

"I love it." There was an envelope on Ryan's bunk. He went to open what turned out to be a Christmas card. On the front, a dark horse wearing a Christmas wreath around his neck galloped through the snow. The printed message read: "Thinking of you at the holidays." The handwritten message read:

Dear Ryan, aka the "nicer" Oakley,
Thank you for turning one of the worst years of my life into one of the best. I thought I'd do something un-grumpy for you to show my gratitude. Do you know why *A Christmas Carol* is so popular? Because it proves that grumps don't stay not-nice forever. Hint, hint. In fact, they might even find something wonderful at Christmas if they take a chance.
Your friend, no longer your rival,

Jo
P.S. Check in your stocking. Ho ho ho!

Ryan looked around the room, taking in all the small touches that must have taken Jo hours to do. And this card… It was to the point and heartfelt, exactly the way Jo was.

He missed her. She hadn't been home when he and Tate had gone riding yesterday.

"I got a candy cane in my stocking." Tate unwrapped it, heading toward the bathroom. "I'm gonna eat this in the shower."

Ryan approached the kitchenette and a red-and-white Christmas stocking with a felt *R* glued to the front. There was a candy cane inside, but also a small piece of paper with neatly printed letters on top. "Dance card?" He turned the square over. "Jane Austen?"

Hours later, Ryan lay in bed. He hadn't turned off the twinkle lights on the tree or his bunk bed. He'd even adjusted the timer on the holiday lights in the main house so that they'd stay on until midnight.

His roommates didn't care. Tate said he had years of holiday nonsense to make up for. Griff said he'd finally found some holiday spirit. They'd gone to sleep almost before their heads hit the pillow.

They didn't realize those lights and holiday

displays had less to do with Christmas and more to do with Jo.

This is a test.

Mom had explained what the dance card and Jane Austen meant.

But if Ryan was going to do anything about it, he had to make peace with Christmas.

And with the idea that he really was no longer his brother's keeper.

CHAPTER TWENTY-NINE

"ARE YOU NERVOUS about tonight?" Ma asked Jo on Saturday afternoon. "You skipped training horses today. And I was out there with the volunteers all afternoon fixing the Santa-palooza wagon without you."

"It's nerves." Jo wore one of the dresses Ronnie had loaned her, along with the silver boots. "I just have to wonder if Tate accepted my date because I seemed different on the outside." He didn't know her well enough to realize she was different on the inside, too. "You know, it's funny. Ryan has looked at me the same way from the day I let him ride Pauper until the day at the feed store." When she'd kissed him.

And then everything changed. She hadn't seen or heard from him since. Was it because of that kiss? Because he thought his brother needed someone like Jo? Because Ryan didn't see them in a relationship?

"Jo, it might be time to face facts." Ma laid her hands on Jo's shoulders. "Scrooge Oakley wasn't ready to embrace Christmas or you. That means you have to go on this date tonight with your heart open to Tate. It's only fair since you'll be staring across the table at him."

"I know."

The house was quiet. The boys had gone into town for a pizza birthday party and sleepover at a buddy's house.

Jo was used to the quiet. She spent most of her days alone with horses. And then Ryan had come into her life, drawing her out and making her long for more conversation. With him.

She shook her head. "Tate. Tonight, it's all about Tate."

"You mean it's all about you." Ma gave her a little shake. "I hear a car on the drive. That's probably Ronnie."

Ronnie had agreed to come over and do both Jo's and Ma's makeup. They both had dates.

Ronnie smoothed Jo's hair with the flat iron, talking nonstop. "I could have arranged this date with Tate. You could have skipped the embarrassing moments."

Jo made a noncommittal noise. All that discomfort, awkwardness and drama had smoothed the relationship she had with Ryan.

If only it had cemented it.

"Tell me the truth, Ronnie." Jo caught Ronnie's gaze in the bathroom mirror. "If

I hired you as my matchmaker, who would you have paired me with?"

"I would have suggested you date Clyde Dabble. He's a mild-mannered schoolteacher." Ronnie fussed with Jo's hair, trying to get it to curve around her cheek. "But the way you've bloomed in the past few weeks... All that confidence..."

"Still not Tate," Jo guessed.

"No." Ronnie sprayed Jo's short locks with hairspray. "I would have asked you about your dream date. And what your goals are. I would have pointed out that you're a homebody. But since then, I've seen you out and about more. Have you enjoyed it?"

"Sometimes." When Ryan was with her.

"The thing about change is that you have to want to embrace something new. It has to make you smile, not cause you stress." Ronnie caught Jo's gaze in the mirror. "You're tense."

"I am."

"Do you like Tate? As a real person, not the idea of him we all had in high school?"

Jo didn't know. "I guess that's what this date is all about."

"YOU LOOK LOVELY." Tate held out a chair for Jo at the Buckboard.

"Thank you. You look pretty, too." *Oh, that*

was wrong. Jo felt hotter than if she'd eaten a jalapeño pepper, seeds and all.

Tate chuckled. "Thanks."

The line dancing had begun. Jo's friends were all out on the dance floor, stomping and clapping.

"You should join your friends if you'd like to," Tate told her.

"No. I'd rather be here, getting to know you." That wasn't entirely true. She'd rather be sitting across from her clean-shaven Oakley, talking about horses or ranching or things that had happened in their past. "How is your mother?"

"She's good. Ryan helped me fix her house so that it's safe inside. All she needs now are alpacas and some of their wool to make yarn."

"Only the best," Jo murmured. "How did you get Ryan to help you? I bet you had to twist his arm."

"Not exactly." Tate grinned, a big smile framed by a thick and scruffy beard.

Jo didn't feel a whit of attraction.

"He volunteered to help," Tate said, waggling thick eyebrows that did nothing for her. "He probably told you we hadn't been getting along lately. But that's all changed. In fact, I don't want to destroy the mood…"

What mood?

"…but I was wondering if you could coach me on Prince the way you coached Ryan."

Jo nodded numbly, mind reeling. There was no mood.

There should be a different Oakley sitting across the table from her, one who could go toe-to-toe with her on any topic. Ryan earned her respect as a cowboy and rodeo man, but he was also great with her kids and her mother. She loved Ryan, whether he was bossy, moody or trying to make her laugh. But most of all, she loved him because he wanted her to live the life she wanted, including with the man she wanted—Tate.

The man I thought I wanted…

Jo gathered the confidence Ryan had been telling her that she had. "I'm sorry, Tate, but I have to go." She stood up to leave just as Ryan appeared at their table.

"Jo, I need to talk to you." Ryan stared at his twin. He was wearing an ugly Christmas sweater and had what looked like white paint in his hair. "Sorry, bro."

Tate's brow furrowed, but only for a moment before he smiled. "Go right ahead."

Ryan brought Jo a few feet away, making her heart pound with anticipation. "I should have thanked you for the Christmas decorations when I got home the other day."

"Oh." That's why he was here? What a let-down. "You're welcome." Had he not read her card? Looked inside his stocking? It would be just like Griff to take those things and not tell Ryan about them. That's what Bess predicted would happen. Jo glanced around, looking for Griff and that mischievous grin. But Griff wasn't nearby and her attention returned to Ryan's ugly Christmas sweater. What was that all about?

"I need something from you," Ryan was saying.

"A horse? A favor?" This evening was not turning out the way Jo had expected. She was ready to go home.

"More than a favor." Ryan squeezed her hands. "I need a happy Christmas, the kind with traditions meant for sharing. And I need a dance." He shifted his feet, glancing at the dance floor, a place she'd seldom seen him. "Maybe more than one dance." He reached into his back pocket and handed her a small square of paper, one she recognized.

Jo began to smile. "It's my dance card." He'd written his name several times on both sides of the paper. "I wasn't sure you'd understand. But…"

"My mom is an avid romance reader." He grinned. "Message received. I'm claiming all your dances tonight. And I want to dance with you for the rest of my life. I love you, Joanna Pierce. I love you in your grubbies. I love you in a dress showing off those fabulous knees. I love you when you're grumpy or bossy or being confident in difficult situations or when you're kind to a man with rough edges."

"You apologized for kissing me," she pointed out, so filled to bursting with joy that she laughed.

"I thought you wanted Tate." He gave her hands a little shake. "If you do, I'll figure it out. But I had to come tell you I love you. And if you know me, you know I don't say those words lightly."

Jo didn't think she could breathe. She managed to draw a shaky breath, eyes brimming with tears. "Hold that thought." She turned to Tate. "I'm sorry to cut this date short, but I don't want to date you, Tate. I'm in love with the best Oakley twin in my books, your brother."

The object of her youthful affection sat back in his chair, laughing.

Jo turned back to Ryan. "I didn't want to ask Tate out the other day. I wanted you…" Her hands ran up the stitching on the appliquéd reindeer and over his broad shoulders until her arms twined around Ryan's neck. "You're the Oakley for me. Turns out, I have a thing for stubborn, protective cowboys who love their family and put up with mine. I could love you till the day I die."

"Why?" Ryan whispered, lips just out of reach. "Why could you love me?"

Her fingers drifted through the hair beneath his hat. "Is this…is this paint?"

He nodded. "I was with the Santapalooza decoration committee today at your ranch. If you'd have come out, you'd have seen me. I wanted to talk to you, but your mother said you needed some time alone."

"To figure out what I really wanted." Jo squeezed her eyes shut and then opened them wide because Ryan was everything she wanted, everything she'd dreamed of.

"Why do you love me?" Ryan said again.

Jo drew a big breath. "Because a man with rough edges hasn't had it easy, and neither have I. A man like you has carried emotional baggage that won't be easy to work through, but neither is mine. You make me laugh. And you're great with the boys. Most of all, I love how you've always seen me just as I am and liked me just as I am. It's us, together, just as we are. Forever."

"Yes." Ryan finally kissed her. And then

kissed her again. "I'm still going to compete in team roping this year, along with Tate." He led her to the dance floor. "But if I don't make it to the postseason, that's it for me competition-wise."

Wise was a good word to describe her Oakley. They joined the line dancers. And Jo didn't care that they were receiving all kinds of curious glances. She was confident in making her feelings about Ryan known. "Ryan, promise me one thing."

"Anything."

"Don't grow a beard."

His laughter caught the attention of everyone on the dance floor.

EPILOGUE

Christmas Eve morning

THERE WERE HUNDREDS of Santas of all shapes, sizes and ages mounted and lining up for Clementine's Annual Santapalooza Ride. The morning was crisp and clear. And carols were being sung by members of the church choir.

White beards ran the gamut from paper to cotton balls. Santa suits ran the gamut, too, from thick, plush red ones to the debut of the silver suits Lois had sewn.

Ryan wore one of the silver suits, as did Chet, who was driving a team of horses pulling the candy-cane-themed wagon with Lois by his side. Ryan and Tate's mother rode in the wagon.

And somewhere up in the front of the line, Jo's father and brothers rode as grand marshals. Well, Eric and Ty were grand marshals. But nobody wanted to tell Herbie Pierce that.

Jo had paid her father on time, an event he'd tried to smile for. And surprisingly, her brothers had provided Jo with referrals from cowboys they'd met at the Nationals. Things were looking up.

"Merry Christmas, Dix!" Ryan called to one of his foster brothers before swinging into the saddle. "Merry Christmas, Allison!"

The couple returned his greeting, and Jo's, as they rode past to their place in line.

"Lila said she and her family are gonna watch the parade from in front of the Buffalo Diner." Max sat atop Bobbin, chattering with Dean, who rode Button. They both wore Santa costumes but with cowboy hats trimmed with red velvet and white faux fur. Their white beards hung beneath their chins.

"You can wave at townies the whole way," Dean said pragmatically. "Every cowboy in eastern Oklahoma is out riding today."

"But I'm going to wave best to Lila," Max said, having fallen hard for his fifth-grade sweetheart.

"Luckily, I don't need to wave to my best girl." Sitting on Pauper, Ryan adjusted his Santa cap and smiled at Jo from behind an impressive white beard that he somehow made look sexy. "My best girl is right here next to me."

"Present and accounted for," Jo said, adjusting her Santa hat and readying to mount up.

She took Tiger's reins from Ryan. The Santas were being called to assemble at the high school rodeo grounds to get the parade started.

"I have a question." Ryan leaned on his saddle horn. "Why do all your pairs of horses have names that go together? Laurel and Hardy. Prince and Pauper. Bobbin and Button. You've told me how training a pair of horses to work together takes years and is an art form. You can't name them when they're born."

"That's right. You can't." She waved to her mom. "But every horse has a nickname that's different from their breeding record. And it's easier to keep the pair straight in my mind when I name them uniquely. Like you and me."

"You and me?" Ryan raised his brows.

"That's right. You're Santa and I'm—" she tossed him her warmest, brightest, most loving smile "—Mrs. Claus."

Ryan nodded, smiling right back at her. He wished another couple on horseback a merry Christmas before turning his attention back to Jo. "You want to drink eggnog and sit in front of the fire later?"

"Can't wait." Jo grinned. "Was that on your Christmas wish list?" He'd made one this year for the first time in decades. And all his Christmas wishes involved spending more time with family and friends.

Ryan fluffed his white whiskers. "Nope. But I figure by the time this ride is over, you're going to want to cuddle up to me and get warm, maybe share a kiss beneath the mistletoe."

"Someone should have told you the benefits of a cozy Christmas sooner." She settled into the saddle, unable to contain her grin. "At this rate, you'll want to hold on to that Christmas spirit all year round."

He laughed a hearty ho ho ho that made the twins giggle and warmed Jo's heart.

Ryan had truly embraced the holiday spirit. And she, in turn, had embraced the idea that loving and being in love wasn't a foolish wish.

Everyone deserved love.

And as she looked at the scene all around her, filled with family and friends, and one particularly handsome cowboy at her side, she realized this would be the best Christmas yet.

* * * * *

For more great romances in this miniseries from acclaimed author Melinda Curtis and Harlequin Heartwarming, visit www.Harlequin.com today!